SHRAPNEL

ISSUE #18   **THE OFFICIAL BATTLETECH MAGAZINE**

SHRAPNEL

THE OFFICIAL BATTLETECH MAGAZINE

Loren L. Coleman, Publisher
John Helfers, Executive Editor
Philip A. Lee, Managing Editor
David A. Kerber, Layout and Graphic Design

Cover art by Tan Ho Sim
Interior art by Alan Blackwell, Jared Blando, Mark Hayden, David A. Kerber, Natán Meléndez, Matt Plog, Klaus Scherwinski, Tan Ho Sim

Published by Pulse Publishing, under licensing by Catalyst Game Labs
5003 Main St. #110 ▪ Tacoma, WA 98407

Shrapnel: The Official BattleTech Magazine is published four times a year, in Spring, Summer, Fall, and Winter.

Available through your favorite online store (Amazon.com, BN.com, Kobo, iBooks, GooglePlay, etc.).

ISBN: 978-1-63861-162-2

COMMANDER'S CALL: FROM THE EDITOR'S DESK 4
Philip A. Lee

SHORT STORIES
NESTING FALCONS. 6
Alex Fairbanks

POTTER'S POUNDERS 29
Ken' Horner

HIDE AND SEEK. 53
Sam Barrett

THE SHADOW OF THE MAD TEA MASTER. 89
James Hauser

METACHROSIS. 156
Giles Gammage

ACE DARWIN AND THE GREAT SMALL WORLD PRANK WAR. 178
James Bixby

ZEALOT'S NEST 205
Bryan Young

SERIAL NOVEL
VIOLENT INCEPTION, PART 2 OF 4 119
Russell Zimmerman

ARTICLES
VOICES OF THE SPHERE: STOLEN LIFE 26
Mike Miller

WHAT NEXT FOR BLUE HOLE?. 47
Lorcan Nagle

C.U.P.P.S. 2: KOWALCZYK GETS AN UPGRADE 65
James Kirtley

BREWER'S HOUSE OF CARDS 107
Eric Salzman

ALL'S FAIR IN LOVE AND INDUSTRIAL ESPIONAGE 146
Matt Larson

GAME FEATURES
TECHNICAL READOUT: TDK-7Z THUNDER HAWK 41
Stephen Toropov

ICEBREAKER: A MECHWARRIOR: DESTINY MISSION BRIEFING 83
Eric Salzman

PLANET DIGEST: LESKOVIK. 113
Zac Schwartz

CHAOS CAMPAIGN SCENARIO: RAID ON TOMANS 152
Luke Robertson

PLANET DIGEST: ANTARES 173
Tom Stanley

UNIT DIGEST: OBERON GUARDS 196
Alex Fauth

CAMPAIGN:
DEATH OF A DREAM—THE BATTLE FOR BARCELONA 199
Eric Salzman

COMMANDER'S CALL
FROM THE EDITOR'S DESK

Get ready for your next mission, MechWarriors, because the instability in the Hinterlands needs seasoned warriors to help forge order out of all that chaos.

That's right: this issue, to commemorate the upcoming November release of *Hot Spots: Hinterlands*, we're taking a deep dive into this ilClan-era region to learn more about what makes it work...and, more often, why it *doesn't* (which is honestly more fun for stories and for tabletop games). We've got some Hinterlands-themed short stories, articles, planet and unit digests, playable scenarios—the works. So throw your lot in with your favorite Hinterlands faction—or read through this issue and find one that speaks to you—and get ready to make some noise!

For fiction, we kick off with "Nesting Falcons" by Alex Fairbanks, whose first story appeared back in *Shrapnel* #9; this story explores the unrest among the Jade Falcons abandoned in their occupation zone. In "Potter's Pounders" by Ken' Horner, a group of Hinterlands mercenaries at the end of a contract are offered a choice between going home for a much-deserved rest or staying on to defend a planet in dire need of protection. (It's worth noting that the character of Lt. John "Potter" Peters is Ken's tribute to a fan who is no longer with us.) "Metachrosis," by Giles Gammage, takes us to the seedy underbelly of the Hinterlands and shows the lengths some people will go to adapt and survive—or not—in the shifting sands of this region. We cap off the issue with "Zealot's Nest," Bryan Young's tale of the Kell Hounds and their newest recruits: a handful of former Jade Falcons struggling to find their place in the legendary mercenary unit. But the *BattleTech* fun doesn't stop there! Sam Barrett's debut story "Hide and Seek" puts us in an icy blizzard in the Magistracy of Canopus, where mercenaries must hunt down dangerous pirates or be hunted themselves. James Hauser, whose stories we've previously seen in *Shrapnel* #11 and #15, takes us on an incredible journey to uncover the lost treasure of House Kurita in "The Shadow of the Mad Tea Master," and James Bixby continues the saga of our favorite pink-*Panther* pilot in "Ace Darwin and the Great Small World Prank War." Finally, we have the continuation of Russell Zimmerman's serial with Part 2 of *Violent Inception*.

For game content, prepare to either level up your existing Hinterlands campaigns or embark on a brand-new adventure in this turbulent region! Get a glimpse into the possible future with articles about Duke Vedet Brewer's Vesper Marches in "Brewer's House of Cards" and the independent world of Blue Hole in "What Next for Blue

Hole?" Let Planet Digests for Antares and Leskovik help you plan your next campaign setting, and Unit Digest: Oberon Guards provides you with some piratical opponents—or untrustworthy allies, depending on your preference. Also included are three playable scenarios: "Icebreaker," a *MechWarrior: Destiny* Mission filled with aquatic misadventure (including stats for submersible combat vehicles); "Raid on Tomans," a *Chaos Campaign* scenario for a Rasalhague Dominion attack on the Tamar Pact; and "Death of a Dream" a fully playable mini-campaign for control of the Barcelona system. Then see how life expectancies have shifted over the years in "Voices of the Sphere: Stolen Life"; learn how industrial espionage can change the course of history in "All's Fair in Love and Industrial Espionage"; and catch up with the latest misadventures of our favorite *UrbanMech*-piloting law-enforcement officer in "C.U.P.P.S. 2: Kowalcyzk Gets an Upgrade," by James Kirtley. And finally, Technical Readout: TDK-7Z *Thunder Hawk* introduces the hard-hitting Thunderbolt-missile-toting variant (which also features the Kickstarter backer character of Joseph Berendt).

One other thing I thought worth mentioning before we kick things off: we're currently celebrating the 40th anniversary of the *BattleTech* universe, and during the assembly of this issue, it occurred to me that this year also marks another truly noteworthy anniversary in *BattleTech* history. Thirty-five years ago, this very month—September of 1989, to be specific—the Clans first arrived on the stage with the publication of Michael A. Stackpole's novel *Lethal Heritage*, the first book in the beloved Blood of Kerensky Trilogy. This novel introduced us to a strange new threat that emerged from the coreward Periphery with truly frightening advanced BattleMechs piloted by peerless warriors, and the arrival of the Clans in the Inner Sphere has affected the landscape of *BattleTech* ever since. Even the Clan Invasion Kickstarter campaign in 2019, which helped create this very magazine you're reading, owes a debt to that pivotal point in *BattleTech* history. So, while we're still observing *BattleTech*'s 40th birthday, feel free to take a moment and drink a fusionnaire—or any saner beverage of choice—to celebrate the 35th anniversary of the arrival of the Clans, and acknowledge the truly monumental impact they've had on *BattleTech* throughout the decades.

—Philip A. Lee, Managing Editor

NESTING FALCONS

ALEX FAIRBANKS

THE EMPYREAN NIGHTCLUB
NEW MEMPHIS
GRACELAND
TAMAR PACT
21 MAY 3152

At least the bourbon wasn't bad, Captain William Tucker thought as he glanced over the gaudy decorum of the Empyrean nightclub. A loud, reverberating bass echoed from the dance floor downstairs, sending pulses through his body. Even upstairs, his eyes were bombarded by bright white-and-scarlet lights of a holovid reflecting off the obsidian walls.

Will and his lancemate, Cameron Pham, arrived right on time, but of course, Donal Malthus, Military Governor of Graceland—and prominent member of the seedy Malthus Confederation—made them wait in the lounge, offering free drinks to soften them up until an attendant arrived to escort them to the office.

Whatever frustrations he felt, Will pushed them aside. After all, money was on the line. Donal had tasked the Bleeding Eagles with protecting New Memphis from attacks by Jade Falcon sympathizers who held onto their old beliefs, and Colonel Barnes had delegated the matter to Will's lance. The job had proven difficult, since the few Jade Falcon followers that remained loyal to the Clans had scattered throughout the populace, striking seemingly at random. Despite mostly being made up of ill-equipped ex-laborer caste members, they were still vicious and deadly.

Last week, the rebels struck a supply depot, stealing countless weapons in a quick raid. Before that, they led a raid on Dunbar, a town a good ways away from New Memphis. Between the Clan sympathizers and civvies, there had been hundreds of deaths. Ugly business.

When the Eagles arrived with a full lance, most of the raiders scattered, fleeing from the carnage. Some died, some were taken prisoner, but the rebellion didn't seem to slow down. This afternoon though, Donal had excitedly called Will, saying he had some intel on how to "cut off the head of the snake." Now they had to meet in person at the crime lord's new nightclub.

Will had low expectations for whatever this new "intel" was. His lack of fondness for Donal was painfully obvious, but as per their agreement with the Tamar Pact, the Bleeding Eagles had to protect the Graceland system. He did his best to keep from complaining too much.

An old merc and MechWarrior, Will felt out of place among the cosmopolitans of New Memphis in his battered duster and heavy boots. While he might have blended right into a weathered and rough bar in Galatea with his bull-like build, long, unkempt hair, and graying beard, he looked like an ancient relic at the high-energy, upbeat club.

While this kind of nightclub was anathema to Will, he couldn't help but notice with slight frustration that Cam seemed to soak in his surroundings. The younger MechWarrior fit in perfectly, wearing an olive-green tank top that showed off the biceps he spent most of his time at base sculpting, further embellished by his tattoo of the Bleeding Eagles insignia: an abstract red eagle with long wings stretched out and dripping with blood, superimposed on a black triangle, the antithesis of the Free Worlds League symbol they had discarded as expatriates of House Marik. Cam even made his cowboy hat work. Although he was a recent recruit picked up on Galatea, he'd proven to be a talented MechWarrior with serious determination under his carefree attitude, and so Will had taken him in under his wing as his right-hand man in the lance.

One of Donal's goons finally fetched them, and as Will walked down the hallway, he watched with horror as Cam continued sipping the drink he'd gotten from the bar downstairs. It was a viscous, bright green, creamy monstrosity topped with a blood-red fruit. The main selling point of the "Dead Falcon," as they called it, was the inclusion of egg white from the nearly extinct Graceland Falcon. Will had seen anti-Clan mentalities spike during their short time stationed on Graceland. He wasn't necessarily surprised by propagandistic symbols that valorized violence, but the gloating nature of it all never sat right with him. "You really gonna finish that thing?"

Cam shrugged mischievously. "It's on the house. Might as well go all in," he said, taking an overly emphatic sip. Green foam still hung on his upper lip as he offered the glass to Will, grinning. "Not too bad, either. Want some?"

"Get that thing out of my face." Will waved away the sweet-smelling sludge. Although he often played the part of the curmudgeon, part of him secretly enjoyed their usual banter.

Behind two large, lavishly engraved wooden doors guarded by security, Donal Malthus awaited them. Sporting well-oiled hair and a small goatee, the man certainly looked the part of a prominent crime family member as he leaned back in his plush chair, his feet resting on a large mahogany desk.

Another man stood beside him, remarkably burly, with his head shaved on the sides. Several large scars ran down his face, the toughened tissue hiding his blue eyes that gleamed like two tiny sapphires, or in this case, pulse lasers. *Is he ex-Clan? A bondsman?* Donal was playing with fire if so, considering their hatred for him—Jade Falcons held particular scorn for him holding the surname Malthus, a prestigious Bloodname among their Clan, without having any actual connections to their society. Will stood a little straighter, refusing to be intimidated.

Donal smiled, apparently amused at the impression his other guest made. "Ah, the Bleeding Eagles have arrived. I hope you weren't too...bothered...by the altercation downstairs." His voice dripped with faux concern.

When they were waiting at the bar, a small fight had erupted. Some loud drunk was making fun of the Clans—something about inbreeding or ridiculing their test-tube breeding programs, whatever typical crap people thought they needed to voice. Will wasn't listening. But he did pay attention when someone came out and decked the loudmouth. The drunk probably would have been killed if security didn't step in as quickly as they did.

"Your men handled it well," Will replied. "Seems like they get plenty of practice."

Donal grinned mercurially at the slight, holding up his hands. "Almost every day there's something. These Falcons, they're just unreasonable. Ungrateful. Do you know how much better the economy has gotten since we moved in? Moreover, most of these...*sympathizers* were miserable little laborers before we liberated them. I just don't understand."

"Maybe they just don't like how you're running the show," Will said. "You could start by holding off on the 'Dead Falcons.'"

Donal paused, searching for the right words, until his eyes flickered to Cam's nearly empty glass. "A little fun to keep the people happy," he said. "Did you enjoy it?"

Cam put the remains of his drink down on the table. "I—it was fine. A bit too sweet, maybe, but not worth stirring up more trouble over. How often does something like that happen?"

Donal sighed and put his hand over his chest. "Trust me, if it were just over a drink, I would be jumping for joy," he said, his eyes narrowing as he spoke. "But I don't think any of this will stop while 'the Talon' is feeding them propaganda, which brings me to my main point." .

He gestured to the large man behind him. "Gentlemen, I'd like you to meet Johan. He'll be working with you on a new mission."

Johan, glaring, nodded with a grunt.

"Oh, will he now? Let's maybe talk things over first." Will took a step toward the table, showing he was still in control of the conversation. Completing assignments for Donal was one thing, but making decisions about the process was stepping over a boundary.

Cam followed his lead, backing him up.

"I don't mean to insist," Donal said, raising a hand to calm Will. "He's just the reason we're meeting today, and I'm offering his services as a gesture of goodwill. I truly believe we now have a chance to wipe out this obsessive Clan sentiment once and for all."

Will grimaced, taking a seat in front of the desk. When he'd set out to become a MechWarrior, he didn't imagine himself cleaning up after a crime lord's mess, but they had to fulfill their part of their contract with the Pact. *Sometimes, you have to give to get*, he told himself. After all, if Donal wasn't happy, he could make things difficult for Governor-General Sarah Regis, since Graceland served as an important location on the border of their newly acquired territory. If they messed up here, the Eagles' place in the Pact would be threatened, and they'd lose their chance at gaining prominence in the merc world. "Explain. Then we'll negotiate. Who's this Talon?"

Donal leaned back and smiled as he pulled out a Thunderstrike cigarette, offering one to Will, but clearly expecting the refusal. "Johan has discovered from some thorough...questioning...that there's a leader among the rabble. We don't know their real name yet—seems they just call them 'the Talon.' The prisoners we've had from the last raid are keeping tight lips, but they seem to worship this agitator as some kind of god-hero. You'd think it was the second coming of Kerensky if you heard how they talk about them."

Will rested his head in his hands and took a moment to think. "You think if we take this Talon out, the resistance will crumble?"

"I do," Donal replied. "The Clans believe might is right. They need to know who's in power now. With their leader dead, they'll lose traction. Unfortunately, we know very little about the Talon's identity or whereabouts. However, Johan knows someone who might. As you may have noticed, my friend here looks like he would fit right in with other Clanners. He's an excellent warrior, but in truth, he's Inner Sphere born and raised, and one of my most trusted soldiers. His appearance has been particularly useful on Graceland, and he's made some acquaintances. One of those acquaintances has reached out to us, saying he'll tell us where the Talon is for a price. I need you to escort Johan to Gallatin and follow his orders. You may need to strike quickly if you find out where this Talon is—I hear they don't stay in one place long."

"We leave tomorrow," Johan explained, curtly and to the point.

"Wait, why do we need to go gather info?" Cam asked. "Isn't this more of a job for your thugs? No offense," he added, glancing at Johan.

Will touched his subordinate's arm, quieting him, though he'd had the same thoughts. This situation sat wrong with him, too. Something was off.

Chuckling, Donal leaned forward. "You're simply making a trade with an informant. If you get the name and location of your target, you may need to act quickly. Believe it or not, there are ex-sympathizers who have grown tired of the constant back and forth, and poverty has made some desperate. If you're concerned about safety, know that you'll be meeting on neutral ground. If something goes wrong, I can send backup."

Will gave Cam a knowing glance. He didn't like the situation either. The morally questionable crime lord was known for leaving out details. Everything they did on Graceland felt painfully slimy, but for Will, this was just another part of the mercenary life. But taking out the Talon could finally put an end to all this civilian violence, at least.

"We'll get this done for you—but it won't be cheap." If he had to accept, he figured he could at least squeeze his employer for every drop.

Will made sure the grin on Donal's face was wiped clean off by the time negotiations were over.

GALLATIN
GRACELAND
TAMAR PACT
22 MAY 3152

Will discovered, to his surprise, that Gallatin was a pleasantly quiet town. Between the domed ferrocrete buildings, specks of white and yellow flowers were scattered throughout the landscape amid crisp green grass. Driving their buggy through the town, he wondered how many of those flowers would be crushed by the feet of BattleMechs stomping forward. How many would be torched by lasers? How much blood would soak those fields? The thought of attacking desperate, poverty-stricken rebels didn't sit right with him; he preferred an old-fashioned showdown. But the life of a mercenary did not allow for many preferences. He turned away and focused on the road. If it took the destruction of 100,000 beautiful fields to get the job done, then that's what it took.

While the cool breeze and clear air of Graceland made for a nice climate, with the orange sun setting overhead, the company was awkwardly quiet, making the trip uncomfortable. It was an especially long drive with Johan awkwardly squeezing himself into the too-small seat in the back, pulling his large frame tight to fit in the narrow space. There was more room up front, but Will made certain Cam sat shotgun, at the very least to slight Johan. Their third lancemate, Haley, sat beside Johan, comfortably cross-legged as her cigarette left a trail of smoke behind them. They made quite the contrary pair—a huge, hulking mass of muscle next to a lithe, erudite mercenary with black lipstick and a shock of pink hair.

As they drove through the city, Will couldn't help but notice glares from pedestrians as they passed by. Things seemed normal enough, though he was shaken when he noticed a family of four walking under graffiti depicting Donal's severed head being carried away by a falcon.

He laughed. "At least they have good taste."

Johan, clearly unamused, pointed to a crossroad. "Turn here," he said flatly.

Finally, they arrived at a squat ferrocrete building. A public library, of all places. Although their surroundings were relatively peaceful, he noticed a few of the building's windows were shattered, and teenagers loitered outside, glaring at the four of them.

"Go around and park in the alley," Johan ordered. "As far as the informant knows, there are just the two of us here. Will, you'll come with me. Say nothing. And you two—" He pointed to Cam and Haley. "—wait out here. If we aren't back in thirty minutes, get backup."

Will got out of the car and handed Cam the keys. He didn't like Johan calling the shots. "I don't trust this one bit," he whispered. "You and Haley drive around. Look for anything suspicious. Be on guard."

Cam nodded solemnly, taking the keys.

As Will and Johan walked through the library, they passed several small chambers containing a console, each one providing the potential to have near-infinite texts. Will wondered what they could actually read, though—if this place hadn't changed since the Clan's occupation, was there a strict list of accepted reading material? Did available texts pertain to your caste? How much had changed since Donal's conquest, and how much had stayed the same?

Will followed Johan to the back, where a thin man was sitting at a console. The man had a solemn look in his eyes and dark gray hair that pointed into a widow's peak, but Will couldn't help but be taken aback by his odd proportions. His head seemed too big for his body, and his eyes too large for his face.

The man turned to Johan. "Today is the day, then?"

Johan took a deep breath. "It is, Simon."

The informant nodded. "I'll tell you what you need to know, but first, would you spare a moment?" he asked, gesturing to the seat next to him.

Johan glanced at Will, nodding as he squatted on a stool clearly made for someone smaller. "What's this about?"

"I was reading about the Golden Century in the Clan's history," Simon said, pointing to the monitor. "They achieved much in those times. There was order, new technology, a society on the cusp of greatness. They all had faith in Kerensky's vision, and they never let go of that faith. Do you not think that such steadfastness, such loyalty, is a virtue unto itself? That the vision of a greater future supersedes temporary setback?"

It seemed as though the informant had forgotten Will existed. "It is never too late to believe in something," Simon continued.

Shaking his head, Johan flushed. A bead of sweat dripped down his forehead. "You said you know where the Talon is. So, get to it."

The hairs on the back of Will's neck stood up; he realized now the danger Donal had put them in. The informant was one of those phenotypes—aerospace. And clearly, he still held some Clan sentiment.

The informant closed his eyes and sighed. "The Talon is here." Responding to Johan's alert expression, he continued, "In Gallatin."

Nervously, Simon stared up at the giant, who stood several heads higher than him. "Do not look so surprised. Did you not think the Talon already knew of your charade? A freeborn, pretending to be True? One ruse begets another."

He held up his hand to halt Johan's advance. "But, despite your treachery, our leader has chosen mercy and offers an audience with you all. If you lay down your weapons, you will be unharmed."

Will surreptitiously reached for his pistol. "And if we don't want an audience?"

A deep, sonorous voice came through the intercom, startling Will. "Then you will die."

Johan erupted with lightning speed. He grabbed Simon by the collar and slammed him into the wall as though he were a ragdoll. "Lying worm," he snarled, pinning the informant. Simon's already large eyes bulged even more as he desperately squirmed.

Will took a deep breath. Peeking out of the cubicle, he saw two soldiers, clad in black, approaching from one side of the hallway. Two more to the other. Bad odds, but maybe he could take them out, using their position to his advantage...

The voice over the intercom interrupted his thoughts. "And do not think the two outside have gone unnoticed. Their lives are in your hands, Captain William Tucker."

"Drop him, Johan," Will commanded. "It's over."

"Not while we have a hostage." Johan grinned, dragging the small man with him. He pulled his gun from his holster. "Tell your men to back down."

The intercom buzzed with the loud static of hoarse laughter. "In truth, I'd hoped Donal's dog would resist."

The first thing Will perceived was glass crashing as the small window slit in the cubicle shattered, and then that his jacket and shirt were covered in thick, viscous gore. Realizing after several moments of agonizing shock that it was not his own blood, bone, and bits of brain matter scattered about, his vision came into focus, and he saw Johan's head had become a mess of carnage. The giant crashed to the ground, eliminated by an unseen sniper.

That was all Will needed. Placing his gun on the floor, he held his hands up as the rebels stormed the room. Someone shoved him to the ground. He felt the sting of a needle, and all went black.

In the morning, Will could barely feel the tight restraints around his wrists as he lifted himself up using his forearms. In fact, he could barely feel his hands at all. In the pale light trickling into the cold, dark cell, he could just make out that the edges of the handcuffs had left a dark red line in his skin, and his fingers, numb and rubbery, had the pallid complexion of the dead. He had seen many bodies in his long career as a mercenary. Will gazed on with the grim realization that he could soon be just another corpse among the many who had failed to see victory through. But then again, why wasn't he dead already?

They kept Cam and Haley in the same cell with him, each restrained in a similar fashion, though they had blood on their faces and their skin was marbled with dark bruises. They all had been changed into simple white garments, flimsy and of little comfort in the night.

Will coughed up some phlegm as he crawled over to his crew. "How are you both holding up?" It was a silly question, he knew, but he craved some kind of normality.

"About to die a horrible death following Malthus' stupid plan. How do you think?" Haley asked. "Why did we think this was a good idea?"

Taking a deep breath, Will wanted to defend himself, but she was right. "It was reckless. Shouldn't have trusted Malthus to do his due diligence. You couldn't get away?"

"By the time we saw them, it was too late," Cam added. "They shot out our tires."

"We got out of the car and put up a fight," Haley noted. "We took out a few of them, but more and more came. Must've been the entire town surrounding us."

"At least you didn't end up like Johan." Will told them his side of the story.

Afterward, they simply waited in silence, each one wondering what horrible fate awaited them.

"Think Donal's actually going to send backup?" Will asked.

With a sudden start, a voice came from the other side of the door. "He tried once already, and to be honest with you, it was a pitiful attempt."

Will turned to see the portal slide open, revealing two soldiers flanking a single figure, whose grandiosity marked him as none other than the Talon. Tall, muscular, and with an air that commanded the room, he wore an obscuring faceplate beneath a helmet decorated with falcon motifs, and he dressed as a Jade Falcon captain of old, bedecked in the majesty of a green, black, and gold one-piece outfit embellished with a long green cape that rose at the shoulders. Even in his current state, Will couldn't help but smirk at the theatrics.

"Captain William Tucker. It is a pleasure," the figure said, in a mellifluously deep and bellowing voice—the same one he'd heard over the intercom.

"The Talon, I presume?" Will muttered.

The figure nodded with a certain genteel dignity. "I apologize for my method of extraction, but I could see no better way to ensure we met on peaceful terms."

Will could hardly call this *peaceful*, but he could see the Talon's point. Reaching out to meet with Donal diplomatically would have led to an assassination attempt.

The Talon walked over to Will. "You must be wondering why you are still alive." With swift grace he unsheathed a combat knife and grabbed Will's wrists, slicing off the restraints. "We have important matters to discuss, you and I."

Will turned toward Cam and Haley. "What about them?"

The Talon paused for a moment, then nodded at his guards, who approached to remove their restraints. "They will be fine."

Shaking his arms as the blood flowed back into his hands, Will followed the Talon out.

The Talon stopped his guards at the elevator. "Leave us. I would like to speak with our guest privately." The two men nodded and stood akimbo at the elevator doors.

The Talon brought Will to the rooftop, where he could see now that they were high above Gallatin, the bright sky making him squint. "Look below us," he said, bringing them to a railing.

Will quickly glanced over the edge. There was the occasional car, some pedestrians—nothing atypical. Things seemed normal enough. Pondering what the Talon wanted him to see, it suddenly occurred to him that the Falcon leader might be planning to throw him off the roof as a public display of execution. He wasn't terribly high up, but a push would kill him. Cautiously, he glanced at the Talon and took a step back.

The Talon let out a deep, throaty laugh. "I am not going to kill you here, Will. If I ever decide I need to end your life, you will know ahead of time. Tell me, what did you see?"

Will shrugged. "Nothing really. Just some town."

"Yes. And do you know what 'some town' contains?"

Will sighed. "I don't know. People? What's your point?"

"Each person you see is resentful of the false Malthus, longing for the Jade Falcons' presence here. Each one knew a different life before that *surat* slithered into power, and while Donal and your Tamar Pact claim life is better now, these people remember the past differently."

"You mean they're all rebels?"

"I do not think 'rebel' is the right word. It makes them sound like miscreants or troublemakers. They are warriors, in heart at least, though most were born into a lower caste. But I admit, the number of those who are willing to fight dwindles, and I fear that all those with fighting spirit might martyr themselves against the walls of the enemy's fortresses. They long to be part of a society that is free from the filth of Donal Malthus' regime. Each one had a purpose. Each was taken care of, and each had their own place in the world. Now, look again, what do you see there? I promise I will not push."

Will looked over again more confidently. He could see a man squatting in an alley, covered in tattered blankets. "Poverty. Wouldn't he have been executed for living like that before though?"

The Talon gestured. "More likely 'reconditioned,' though Malvina's rule grew harsher. With Khan Jiyi Chistu in control, I have confidence things will be better. Our world before may not have been perfect. But that man would have been given a chance. Here, you must plot and connive to make anything of yourself, and even then, only if Donal finds you useful. Do you know what the 'Malthus' Confederation traffics? What vices they push onto the youth here? And your Tamar Pact turns a blind eye to it, all for a little more foothold in the Hinterlands. Donal has diminished our sense of honor, our sense of hope. And every chance he gets, he insults us. Now, he twists the dagger as he opens places like his Empyrean to suck in our wealth, pleasing his patrons with disgusting displays of excess."

Will shook his head. "What the hell does this have to do with me? The way I see it, both societies rely on someone's misery. You're stuck as a servant for the Falcons if you're born into the wrong caste."

The Talon shook his head. "Perhaps. But can things be worse than what we have now? The top of the food chain is some slimy, uncompassionate, self-serving *surat*, while noble and true warriors who wanted to create a better and more peaceful society ruled before. Back then, all were taken care of with respect, as long as respect was shown."

Will frowned. "Some would say the Falcon warriors were overbearing tyrants who forced their ideals on others. I've heard of plenty of people who were pleased to be free of the Clan."

The Talon pounded his fist on the railing. "*Stravag*! Someone will always complain. But those who remember reject Donal. This town, this planet—" He gestured toward the horizon. "—we want to rule it our way again."

Will noticed the sun shining over the bare and utilitarian buildings that made up the town, stretching out beneath the blue-yellow sky of Graceland. Even in his current situation, he could appreciate, in some way, the quiet respite compared to the overwhelming barrage of advertising in New Memphis.

Suppressing a chuckle, he replied, "You can't really be that sentimental. Sure, you might kill us off, but there's the whole Malthus Confederation and the Tamar Pact for you to face. Your Clan is waning and weak, and even if we didn't succeed, there're the Vesper Marches and Hell's Horses to clean things up."

The Talon moved as if to slap Will across the face, but let his hand fall. "You think I do not know this? That is why you are here.

"We had some fighting chance before you came, but now that the Pact has joined Malthus in holding Graceland, I fear all hope is lost. My death is certain. I could run and hide, but I am not interested in that. Still, these people can survive, even if most of them also want to go out in a blaze of glory. I have brought you here to propose an offer. We will see what fate decides.

"My offer is this: tonight, you will challenge me to a Trial of Possession for command over the Jade Falcon forces of Graceland, and I will accept. If I win, I will kill the rest of your crew and we will march to New Memphis for one final battle. If you win, you report my death and say that the uprising has been put down, and you will tell my followers to end their crusade, for now. The people here will listen to you because you defeated me in honorable combat, and you will tell them to keep the peace. It is not ideal, but it is the best option I can see. If you refuse to do this, you must understand you are useless to me."

Will breathed heavily. *What kind of sick game is this?* "Why don't you just decide now?"

The Talon shook his head as if he heard Will's thoughts. "I would not expect a Spheroid to understand. A Trial of Possession is fitting. I want our fate decided by a fair fight. You hear me? Fair. Not like Tukayyid, or any of your other Spheroid schemes. We will battle in a Circle of Equals."

Will leaned against the railing, thinking. The Talon was right: it made little sense to him, but then again, he had never seen much sense in the Clans to begin with. "Why me, though? I'm a mercenary. The plight of the ex-Falcons is sad, sure, but there's a lot of crap in the Inner Sphere, and this case doesn't particularly concern me. I'm just interested in getting paid."

The Talon shook his head. "In truth, between the false Malthus' forces and your outfit, you are the best option among a batch of poor choices. I have needed someone who can give me a decent fight. When I found you were investigating us, I ordered your capture, not your death. It is in your best interest as a mercenary to follow this plan. You can tell them you killed me and quelled the Jade Falcon sympathizers, and then you will get your pay. I just ask you, warrior to warrior, to let the others live. If they continue to believe, maybe when the true Falcons return—"

Will nodded. If this did stop the rebellion, it would mean, at least for the time being, that there could be some relative peace, and more importantly, the lives of Cam and Haley were on the line. "It's a deal," he confirmed.

To Will, the Talon sounded like a man defeated, as if he wished to lose the battle. But he knew at least enough about the Clans to know honor and combat were things not to be taken lightly. This trial, in the Talon's mind, would be the judge between right and wrong. For Will, it was just a chance to keep his crew alive.

The Talon tensed. "This will be a battle to the death, you are aware."

Will let out a breath. "Fine, if that's what you want. What will I be piloting?"

"We do not have many choices. But you can pilot the *Hunchback* or *Griffin*—Clan upgrades. I will fight in my *Pinion 3*."

Will raised his eyebrows. Those 'Mechs were not impressive choices. So, the opposition they'd met was their entire force? At first, he wanted to laugh at the Talon's confident claim to a 'Mech like the *Pinion* as though it were something worth gloating over. But then, a surprisingly deep sadness hit him. In an instant, he realized the reason for all the grandeur, the symbolism, and the sentiment. This was the best they had to offer—the mighty Jade Falcon forces had three mediocre 'Mechs. All the showiness was a facade, hiding profound shame. It was the crushing despair of dwindling to nothing while tightly gripping a sense of undying pride.

"I'll take the *Hunchback*, then. And I will accept—on two conditions."

"Name them."

"Keep my crew imprisoned if you need to, but do not kill them. You can kill me. That's fine, but they don't deserve to die."

The Talon looked upward, his mask reflecting the sun. "On the condition that you uphold your bargain and fight honorably, *quiaff*? The second?"

"Throw in a last cigarette and we're good."

The Talon nodded. "Well bargained and done."

Will, Cam, and Haley were taken to an old factory on the outskirts of town. Both 'Mechs, the *Pinion* and the *Hunchback IIC*, towered above the large gate entrance like guardian statues. Time and battle had chipped away at the green paint that coated each metal monstrosity, revealing the scars of many encounters. Maybe he was being trivial, but the thought crossed Will's mind that he would've preferred to fight in his unit's parade colors: teal with orange-red accents.

Entering the factory, he walked past crowds of people, each staring at him with anticipation. Some climbed on top of the old, rusty machines scattered throughout, watching from above. They were escorted toward a large wooden stage raised at the far end of the building. Roughly, the guards pushed them to the dais, denying Will any further observations.

Large spotlights illuminated the enormous space, revealing the massive crowd. Shoulder to shoulder, desperate and adoring fanatics waiting in eerie silence. Some were even gathered around outside the large warehouse doors, leaning in as much as they could. *Did all of Graceland come to watch the Talon speak?*

Will stood, feeling the eyes of the throng boring into him with disdain.

Finally, the Talon appeared, walking past them to a pedestal in the center of the stage. "Welcome, one and all. We are here, once again, together in action. But today is different. There will be no battle plans, no sabotage attempts. Today, we have a challenge to address!

"We are, I regret to tell you, in a trying time. The Tamar Pact hunts us down, Donal continues to control us, bringing his crime syndicate's affairs into our daily lives, and Clan Hell's Horses stand at our gates."

The crowd seemed to sober, the anticipatory energy dying out at the Talon's words.

"This is not what you wish to hear, I know. But do not lose hope—I have one last gift for you before the night ends."

He held up his hand, quieting the excited rumblings in the audience. "In the tradition of Clan Jade Falcon, we will leave our fate to a contest of warriors. Tonight, you will all be witnesses to a moment of destiny. Captain William Tucker of the Bleeding Eagles has challenged me to a Trial of Possession for the remnant forces we have collected. Though

he is a mercenary, I have deemed him worthy of this trial. If I win, we will fight to the last and leave a scar upon the false Malthus' holdings here, but we will go out gloriously in the name of Clan Jade Falcon."

The crowd erupted with cheers. Such revelry made Will wonder what would really happen if he defeated the Talon. Would they really stand down, or would they tear him to pieces?

The Talon held up his hand, silencing the audience. "If Captain Tucker wins, you will obey his order to stand down, for now. But I believe our cause will rise from the ashes like a phoenix when Khan Jiyi Chistu returns. In the meantime, be patient. Do not commit *bondsref*. You will not throw your lives away. You will survive. You will wait. Remember that one day, your place will be restored in Clan Jade Falcon!"

The crowd grew quiet, anticipating his next words.

"This is our way. It must be done through trial. Stand forward, Captain William Tucker."

Will walked forward, trying not to show the pain he felt from his beating earlier.

The Talon said, "I, Star Captain of Graceland, accept your *batchall*, Captain William Tucker of the Bleeding Eagles, for command of Graceland's forces. With your victory, they will disband until they may return to Jade Falcon space. If I win, we will lay siege to the forces of New Memphis, fighting to the last breath."

Will just walked forward and shook the Talon's hand. He saw, in the corner of his eye, that Cam and Haley looked shocked at the announcement. In truth, he felt some excitement. There had been little true combat on Graceland; a test of honor in an old-fashioned showdown quickened his blood. If he could take out the Talon, he wouldn't have to deal with this dissent anymore—at least he hoped that would be the case.

Still, contrary to his cold pragmatism, he did feel a semblance of pity as he looked down on the crowd. Picking out a few individuals, he could see they were ragged, worn down, tired. Any energy they showed at the beginning of the rally had faded, despite their quiet anticipation; these were people continually crushed by the remorseless nature of the universe.

After boarding the 'Mech, Will traveled to the designated location in the *Hunchback IIC*. As he piloted the machine, he couldn't help noticing it felt slightly uncalibrated. There was a strange hum under his seat, and the movement felt a little jerky. Though he had never piloted a Clan 'Mech before, he imagined they were supposed to run a bit smoother. The smell wasn't great either. He was pretty sure at least two *solahma* had died in the cockpit at some point. *Did they have techs or the resources to maintain a 'Mech?*

He just hoped the Talon's *Pinion* was in a similar state. Longing for his *Quickdraw*, Will accepted that this would just have to do. At least, as far as the *Hunchback IIC*'s monitors showed, all systems were operational.

"Is your 'Mech satisfactory?" he heard the Talon's voice crackle through the grainy comm system.

"Not in the best shape, but it'll do."

"Trust that you have the best we can offer."

For assurance, Will tested one of the medium pulse lasers. A yellow beam flickered, scorching great gashes in the grassland. "Weapons seem operational. I have no complaints. By the way, since one of us is dying tonight, care to tell me what that 'gift' you mentioned is?"

The Talon chuckled ominously. "You will have to survive if you want to find out. Trust that no harm will come to your company, however."

After a short pause, the Talon announced, "Let the battle commence."

Will took a deep breath, his hands tightening on the controls. His neurohelmet pressed on his bruises uncomfortably, and his body ached. He closed his eyes for a moment and tried to ignore the pain—he needed to focus if he wanted to live.

The comms grew quiet. Will maneuvered the top-heavy humanoid 'Mech toward some forest. Using the cover of the night, he would try to use stealth to his advantage as best he could, at least until they engaged in combat. An odd calm came over him while he anticipated the moment to strike, like a serpent waiting for its prey.

Crackling, the Talon's calm voice came through the comm system. "We cannot sit and wait for each other all night. If you will not come out, I will just take the first shot."

Does he see me? Will wondered. He moved backward to get a better sight, and from a vantage point on a hill, he spotted the squat, humanoid *Pinion*. Will fired his pulse lasers, but missed as the *Pinion* launched into the air on its jump jets. From above, its arm ignited with a crimson laser, streaking across the grassland and cutting across his body.

Will took a step back. Heat seeped through the cockpit. Sweat dripped down his forehead. *How is it already hot as hell?* The damn heat sinks were probably out of order. He wondered if they were even all installed. The *Pinion* was too fast and too far away for the massive Ultra-class autocannons mounted on his 'Mech's shoulders to be effective. Besides, he was certain they'd jam after a few shots if they were even operational to begin with. Instead, he fell back further into the forest.

Another laser shot from the *Pinion*'s other arm, igniting one of the trees.

"How much do you know about Tukayyid?" the Talon asked. "When ComStar did battle with the Ghost Bears, they decided to use the forest to their advantage, turning it ablaze, trying to force a retreat. But the Bears pressed on and paid dearly for it." Another red beam hit the base of a tree, making a small fire. Smoke would start to billow soon, impairing his vision.

"So now you're using ComStar's tactics?" Will asked.

"If you will not fight out in the open, then I will use your dirty tricks. It is only fair, *quiaff*?" Another beam ignited a tree. The fire was slowly growing. Though Will couldn't feel the effects of the heat yet, he would soon enough. "Come out, and we can fight like warriors." Even through the grainy comm system, he could hear agitation in the Talon's voice.

"You want a fight? You got one." Will felt his blood boil, the rush of adrenaline hitting his system. He pushed the throttle forward toward the tree that burned brightest for cover.

The *Pinion* turned toward him. Will could see the massive barrel of the heavy large laser that made up its right arm jerk erratically. He prayed it would miss, but the bright blue beam slashed across his left torso, making the armor melt off like hot butter.

"Hard to see me on the sensors now, huh?" Will said, hoping that standing near the flames to disrupt his foe's vision was worth the risk. He fired a pulse laser barrage. Slag melted as the flashing yellow lasers bore into the protruding chest of the *Pinion*.

The *Pinion* strayed to the side and launched its jets again. Will imagined it was getting hot, but it couldn't have been as sweltering as his own cockpit. He tried to ignore the thick beads of sweat that threatened to drench his eyes and the stench that grew worse every moment.

"How unClanlike. I am not sure your companions will get to live, based on our terms," the Talon goaded. The *Pinion* fired lasers from each arm this time. One beam narrowly missed the cockpit, but Will flinched as the Ultra autocannon on his right side creaked loudly as its interior melted away.

Will pushed forward, resisting the impulse to fire any more weapons until he was close enough. Pushing the *Hunchback IIC* too hard could lead to a shutdown.

Now out in the open field, the *Pinion* fired again; this time both lasers went for his left side. As quickly as he could, Will twisted to the right, trying to shield his already weakened left. Despite his best efforts, his 'Mech staggered back as it took another full blast. A loud screech signified internal damage—if any of those lasers even touched his ammunition bin, the explosion would make a crater the size of New Memphis.

Traces of smoke rose into the canopy. Heat was going critical, and his control over the *Hunchback IIC* seemed laggy and less responsive. He fired another volley of pulse lasers, this time both hit, boring into the enemy 'Mech's chest. He hoped he had at least damaged a heat sink.

The *Pinion* took to the skies again, this time flying backward, landing heavily on a grassy mound. Will jostled to the side, just barely avoiding another heavy laser shot. He fired back, each beam from his pulse laser traveling up the left side of the *Pinion* to its arm. He was relieved to see smoke coming up from the 'Mech's side.

Strafing right, he forced the *Pinion* to turn toward him. Another laser from the right arm melted armor away from his right leg. Will could almost feel the machinery slowing down as his 'Mech began to limp toward the *Pinion*. But now, as he approached, he could fire his remaining autocannon accurately enough. He aimed just above the *Pinion*, waiting for it to fly again. As soon as he saw the jets ignite, he pulled the trigger.

Nothing.

"Dammit," he muttered, jostling the controls and pulling the trigger rapidly. Wiggling the 'Mech's torso back and forth must have shifted something. A loud explosion startled him as a burst of high-powered rounds exploded out of the massive shoulder-mounted cannon. The delay caused the weapon to miss the torso as the *Pinion* soared, hitting its leg instead. Chunks of metal blew off the limb, raining down in burning arcs.

The *Pinion* spun in midair, twirling toward the ground at high speeds. Its leg, barely hanging on by myomer cords, collapsed as it hit the ground, forcing the 'Mech down in a smoking heap.

Will inched forward, holding back another shot. "It's over."

There was silence. He wondered if the Talon had passed out. But as he came closer, he heard a crackle.

"Finish...what you started."

The *Pinion* started to rise, using its one good arm to lift itself. It swayed, trying to point its weapons at Will.

Will shook his head. He wasn't sure if it was going to fall again, but even the slightest bit of damage to his 'Mech could be lethal. He'd been in the business long enough to know not to take his chances. Mercy had led to the deaths of too many friends.

With quiet respect, he fired his autocannon square into the chest of the *Pinion*.

The Ultra autocannon burst ripped through the torso. Metal exploded in a plume of fire. The 'Mech, barely held together, careened to the side as the arm holding it began to give until finally, it collapsed.

"The falcon...leaves its nest," the Talon's voice crackled, almost serenely.

The comm buzzed out with a sense of finality as the *Pinion* crashed to the earth.

After the battle, Will returned to the factory. He thanked the stars that the rebels honored their posthumous leader's wishes. There was no rage: the air hung only with grief. Gray faces stared at him with tearless eyes. Rebel soldiers had found the Talon's ravaged body and set it up on a table, draping him in white cloth.

Will quietly came to pay respects, and frankly, to satisfy his curiosity. He wondered if the Talon was someone he knew or had heard of. But no, as he gazed at the face of this man, with his helmet removed, he was astounded by the ordinariness, the plainness of his visage. He could have been anyone. Though the Talon had a strong jaw and powerful features, and from his build was likely at one point a Clan warrior, Will could not help but notice the man was old—graying hair, wrinkles, a few battle scars, all the signs of an aged soldier. He would have been considered *solahma*, by Clan standards.

"Who was he?" Will asked one of the fighters.

The rebel shook his head. "An old warrior. I do not know."

Will nodded, wondering if the Talon had been stationed here as a garrison trooper. Though he imagined he would find a young warrior, he wasn't surprised. The Talon seemed too desperate—too attached to his worldview.

Will walked up to the stage, watching the crowd. Cam and Haley stood nearby. They looked confused more than anything. The crowd seemed broken in spirit, waiting in silence, eager for his words. He was no orator, but he would do his best.

"You know what you need to do. Comply with Malth—er, Donal. Go back to living a normal life. Survive. It's what the Talon wanted. Just know that if you cause problems, there will be no mercy from either the Confederation or the Pact. I officially disband this rebellion."

The crowd sat waiting for more. For something to cling to, but Will didn't have anything to add. He quietly walked off the stage alongside his crew. It was time to go home.

NEW MEMPHIS
GRACELAND
TAMAR PACT
30 MAY 3152

Will decided to pay the Empyrean's remains a visit while on an errand. Construction workers busily cleared away rubble and debris as he passed by, making way for the new building that would take its place.

When he had returned to base after the ordeal in Gallatin, Will discovered the nature of the Talon's "gift." Colonel Chester Barnes informed him that on the very night of his duel, Falcon sympathizers had bombed the Empyrean. It turned out a significant number of staff members were undercover rebels, and had hidden explosives throughout the nightclub. Casualties were high, but Malthus had managed to weasel away. Still, Will and his crew were paid well for the job. As far as anyone was concerned, any large-scale rebellions had come to an end.

The futility of the Talon's plans bothered Will more than it should. On some level, he thought he should be glad his realist outlook trumped those bizarre ideals, but to see hope die brought him no joy.

While he once saw the rebels as "just another problem" for the Bleeding Eagles, he could not help but see how Donal's society supplanted the old. Will certainly wasn't ready to give up his life's career for some humanitarian effort, but something bore into the back of his mind: a gnawing discomfort, trying to weigh right and wrong. It distracted him more often than he liked, and he tried his best to remind himself that he was a merc, and a job was a job.

On a street corner across from the new construction site, Will happened to see an old man peddling kitschy merchandise. Despite the colorful array of T-shirts, dolls, magnets, and other eclectic goods, Will wondered if behind the bright smile the man wore, he hid the severest feelings of hatred and pride, ready to erupt. He hadn't believed in much of anything in his life, and he always thought anyone who put too much faith in anything was a fool. But now he couldn't help but admire, at least on some level, the Talon's faith that the world could be better, even if he thought the Clan's ways were misguided.

He imagined he would soon discover if killing the Talon had truly ended their resistance, or if he had merely created a martyr.

Maybe, he thought, *these Falcons are just nesting.*

VOICES OF THE SPHERE: STOLEN LIFE

MIKE MILLER

17 JANUARY 3152

In my forty-two years, I worked my way up to grade 15, secured a place in a merchant JumpShip crew, and praised the Falcons and the Clan way of life all the way. Now I have done something Malvina Hazen would have shot me for: I learned. I learned about foreigners, and I learned they had something we do not: long lives. Good lives, too.

My eyes were opened by a random coupling. At port on Mizar around 3145, I caught the eye of a Terran spacer, and we had a good weekend in a little budget hotel. (Weathertight, dependable plumbing, working climate control, and larger than my apartment, the room she called "cheap and sleazy" was better than any Alyinian apartment below a rank 20's.) At the end, I asked her why she'd pick someone old enough to be her father. She laughed. I was confused. Then she showed me her passport. No, she was old enough to be my mother. Grandmother, if she started young. I still did not believe her, so she bought day access to Mizar's central library, and I learned about human lifespans.

By the end of the Western Alliance, humans had an average lifespan of 100 years. Many colonies regressed for lack of Terra's healthcare system, but by the end of the first Star League, the humanity-wide average was 120. Advanced worlds, like Terra, averaged 150, and that's an average. Think how far out a few sigmas would go on the high end of the bell curve. When we invaded the Inner Sphere, the Spheroid average had dropped to eighty-nine, but there were still worlds like Terra that had lifespans over the Star League average. My beautiful Terran spacer said twelve decades of technological recovery meant the

Spheroid average in 3145 was back to 100, and a dozen worlds have surpassed the Star League in...whatsit...gerontology.

Us Clans? The inheritors of the Star League and the most advanced civilization in human history? Before the Invasion, the average Homeworld civilian lived to sixty-two. Medicine went to the young, not the burdensome elderly, as Nicholas specified. What a pfennig-wise, kroner-foolish way of saving resources, especially once you see how skilled the elderly get in their fields. The Clans—at least the Falcons and Horses—imposed Clan ways on captive populations, too. They stole those years, so they did not have to deal with long, rebellious memories of conquest. Billions of us will be dying just as most Spheroid civilians are peaking in their careers or starting another. (I'm told the Wolves and Bears prefer a lighter hand and leave conquered worlds' healthcare systems alone.)

If Syndic Marena does anything useful with her mad reforms besides getting lynched for putting everyone out of work, it will be to give us back those decades.

—Technician Rogers, Alyina, Alyina Mercantile League

Scientist (Geneticist Subcaste) Gregerton, ArcShip *Poseidon*, Clan Sea Fox: In the low-mass, low-volume, high-value form, Spheroid gerontological treatments are ideal interstellar trade goods because of their recurring need. Obviously, control over distribution would be a source of significant authority. However, traditionalist Merchant Council members would need to overcome their objections to extended civilian lifespans to spread sales beyond test markets like Euclid and Annapolis.

Agent Smith, location withheld, Clan Wolf Watch: The good news among all the studies of Inner Sphere productivity advantages due to mature, skilled personnel is that the morally acceptable gerontological protocols (those avoiding genetic treatments) require years-long drug regimens in childhood and adulthood, plus continuous medical monitoring and treatment for dementia, cancer, cardiological issues, and so on. Many Spheroid interstellar travelers—soldiers, political leaders, and merchants—are unable to adhere to the treatments and monitoring, so we are usually spared the threat of healthy, long-lived rivals in leadership and military positions.

Countess Johanna Zibler IV, Euclid, Federated Suns: Beware of Sea Foxes bearing gifts. As of last count, there were 1,127 cases of birth defects, stillbirths, and spontaneous abortions related to their "immortality pills," plus lowered male fertility. And the magic pills were just repackaged El Doradan gerontology treatments we could've ordered directly. Repackaging those pills into blister packs allegedly made it simpler for us "Skid Row hicks" to stick the lifelong regimen, but the Foxes also dropped the "alarming" original instruction guides that would've warned women to pause treatment around pregnancies, and the Foxes certainly didn't offer to train our pharmacists. We wasted three years chasing water filter and greenhouse contamination, which caused similar reproductive problems during the Third Succession War. Honestly, I don't think the damned Foxes realized what they did because the Clans know squat about medicines like these.

Baroness Lucy Small, Terra, Clan Wolf: An excellent method of establishing non-collaborationist credentials among fellow Terrans is to correct a Wolf Star Captain on their pronunciation and grammar of Star League Standard English. They've rather got the idea that they're the defenders of the language. I ended the factual element of the debate by providing numerous family holovids of my late grandfather chumming about with his classmate, future First Lord Richard Cameron, and both of them were using a plethora of contractions and curses. But the evidence was apparently enraging. I don't think the puppy considered what "one hundred years of fencing practice" meant before insisting on a physical resolution with weapons of my choice. The wait for a cloned replacement nose was instructive to the puppy, anyway.

Technician [name withheld on request], Csesztreg, Clan Hell's Horses: Chingis Khan Hazen is the greatest of Khans. She is not dead, you know. She just had to go undercover to fight the Belters when ilSurat Alaric sold out for the Belter immortality serum. They make that from Trueborn babies, which are the only source of pure enough genes. It's right on the Chatterweb, do your research.

POTTER'S POUNDERS

KEN' HORNER

YPIR HILLS
RAMPART
BALLYNURE
24 MARCH 3152

Sophia Allegrante nervously tapped her aiming joystick, waiting for the cue to spring the trap as she watched her compressed 360-degree viewscreen in her *Nightstar*. Her main focus lay ahead, but on the field of battle, she knew things didn't always happen where they were expected.

She'd dealt with the unexpected before, though. If she could just make it through this one last battle, she and the rest of Potter's Pounders could finally go home for some much-needed R&R.

"Hound, this is Rabbit…" a breathless voice said through the speakers in her neurohelmet. "The Fox is on our tail, see you in a few seconds!"

She did one last check of her systems while toggling communications to her lance network. "Guys, contact incoming!" Everything looked ready to go.

Three 'Mechs from Rabbit Lance burst through an opening in the trees. An ancient *Shadow Hawk*, a *Griffin*, and a *Valkyrie* all bore recent damage on their armor as they ran past Sophia's 'Mech hidden in the foliage. Rabbit Lance fired a few poorly aimed shots behind them, mostly to distract their pursuers than to do any actual damage.

Once the three friendlies passed her position, a *Black Hawk* and an *Uller* in faded Jade Falcon colors ran after Rabbit Lance, quickly followed by a *Mad Cat* and another *Uller*. As per the plan, Sophia surged her *Nightstar* forward just as a *Loki* trotted into the clearing. The Clan

'Mech slowed, as if sharing the surprise of its pilot. Her ambush had cut it off from its Starmates.

She pulled the trigger, unleashing all her weapons except for the small laser. The two Gauss rifle slugs smashed into the smaller 'Mech. One gouged a massive hole in the left leg while the other ripped a gaping wound in the right torso, knocking its shoulder-mounted missile launcher askew, its payload facing the cockpit as if to highlight the misery of the surprised Clanner. Her particle projection cannon continued the assault, melting armor off the *Loki*'s left arm, but only one of her pulse lasers hit the center of the enemy's chest.

The *Loki* retaliated, firing both PPCs and a pair of medium lasers. One of the particle beams hit a tree to Sophia's left, sending a small storm of splinters into the air, while the other gouged a deep trench up her right leg. The lasers stitched across her torso as she steadied the machine.

The *Loki* turned to run, but didn't make it far as she continued the fight. One of her Gauss rifle slugs and a laser ripped through the soft back armor on her opponent's right side, causing the arm to fall off, while the other Gauss round caught the left knee, severing the limb. The *Loki* crashed to the ground, and Sophia turned to join the rest of her lance.

One *Uller* was on the ground while the remaining three raiders were surrounded by the rest of her lance, Potter's *Devastator*, Max's *Thunder Hawk*, and finally the smallest of Potter's Pounders, Xavier's *Zeus*. Almost a half a kilometer past them, the rest of Rabbit Lance was supporting the Pounders with long-range-missile fire, keeping well clear of the Clan firepower.

"Take down that '*Cat*,'" commanded Potter.

The *Mad Cat*, already damaged in the initial ambush, was the target of seven Gauss rifles, four particle cannons, fifteen long-range missiles, and one large laser. Only about two-thirds of that firepower landed, but the terror of the Clan Invasion was no match for an entire assault lance at close range. Armor plating flew everywhere as the assault turned the 'Mech into the universe's largest piñata.

The battered *Black Hawk* shut down its engine, a universal sign of surrender, a rarity from a Clan warrior. The *Uller* attempted to leap over the *Devastator* with its jump jets, but Potter's salvo left just a hulk to crash to the ground.

"Great job, everyone," Potter said. "Let's grab what we can and head back to camp."

Sophia exhaled with relief.

The job was done. Home awaited.

BASECAMP
RAMPART
BALLYNURE
24 MARCH 3152

"Cheers!"

Sophia raised her glass of local brew and toasted glasses with her commander, John "Potter" Peters. His shaggy hair, big glasses, and even bigger smile were how most saw him and led more than one person to underestimate what he became in the cockpit: not just an ace shot, but an inspiring leader. In fact, despite upgrading the Gauss rifles in his *Devastator*, *Nina*, to Clan-spec models, he didn't make up for that with more weapons or armor, but more communications equipment so he could be more aware of what was happening on the battlefield.

"Are you ready to get back home?" he asked, raising his voice slightly over the music from a portable music player one of the locals brought.

"Hells yes," Sophia replied. "My sister is about to pop, and I don't want to miss my first niece. Plus, Tommy's boy is about to start running the AgroMech for the first time. Carson will do so much better if I'm there to teach him instead of his dad. How that man hasn't destroyed a barn yet is beyond me..."

John laughed. "I feel you. So many people I haven't gotten to see in a long time. They're probably missing me as bad as I'm missing them."

Xavier plopped down next to them. His swarthy features made him look mysterious in the flickering firelight. "I'm glad this is over. This whole tour has been us one step ahead of the Grim Reaper."

Potter nodded. "It's certainly been a grind. Our spares are running low, our munitions are almost gone, and worst of all, the liquor cabinet is empty!"

Sophia groaned. "My dream vacation is now getting back to boring old home."

"Well, I wouldn't say no to a swing by a Pleasure Circus," Xavier grumbled, "but yeah, I'd rather retire than do another fight right now."

Potter slapped the table. "C'mon, guys, we've made it through. Just a few weeks of boring transit now. Keep focusing on getting back home."

"And all the loot to spend!" Sophia whooped.

"Yeah, I didn't expect to get out so easily against Clanners. Plus, that *Black Hawk* still moving will make selling it a lot easier. Maybe the baron will give us a fair price to leave it here. Either way, I figure we get three months' paid leave before we need to start finding the next contract."

Sophia nodded. She was about to continue the conversation, but the music and dancing suddenly stopped. Kommandant Ostberg's noteputer was beeping. As the head of Ballynure's armed forces, he was their liaison to Baron Singh, the local noble.

"Everyone gather about," Ostberg called in his deep voice with a Swedenese accent.

The group of mercenaries and Ballynurites formed a semicircle as Ostberg stood up his 'puter on a collapsible table.

The face of Baron Singh appeared on the screen, his long beard and ornate crown unable to both fit on the screen at the same time. "Congratulations on your success! These Clan raiders have been a plague upon our society ever since we won our freedom from them, acting more like pirates than conquerors. Tamar was unable to assist us, but our armed forces, along with these wonderful mercenaries, finally defeated them! We will enjoy our respite from them with a banquet when you all return to the palace!"

The camp cheered and clapped, and the baron paused until the group quieted down.

"Now the current threat is gone, but we will certainly face future challenges. It is apparent that the people of Ballynure need an increase in defensive firepower. To that end, I am inviting Potter's Pounders to become official members of the Ballynure Defense Force!"

He waited for more applause, but was met with silence and an exchange of glances among the gathered group.

He cleared his throat and said, "I know your worth. You will each be paid three thousand ryu per month!"

Potter stood up and moved a little closer to the 'puter. "Thank you for your, uh, generous offer, Lord Singh, but we have families elsewhere. We were glad to help your defense, but now that the contract is finished, we'll be returning home."

"Ryu?" Max muttered under his breath. "I'll have to go to New Samarkand to get groceries!"

"Nonsense. Your families are more than welcome here."

Potter shook his head. "I'm sorry, but no. We have obligations back home, and we're already scheduled to ship out tomorrow."

"*No*?" Baron's Singh's face reddened with rage. "How dare you turn down such an opportunity when presented with a challenge!"

"Again, thank you, but as we discussed with your representatives, we're just here to fulfill the contract."

"Cowardly thieves! You will join us as comrades or as prisoners, your choice!"

The transmission ended.

Kommandant Ostberg looked paler than usual and glanced around, as if looking for someone to take command of the situation.

The four mercenaries, along with their field technicians, quickly retreated from the party.

"Max, I want you on overwatch," Potter ordered.

Max Rogers was the most athletic of the MechWarriors. His hair was cut short in the Steiner style both for ease of care in the field and a better connection with his neurohelmet. He would be the best of the Pounders in a gunfight, but he had replaced one of the medium lasers on his *Thunder Hawk* with a flamer, making it the ultimate deterrent for both dismounted soldiers and the 'Mechs of Ballynure's militia.

"Sophia, Xavier, grab a rifle and keep an eye out." Potter hesitated a second. "And grab a headset. I want you guys looped in."

"Rach," he continued to the senior field tech, "take your crew and grab anything that's super valuable. We want to be out of here in thirty. I'm going to fire up *Nina* and get in contact with the DropShip."

Sophia grabbed an assault rifle and kept an eye out while the technicians were packing, but she listened in as Potter and Ostberg conversed.

"Lieutenant Peters," Ostberg said, "our lord was a bit hasty in his request—"

"You got that right."

"—but we have suffered a long time under the yoke of the Clans, and he was rather excited at the possibility of long-term peace. Please accept my apologies, and let us discuss this between us as brothers-in-arms, with less animosity."

"I thank you for your words, Kommandant, but we're just going to cut this trip short. The contract is complete. We upheld our end of the agreement, so you can just let us be."

"Please, Jonathan. I can work this out, but I cannot just let you leave. I have strict orders to—"

Potter unsnapped the strap holding his pistol in its holster. "Kommandant, I appreciate that you have your orders. They are illegal orders, a direct violation of the merc board's rules your employer agreed to. You can either let us go or we can fight our way back, but right now you need to leave us be."

"Look," Ostberg said, "this is a great opportunity. You could really be someone important here. If you can't open yourself up to that, then just leave your 'Mechs and head back home. I'll get the baron to reimburse you for them. You've seen what we're up against, we *need* those 'Mechs."

Potter shook his head. "Kommandant, I don't want to insult you, but you haven't been true to your word about anything here. And those 'Mechs...they're our *livelihood*! We aren't going to leave them here to your empty promises. If the baron needs 'Mechs so badly, why doesn't he just go buy more himself?"

The kommandant sputtered, grasping for words that would solve the issue.

"Just as I thought," Potter said, shaking his head. "Even if we did leave our 'Mechs, we'd never see a single C-bill for them, would we? The baron could never afford our asking price."

Ostberg's face paled as he gave up, turned around, and left.

Sophia gripped her rifle tighter. She was glad to see him go.

UNKNOWN VALLEY
RAMPART
BALLYNURE
24 MARCH 3152

The march was quiet, Sophia noticed from the cockpit of her *Nightstar*. Radar, sensor sweeps, and eyesight were the best way to detect the opposition, yet psychologically, silence seemed beneficial. Sophia and Max led the way, with the other pair in the rear and three armored crawlers between them. Armored against insurgents or an infantry squad, the vehicles would, at best, only be able to withstand a couple salvos from one of the BDF's 'Mechs.

Alarms quickly shattered the quiet, alerting her to the incoming missile spread. Over two dozen flew at them, about half peppering the side of Max's *Thunder Hawk*.

Tracing back the path of the missiles, Sophia saw the pursuing BDF 'Mechs in a grove of pine-like trees, over half a kilometer away up on a ridge. PPCs and Gauss rifles fired as the locals let fly another salvo and melted back into the trees. Eight more missiles chipped away at Max's 'Mech. Neither salvo was devastating, but with no time to repair, the Pounders couldn't endure this the entire way back to their DropShip. Especially if their opponents managed to hobble one of their already-slow assault 'Mechs.

Twenty minutes later, the scene replayed itself. BDF 'Mechs had found a hiding spot ahead of the Pounders' advance, waited, fired a pair of salvos, and then retreated before Sophia or Max could get a good return shot. And a half hour after that, they were ambushed again, this time targeting Xavier's *Zeus*, since Potter had had the 'Mechs switch sides.

After scaring off the BDF, the lieutenant called a brief halt. "All right, peeps," he said, "it's time to go bold or we don't go home."

An overhead map of the valley popped up on Sophia's display. A red circle appeared around the attackers' last known position.

"They were here, the next good spot they can get to is...here." A blue circle appeared on the map, fourteen kilometers farther down the valley. "There is a small incline up there."

"There's no way we'll make it up there before they see us and pull back out," Max groused.

"I agree," Potter responded. "That's why we're going to split up. They can either deal with the forces chasing them or the remainder of our convoy. Sophia and Xavier, you'll escort the vehicles. Max, you're with me."

Sophia's stomach felt like she'd just started an orbital drop. She was nominally second-in-command, but that was typically filling out paperwork when John was otherwise busy.

"Yes, sir," came a chorus of voices.

"Soph, get our people back to the DropShip, mission number one. Stick around a bit if you can, but don't let anyone else die."

The march continued, in a different kind of silence this time, not of fear, but of sorrow.

TAIO FOOTHILLS
RAMPART
BALLYNURE
25 MARCH 3152

Sophia gently pushed on the back of the armored vehicle, at least as gently as a 95-ton war machine could. Recent rains had left muddy puddles everywhere, but one turned out to be a meter-deep hole, unfortunately found by one of the wheeled transports. On the bright side, Sophia hadn't yet seen any members of the Ballynure Defense Force after the Pounders had split up yesterday.

"Hey, Soph," Xavier's voice whispered into her speaker.

"Yeah," she replied.

He cleared his throat. "Maybe we should see if we can contact Potter. He's got that communication array..."

She sighed. "But we don't. Maybe we reach him, maybe we don't, but odds are the locals will pick up on that signal and give them a good clue where we are. Just stick to the tight-beam communication until we get to the dropper."

Unsaid was the possibility that the lieutenant's 'Mech wasn't even capable of receiving a transmission.

Potter had contacted the DropShip and had it move to a more remote location. The inhabitants of Ballynure would no doubt be able to track the plasma plume, but their ability to do anything about it was another question. The BDF would probably just wait for the DropShip crew to run low on food and leave.

The boredom continued. It wasn't fun, but it was far better than combat, especially since the Pounders weren't looking to initiate it. The hills grew flatter, and Sophia spotted the occasional farm in the distance, but the atmosphere of her cockpit had degraded after almost a day and a half strapped inside. Finally, the egg-shaped silhouette of their *Seeker*-class DropShip appeared on the horizon, a few kilometers away.

Behind the four BattleMechs walking toward them.

The heavy lance of BDF 'Mechs contained most of their new technology, weapons, and armor. It had been far too slow to be a threat to the persistent Clan raiders, but it was fast enough to outpace the Pounders' assault 'Mechs. A *Thunderbolt*, *Archer*, *Nightsky*, and *Eisenfaust* were arrayed between the Pounders and the DropShip, about a kilometer away.

"All right, Xavier," Sophia said, "let's see if we can wall them off to the left and get the techs a free shot to the dropper."

"Soph, that's a lot of firepower..." Xavier responded, clearly worried.

Sophia was equally worried, but she kept her voice calm, like Potter would do when things were getting crazy. "We'll focus fire on the smaller 'Mechs first. They might not have the stomach to continue this if it'll going to cost them two or three 'Mechs."

A moment later, several pings lit up her targeting system, and she gasped in surprise. Four more BDF 'Mechs appeared, two on either side of the heavy lance—four lighter, faster 'Mechs.

Rabbit Lance.

She wasn't upset because of the increased firepower or Rabbit's ability to flank her and Xavier. The appearance of the lance meant Max and Potter hadn't taken Rabbit down with them.

It was just her, Xavier, and the techs now...

She took a breath and tried to undo the damage her reaction had caused. "All right, Xavier, we're going to stick to the plan."

"But..."

"Stay with me. We can do this, you and I. Look at the *Griffin*—the right side is missing, all it can do is try to kick us. Just don't let it get next to one of the vehicles."

"Yes. Yes, ma'am."

"Remember, move to the right. Let's hit that *Eisenfaust* first. It's small, and we don't need a plasma weapon impinging our firepower."

The *Zeus* followed her lead. The Ballynurites split into two groups, with the *Archer*, *Shadow Hawk*, and *Valkyrie* hanging back while the other five advanced. Sophia and Xavier moved forward as well. At the edge of effective weapons range, the pair stopped. The advancing enemy slowed to a walk, cautious of what the two were doing. Taking aim, Sophia unleashed a salvo at the *Eisenfaust* just moments before

Xavier did. One of Sophia's Gauss rifles connected, along with her PPC. Xavier landed his extended-range large laser along with a dozen missiles.

The smaller 'Mech rocked under their assault, wobbling and then tripping on a small patch of rocks. The return fire was an errant large laser from the *Eisenfaust* and a particle cannon stitching across the right side of Xavier's *Zeus*. The missile-support 'Mechs were too far back to hit the Pounders.

The natives pulled back to their right, away from the Pounders as they still slowly advanced toward the DropShip. A few small, green hills offered decent cover for the armored cars as Sophia kept her 'Mech between the enemy and the technicians. Xavier's slightly faster *Zeus* advanced ahead of her, trying to turn the enemy's flank.

After the first hesitation, the Ballynurites must have realized they had to commit to the attack, and surged again. Lasers, PPC beams, and missiles bathed the *Zeus*, adding to the previous damage. The left leg armor was completely torn open now, and a laser severed the artificial muscle there, causing Xavier's ride to stumble and almost fall.

The pair still concentrated their attacks on the *Eisenfaust*, sending the machine once again tumbling to the ground, unlikely to rise again. The BDF continued to close as Xavier limped sideways, trying to keep distance and protect the noncombatants.

"I'm out of missiles," he told her, his voice carrying a weight of stress the young man had never experienced before.

Sophia checked her own ammunition status to find only four shots left for her Gauss rifles. She kept her voice calm and slow. "Roger. You probably won't need them at this range. Concentrate on the *Nightsky*." The 'Mech with a similar name to hers was nothing alike: it was half her mass and made for getting in close.

As if on cue, a barrage of smaller laser pulses came from the *Nightsky*, along with the continuing barrage of long-range missiles and laser fire. The *Zeus* wobbled and fell to a knee, green steam shooting from damaged heat sinks as their coolant vaporized.

One of Sophia's Gauss rounds went wide, but the other firmly hit the smaller 'Mech square in the chest, briefly stopping it as her PPC etched a crater in its leg. A laser from Xavier melted the armor around the reinforced hatchet the attacker wielded.

Sophia imposed herself between the natives and Xavier's wounded 'Mech. The last of her Gauss rounds clipped the *Nightsky*'s right side, shattering the arm and the hatchet. The *Zeus*' PPC and lasers continued to melt armor off the rest of the Ballynurite as Xavier stood his 'Mech. Sophia widened her stance to keep her *Nightstar* from falling backward as she took the brunt of so much collective firepower.

The enemy *Griffin* ran to cut off the convoy while their *Commando* sprinted in to block the Pounders' retreat. With their foes closer, Sophia

fired her pulse lasers instead of her empty Gauss rifles, making the cockpit warmer and even more uncomfortable as the waste heat flowed in. The *Nightsky* faltered under the combined fire of the two Pounders, but the *Thunderbolt* unloaded its PPC and lasers, melting through armor on the *Zeus'* left arm, reducing its PPC's focusing chamber to slag. Missiles from farther out continued to rain down, as did harder-hitting short-range missiles from the little *Commando*.

The armor diagrams for the *Zeus* and *Nightstar* were full of yellow, red, and black, with a splash of green across their backs. The incoming enemy *Thunderbolt* and *Archer* were untouched while the *Griffin* blocked their technicians and the *Shadow Hawk* advanced to bring more firepower to the front.

"Xavier, get that *Griff* out of the way and get those civvies back to the dropper!" Sophia ordered.

Xavier struggled to get his damaged machine moving, but it limped toward the convoy while Sophia continued her anemic pulse-laser assault on the *Thunderbolt*, hoping for a lucky shot. It responded, along with its lancemates, rocking her 'Mech once again and opening holes up in her armor. She hit the shutdown on her ammo-less Gauss rifles, preventing the capacitors from exploding if they were hit.

The *Archer* and *Shadow Hawk* dropped another barrage of missiles onto Xavier's *Zeus*, like dozens of fiery arrows. He was unable to keep the injured 'Mech upright, and it crashed to the ground, almost directly at the feet of the *Griffin*. The Ballynurite raised a foot and brought it down on the cockpit of the fallen *Zeus*.

"Xavier!" Sophia screamed.

She had failed them all. Xavier, the technicians, the Pounders. Now only she was left.

In that moment, she knew she'd never see home again. Never meet her niece.

The foes closing on her again fired, giving no quarter.

Then there was an explosion. Not her Gauss rifles but the *Commando*. The Ballynurites began retreating.

Sophia checked her radar and saw two blue dots behind her, exiting a rocky crevasse.

She had never felt so relieved. "Potter! You're alive!"

"You're never dead if someone still remembers you, right?" he responded with a chuckle.

She triggered her PPC at the *Thunderbolt* as Gauss slugs from the newcomers peppered it, nearly knocking it off its feet. The machine turned and began a full retreat. The unarmed *Griffin* likewise fled, having no appetite to deal with the two arriving assault 'Mechs that, though battered, were still dangerous in a fight.

Nina's left arm hung limp from a destroyed shoulder actuator, and Max's *Thunder Hawk* had a limp.

"Hi, Max, glad to see you're still alive," Max said into the channel, his voice dripping with sarcasm. "We missed you greatly."

"When you get a cute nickname, I'll miss you," Sophia shot back as she returned to the convoy, which had started moving again.

"This is a lovely kumbaya moment," Potter said, "but let's save it for when we're en route to the JumpShip. I can't wait to leave this damned planet and report this sinkhole of a job."

Max's *Thunder Hawk* limped over to the wreck of Xavier's *Zeus* and grabbed its leg with his lone hand. He wasn't going to leave Xavier's body or ride for the buzzards of this planet. He started dragging the 'Mech, and the rest of the group moved slowly toward the DropShip.

Potter switched channels to include the technicians and their *Seeker*. "All right folks, we'll need to load quickly and do some repairs while in transit. Start getting that planned out. Do we have enough armor to fix all these holes?"

"No, sir," came a response from Rachel Izetbegović, their lead tech. "We had to leave about ten tons of armor back at the camp."

"What?" cried Potter.

"You told us to grab the most valuable stuff. There was this arm from a *Loki* among our salvage…"

Somber cheers from the Pounders, a relief for something finally going right, poured through the speakers.

"Good job, guys," Potter said. "Let's go home. There are some people I haven't seen in a good long while."

"Amen to that," Sophia agreed.

It looked like she'd meet her new niece after all.

TDK-7Z THUNDER HAWK

Mass: 100 tons
Chassis: Norse Heavy XTI-5 Composite
Power Plant: Vlar 300 XL
Cruising Speed: 32 kph
Maximum Speed: 54 kph
Jump Jets: None
    Jump Capacity: None
Armor: ArcShield Heavy Type K
Armament:
    3 Magna Strongbow Thunderbolt-20 Missile Launchers
    4 Defiance Model XII Extended-Range Medium Lasers
Manufacturer: Norse-Storm BattleMechs Inc.
    Primary Factory: Loxley
Communications System: Tek BattleCom
Targeting and Tracking System: DLK Type Phased Array Sensor System

Though Norse-Storm's reintroduction of the *Thunder Hawk* garnered lavish praise in the wake of the Clan Invasion, the Star League brute's second lease on life proved turbulent. Intended as the young company's flagship design, the Loxley manufacturing plant struggled to meet demand for new orders and spare parts. The *Thunder Hawk*'s firepower and excellent computer systems remained very popular with MechWarriors lucky enough to procure one, but frustrated quartermasters began to lose interest. The *Thunder Hawk* steadily bled market share to competitors, such as Defiance Industries' venerable *Atlas* and Arc-Royal MechWorks' licensed *Viking IIC*, until the chaos of the Blackout compelled Norse-Storm to substantially reimagine their standby design.

Capabilities

Taking their cue from the popular -7KMA variant, Norse-Storm's design team opted to move the *Thunder Hawk* out of the direct battle line and into a fire-support role. This justified a radical rework of the ancient 'Mech's internal architecture with modern composite structural components to make room for a main battery that would truly stand out: three mammoth class-20 Thunderbolt missile launchers. These allow the new TDK-7Z to hurl 'Mech-shattering projectiles at standoff ranges: marketing films feature a lance of *Thunder Hawks* obliterating an entire company of opponents in a single salvo. While it meets the brief for uniqueness, considerable compromises are inherent in the -7Z's design. Even a team of 32nd-century designers proved unable to overcome idiosyncrasies in the *Thunder Hawk* that preclude mounting

CASE, leaving the ammunition unprotected within the fragile composite framework. When pressed on this point by industry observers, Norse-Storm's customer-relations representative posited that innovation requires a willingness to test the envelope, and stressed that when properly used in the intended fire support capacity, the -7Z should be exposed to very little return fire before an enemy is crushed by the volume of fire sent downrange.

Battle History

The very first of the new *Thunder Hawk*s to walk off the assembly line was purchased via popular subscription by supporters of Loxley's widely beloved Estates General Representative, Rolf Christian Steiner. When word reached his campaign staff that Representative Steiner was forced to withdraw from several honor duels due to faults in his Hesperus-produced *Atlas*, they made hay in the local press about how the bold warrior fighting for Loxley's interests needed a Loxley-produced steed. Prominently displayed at political rallies, the so-called *Loxley Lionheart* is being held in trust until the representative returns from Tharkad to claim it. Baroness Iseabail MacClellen, his locally despised regent, has recently insisted the BattleMech be remanded to the Eleventh Loxley Armor to bolster the planet's defenses, given their proximity to the unstable Hinterlands, but so far, she has been unable to affect the transfer without starting a riot among Steiner's feverish supporters.

Renowned masters in the use of assault 'Mechs, the IX Legion were settling into a garrison contract on Pasig when BattleMech raiders burst from a DropShip that had passed itself off as a merchant vessel to get landing clearance. Running loose within the walls of the planet's main DropPort, the raiders compelled legitimate traders to load valuable cargo into their ship's hold at the point of their 'Mech's guns. The IX Legion's patrolling lance responded quickly, but damage to the compound's main gate locked them out. Thinking quickly, the mercenaries established radio contact with the DropPort control tower, which coordinated a hail of indirect fire from the unit's new *Thunder Hawk* TDK-7Z. The first salvo felled a *Night Stalker* menacing the tower, and subsequent volleys lobbed at the duplicitous DropShip forced the raiders to rush back aboard and burn for orbit. This expert defense of profitable trade assets impressed the head of the planet's AML merchant conclave, who authorized a bonus for the IX Legion and bankrolled a purchase of several *Thunder Hawk*s for the growing Mercantile Militia.

Variants

Norse-Storm technicians sought to expand on the *Thunder Hawk* TDK-7X's popularity as a command BattleMech during the Republic Era by experimenting with mating its standout computer system to a full

C3 network. The resulting TDK-7XEM variant drops one medium laser and one ton of ammunition from the base model to fit a C3 Emergency Master unit, making up for the loss of firepower by switching the remaining lasers to extended-range models and fitting double heat sinks. Tight limits on the supply of Emergency Master units imposed by the Republic of the Sphere kept production of this variant low until the Blackout. With such limitations now removed, Norse-Storm is field-testing an equivalent upgrade kit for the new -7Z variant, dubbed the -7ZEM, which drops two tons of Thunderbolt reloads to make room for the advanced computer unit.

Notable 'Mechs and MechWarriors

Captain Joseph Berendt: Born to a family who served in the Lyran military for generations after their ancestral homeworld of Roadside was conquered by the Jade Falcons, Joseph Berendt was predisposed to hate the Clans even before his unit was destroyed by the Chingis Khan's forces on Freedom. He led what survivors he could to Galatea and set up the Black Phoenix mercenary company, forever claiming the Lyran Commonwealth Armed Forces had deserted him rather than the other way around. Hearing rumors of the Falcons' collapse, he cashed out every investment, called in every favor, armed the unit to the teeth, and set out on a journey to the Hinterlands. There he means partly to advance Lyran interests and mostly to crush as many of the remaining Jade Falcons as he can. His newly acquired *Thunder Hawk* is decorated with a large phoenix mural on its chest, where Berendt paints one feather green for each Jade Falcon BattleMech he destroys.

Type: **Thunder Hawk TDK-7Z**
Technology Base: Inner Sphere
Tonnage: 100
Role: Missile Boat
Battle Value: 2419

Equipment		Mass
Internal Structure:	Composite	5
Engine:	300 XL	9.5
Walking MP:	3	
Running MP:	5	
Jumping MP:	0	
Heat Sinks:	11 [22]	1
Gyro:		3
Cockpit:		3
Armor Factor:	307	19.5

	Internal Structure	Armor Value
Head	3	9
Center Torso	31	50
Center Torso (rear)		12
R/L Torso	21	32
R/L Torso (rear)		10
R/L Arm	17	34
R/L Leg	21	42

Weapons and Ammo	Location	Critical	Tonnage
Thunderbolt 20	RA	5	15
Ammo (Thunderbolt) 6	RA	2	2
ER Medium Laser	RA	1	1
Thunderbolt 20	RT	5	15
Ammo (Thunderbolt) 12	RT	4	4
ER Medium Laser	H	1	1
Thunderbolt 20	LT	5	15
Ammo (Thunderbolt) 12	LT	4	4
2 ER Medium Lasers	LA	2	2

Notes: Features the following Design Quirks: Command 'Mech, Good Reputation (1), Variable Range Targeting, Difficult To Maintain.

Type: **Thunder Hawk TDK-7ZEM**
Technology Base: Inner Sphere
Tonnage: 100
Role: Missile Boat
Battle Value: 2379

Equipment		Mass
Internal Structure:	Composite	5
Engine:	300 XL	9.5
Walking MP:	3	
Running MP:	5	
Jumping MP:	0	
Heat Sinks:	11 [22]	1
Gyro:		3
Cockpit:		3
Armor Factor:	307	19.5

	Internal Structure	Armor Value
Head	3	9
Center Torso	31	50
Center Torso (rear)		12
R/L Torso	21	32
R/L Torso (rear)		10
R/L Arm	17	34
R/L Leg	21	42

Weapons and Ammo	Location	Critical	Tonnage
Thunderbolt 20	RA	5	15
Ammo (Thunderbolt) 6	RA	2	2
ER Medium Laser	RA	1	1
Thunderbolt 20	RT	5	15
Ammo (Thunderbolt) 9	RT	3	3
ER Medium Laser	H	1	1
C3 Emergency Master	CT	2	2
Thunderbolt 20	LT	5	15
Ammo (Thunderbolt) 9	LT	3	3
2 ER Medium Lasers	LA	2	2

Notes: Features the following Design Quirks: Command 'Mech, Good Reputation (1), Variable Range Targeting, Difficult To Maintain.

Type: **Thunder Hawk TDK-7XEM**
Technology Base: Inner Sphere
Tonnage: 100
Role: Sniper
Battle Value: 2499

Equipment		Mass
Internal Structure:	Standard	10
Engine:	300 XL	9.5
Walking MP:	3	
Running MP:	5	
Jumping MP:	0	
Heat Sinks:	10 [20]	1
Gyro:		3
Cockpit:		3
Armor Factor:	307	19.5

	Internal Structure	Armor Value
Head	3	9
Center Torso	31	50
Center Torso (rear)		12
R/L Torso	21	32
R/L Torso (rear)		10
R/L Arm	17	34
R/L Leg	21	42

Weapons and Ammo	Location	Critical	Tonnage
Gauss Rifle	RA	7	15
ER Medium Laser	RA	1	1
Gauss Rifle	RT	7	15
Ammo (Gauss) 16	RT	2	2
ER Medium Laser	H	1	1
C3 Emergency Master	CT	2	2
Gauss Rifle	LT	5	15
Ammo (Gauss) 16	LT	2	2
ER Medium Laser	LA	1	1

Notes: Features the following Design Quirks: Command 'Mech, Good Reputation (1), Variable Range Targeting, Difficult To Maintain.

WHAT NEXT FOR BLUE HOLE?

LORCAN NAGLE

Chat log from Chatterweb hidden space apparently containing leaders of the world's civilian castes on Blue Hole. Retrieved by automated Jade Falcon Watch forensic software and stored on 22 May 3152.

Francis_Crick (Suspected to be scientist caste): The room is now secure; nobody can access this space for now. I trust we have all read the report Merchant Soufiane has prepared on his travels through our nearby systems. It is clear the warriors Khan Malvina led to Terra are not returning anytime soon, if ever, and we are surrounded, with the Hell's Horses, Vesper Marches, and Alyina Merchant League each one jump away from us. We cannot rely on Star Commander Forster to protect us—it is only a matter of time before we are forced at gunpoint to join one of the nations we border, and it might behoove us all to pick one to approach now and assure Blue Hole's safety. With that in mind, I believe we should invite the Hell's Horses here. They are the only Clan left near us, they have a strong warrior caste, and they will protect us and allow life to continue as it is.

Prime Mover (Suspected to be merchant caste): Life cannot continue as it is. The warriors have failed us. Can we expect another Clan's warrior caste will not fail us as disastrously? For this reason, I propose we join the Alyina Merchant League.

Francis_Crick: Of course you do. You have been engaging in *chalcas* behavior for some time.

Prime Mover: If anyone was *chalcas*, it was Malvina, who abandoned us for her foolish errand. It is past time for someone else to lead. The reports of Syndic Marena's leadership are glowing, as we can see from Merchant Soufiane's own testimony. She has been raising a military that is not in a position to take control of their society; she is looking not to maintain Clan society but reforge it, to give us more of a voice in the running of the nation. The Sea Foxes have had a similar system for almost a century—the Merchant League just changes the Fox paradigm slightly in that the merchants control and the warriors serve. In this new order, we would not have to meet like this in fear of the warriors and constabulary even though we vastly outnumber them, for instance.

Salt of the Earth (Suspected to be laborer caste): Well, the merchants might not, but how about the rest of us? Is there any evidence the other castes have a stronger voice, because *Merchant* Soufiane spent so much time engaging with his fellow caste members instead of filing a comprehensive report. If the merchants are free to trade and earn a profit, how does that pass down to everyone else? Would the laborers be provided for in the same way as with the current system, or would we suddenly have to earn wages, and scrimp and save like the Spheroids?

Prime Mover: I am sure Marena's new order will have more of a place and voice for all the castes.

Francis_Crick: But you cannot guarantee that. What use is a new order that exchanges the warriors for an unknown quantity in merchant rule? Why would warriors protect the other castes in this society? For *money*? Would we be relying on mercenaries for safety?

Salt of the Earth: We have all read the report. You can make your point clearly without these theatrics.

Francis_Crick: Very well. We do know the answer to my rhetorical question: both Marena and Jiyi Chistu on Sudeten have contracted mercenaries—a sign of weakness if ever I saw one. A Clan that cannot stand on the strength of its *touman* is no Clan at all. We will lose who we are to the culture of the Spheroids if we ally with any of these lesser factions.

Problem Extractor (Suspected to be technician caste): Your caste has been terrified of the warriors since the Wars of Reaving. You will toe their line so long as it is less of a threat than acceding to their wishes. You fear that if we ally with Marena, and then the Hell's Horses attack and conquer this world, the Horses will kill you for disloyalty. And yet they could not even defeat Khan Jiyi, a leader you claim to be weak! With the Horses, Blue Hole will be one world among many. We have been an important enclave; we can leverage that concentration of knowledge and logistics to a far more important position with one of the other powers.

Salt of the Earth: An uncomfortable truth is that even though we have held this world for almost a century, much of the civilian castes have not fully abandoned their Lyran roots. They may speak like us and submit to the eugenics program, but the farther out into the countryside you go, the places where those of us whose genelines stretch back to the Homeworlds are the minority. We do not bother to move them so long as they remain productive, and that means their local merchants are descended from the old business owners, the same for their laborers, their technicians. Without the warrior caste keeping them in line, can we rely on them to remain passive? Negotiating a treaty with the Vesper Marches, which allows us to keep our culture intact while giving a connection to the Lyran Commonwealth for the people who want it, might be safer for us personally—we would do well to avoid the fate of Chapultepec's caste leaders. Duke Vedet Brewer can no more enforce his way of life on the people he now commands than we can.

Problem Extractor: And yet, that option opens us up to decay from the Lyran part of his nation, or what happens if he decides to rejoin them?

Repairman (Suspected to be technician caste): Only a minute ago you complained that your laborers may have to earn money instead of having their needs provided for. Now you advocate for joining a society that practically worships money!

Salt of the Earth: You do not understand. For a lot of our people, there is no decay to be had, and we need to take that into account. Just like we could have found ourselves taken to another Clan and integrated quickly, they can do the same to a Spheroid nation. The report states multiple worlds have fallen to rebellion, some apparently instigated by the Lyrans, some spontaneous. And senior caste leaders have been killed during many of them. Letting them *feel* Lyran again may well save our lives.

Francis_Crick: Another problem that would be solved by simply aligning ourselves with the only actual Clan left in the region!

Problem Extractor: There is another choice... The Malthus Confederation has extensive connections throughout the area. They would protect us.

Francis_Crick: The Malthuses are criminals! How is allying ourselves with the Dark Caste meant to protect us and our world?

Problem Extractor: They have ties to the Vesper Marches, the Tamar Pact, and many of the still-independent worlds. We can use their leverage to remain an independent world and forge our own path.

Salt of the Earth: We would not be independent though, would we? We would be beholden to these...hoodlums. What would they demand of us? Money? Resources? People?

Problem Extractor: Does it hurt us to ask the price?

Salt of the Earth: Yes! As soon as people like this discover a weakness, they will exploit it. If we ask the price, the answer may well be "We will take what we want," because we cannot stop them, and will be admitting that by reaching out to them. In fact, it is more than likely they are already operating on this world out of our sight, so finding a partner is important to prevent their predation and influence from expanding.

Prime Mover: Can we point the paramilitaries at the Malthus Confederation then? Rooting them out would be a boon for the world. And if they are not here, then it would distract them from potentially investigating our meetings.

Arrested (Suspected to be scientist caste): Trying to create intrigue could easily backfire on us. We are not Spheroid politicians, thank the Founder. This kind of scheming should be alien to us.

Salt of the Earth: This is hopeless naivete. The leadership of every caste engages in schemes. Do you think I reached my position through hard work and honesty? Or any of the senior scientists? We Clanspeople live and breathe politics regardless of caste, and learning that now would do you well if you want to attain high rank.

Francis_Crick: Wait...damn. Security software is starting to notice this room. We will have to postpone the rest of this discussion until we can safely set the space up again. Disconnecting now...

HIDE AND SEEK

SAM BARRETT

**CLAYBORNE'S COMMANDOS HANGAR FACILITY
THRAXA
MAGISTRACY OF CANOPUS
17 SEPTEMBER 3057**

"What do you think?"

"Honestly?"

"Honestly."

Lieutenant Mira DuMont palmed a cigarette, cupped it between her fingers, and took a long, slow drag. The nicotine helped steel her against the hideous reality of the machine she was about to pilot.

"I think it looks like a death trap."

Major Tabitha Primm crossed her arms and stared up at the *UrbanMech*, watching the techs clamber across it like insects. Jets of neon flame kissed its surface as they set to work finalizing whatever finishing touches they could make before it lumbered into battle.

"It's...certainly got character."

The *Urbie* was a recent acquisition. Primm had haggled it off a merchant ship passing by on their way to Vixen. The last owner had apparently been an aspiring gladiator with little piloting skill and even less aesthetic taste. Mira watched the techs scrub the last of the decals off the side, erasing the head of a coquettish geisha. She was pretty certain Kuritan women didn't actually dress like that.

Mira scoffed. "It's an IndustrialMech with pretensions, Major. If that thing could talk, I'm fairly certain it'd beg me to put it down."

Primm's brow furrowed. "It's not ideal, Lieutenant. I know. None of this is. What I'm asking is—are you ready enough to pilot it?"

She turned, suddenly a little ashamed of her flippancy. She snapped a salute, mindful of the ash that spilled from her cigarette. "Yeah. I'm ready. When you need me, you have me."

"Good." Primm's smile was warm and almost motherly. It was an odd quality in a woman who'd spent a lifetime fighting for coin. "I'm sorry about your *Commando*, Mira. I know you loved that 'Mech. But we need every ton we can spare for this. So: I ask again. Are you ready?"

Mira blew a billowing cloud of smoke into the air and cracked a self-assured smirk. "For you, boss? I'll drag this ugly bastard through hell and back."

The pirates had made landfall near Thraxa's North Pole. By the time Clayborne's Commandos could load and prepare their carriers, the pirates had already conducted hit-and-run attacks on a few scattered research outposts nearby. What little data made it out was frustratingly inconclusive about the exact size or composition of the enemy forces. They were flying in the dark.

And here I am, strapped into a million-C-bill targeting drone.

Through the canopy of her *UrbanMech*, her three lancemates were smears of infrared violet. The footfalls of their nimble, purpose-built scouting 'Mechs were feather-light in comparison to her own slow, ungainly stomping. She could almost feel the indignation radiating from the other MechWarriors that their pace would be constrained by her own.

Her fingers danced across her controls, switching her display from vislight, to infrared, to mag-scan, to vislight again. Nothing. Somewhere deep in all that snow, enemy BattleMechs stalked like hungry wolves. On vislight scans, the sky was gray and heavy and threatened a storm. *Bad omen.*

Up ahead, Jannic's *Stinger* slowly swept the barrel of its laser over the snow-covered ridge. The 'Mech's design was humanoid enough to almost imbue it with a personality: DuMont couldn't help but imagine the thing looked nervous.

She'd been assigned to a scouting lance, though her 'Mech was hardly agile. As Primm had explained it, her role was to locate the enemy, then settle into an ambush position to provide fire support when the battle broke out.

Mira suspected another reason: her lancemates. Of the three, only Youta had any actual combat experience. Jannic and Alvar were entirely green: they'd excelled in simulators and training exercises, but had never seen actual combat. Until the moment when lead and lasers started flying, you never actually knew the make of a MechWarrior, and she suspected Primm had attached her to the lance to corral the rookies if things went sour.

Still no sign of the enemy. Their lance formed a loose diamond—her *UrbanMech* taking the rear, Youta's *Panther* and Alvar's *Spider* fanning out to the sides. As they walked, snow erupted in great plumes beneath their footfalls, only to be immediately torn away by the frigid winds. Something shifted in the sky—a darkening, clouds collecting and spilling thick across the open air. *Storm?*

A crackle on her comms. "Marians." It was Jannic. Her tone was bitter, a current of anxiety in the contours of her voice. "Gotta be. Hundred C-bills says I'm right."

Alvar laughed, curt and forced. "Marians? How do you figure?"

"Honorless shit like this is their MO. They want us dead, but are too godsdamned cowardly to do it themselves. I had family on Logan Prime—"

She reached up to flick open the channel and cut Jannic off. "Hush. Keep unnecessary chatter down. We don't know who's listening in."

Despite herself, Mira couldn't help wondering if Jannic was correct in her guess. Pirate raids were far from unknown in the Magistracy; one of the consequences of living at the fringes of civilized space. Every decade or two, some ambitious pirate warband would tear across the frontier worlds of Canopian space until their mad spree finally brought the full attention of the core worlds on them and the MAF crushed them beneath their collective bootheel. In general, the Magestrix and her generals were loath to commit military forces unnecessarily, which Mira supposed was probably a good thing. Humanity's long nightmare of the Succession Wars was proof enough of the dangers of unchecked militarism. As a result, though, many in the outlying colonies felt the core government would do little to protect their interests, leaving a gap in security that private mercenary companies like Clayborne's Commandos were employed to fill. Their retainer with the duchess had proven beneficial to both the Commandos and the Thraxan planetary government, giving the former a modicum of financial security and increasing the latter's popularity with its constituents.

This new wave of raiding was different, however. Courier JumpShips arriving in-system brought stories of merciless killers striking with unparalleled ferocity and coordination. Often they seemed to have little interest in valuables, choosing to simply torch whole settlements or turn life-support facilities into slag before moving on. The grainy combat footage and IFF data recovered from their raids suggested their equipment was unusually sophisticated and expensive: a class far above typical pirates, who typically employed whatever guns and 'Mechs they could haul off the battlefield in one piece.

Rumors abounded. Everyone had a theory. The Marian Hegemony was the most likely culprit, but in the last few weeks Mira had also heard the attacks attributed to the Taurians, Capellans, Clanners, and even ComStar, improbably enough. The ambiguity of the situation made her uneasy. Without good intel, the battlefield became a swampy haze of possibilities and guesswork.

She switched channels and opened a line with Primm. Above, the sky continued to darken. Ahead, the formation squeezed closer together as the lance moved through a crevasse between two tall ridges of snow. Little eddies of white powder whipped around the legs of the 'Mechs ahead of her.

"DuMont calling in. Do you copy?"

"I copy, Lieutenant. What's your status?" Primm's voice, sharp as the ice around her. Static murmured in the shadows of the connection.

"Weather out here's starting to get ugly. Getting minor comms interference, lowered visibility. If it gets much worse, we'll be fighting blind. Should we still proceed? Over."

A brief silence—Primm switching over to speak to another officer. Then, again:

"Affirmative. Proceed as planned. If the situation gets any worse, contact me and—"

There was a long, drawn-out whine, and the *UrbanMech* stopped in its tracks. The machine slumped forward, the whole cockpit listing so that the viewport was filled with a blank white expanse of snow. The cockpit lights turned the dull amber of reserve power.

Electrical short. Mira hissed, spitting every curse she could think of as her fingers danced across the console to coax the machine's fusion engine back to life. She couldn't imagine what kind of nightmarishly shoddy wiring the 'Mech's former owner had threaded into the guts of this junkheap. As she worked, she calmed herself by vividly imagining the Orguss Industries engineer responsible for this particular insult to the concept of good taste in Hell.

She tried the comms. Dead. Cursing, she thumped the radio once, twice, finally grit her teeth and urged her 'Mech to boot quicker. Climbing into the cockpit of this machine might as well have been putting her head into a noose.

Ahead, past the crossing, Jannic's *Stinger* turned back to face her. She wanted to shout. *Keep moving, you idiots!*

Jannic flicked on her 'Mech's external speakers and moved to speak. A barrage of lasers kissed her back.

Where the bolts hit they rent armor and structure as if they were the claws of some immense beast. Drops of molten metal sprayed like buckshot, hardening instantly the moment they touched the freezing snow. Jannic screamed over the cockpit mic and turned to face her aggressor, at which point another bolt stretched out from the white and sliced into the *Stinger*'s leg at the knee. Youta triggered his jump jets and leaped, vanishing back into the storm. Alvar followed moments behind. *Good. Get out.*

The *Urbie*'s internals thrummed with fierce purpose as the ancient war machine rebooted itself. In her *Stinger,* Jannic desperately traded fire with her aggressor, her arm-mounted medium laser crackling as it fired blast after blast.

Mira gritted her teeth. *Idiot! She's going to get herself killed.*

She thrust the *Urbie* into action and wheeled it east, up around the side of the incline to flank the attacker. It was hazy on the mag-scan: quick, nimble, a thing that vanished in and out of the snowstorm haze and occasionally flared with killing heat. She drove the *Urbie* over the edge of the dune, feeling its underpowered engine strain to accommodate the climb.

Another laser lanced out from the white and tore one of the machine guns from the *Stinger*'s side. In her head, Mira ran through angles, estimating where the damage to the *Stinger* had originated, desperately trying to prejudge where the intruder might be next. She braced her 'Mech in place, switching her viewscreen over to infrared.

Gods, please, give me something—anything—

There! Another laser lanced out from the edge of the storm, a subtle bloom of heat on the monitor. As Jannic desperately tried to limp her *Stinger* away from her unseen foe, Mira squeezed the trigger on her Imperator-B and spat a volley of shells into the enemy 'Mech's side.

The 'Mech stumbled, reeled. With what remained of her jump jets, Jannic and her *Stinger* hopped over one of the dunes and out of sight. Mira roared and fired again. Her aim was off—the aggressor skirted the shells as they kicked up plumes of white about its feet. As the unseen 'Mech turned to face her, it spat a laser that cleaved clear over her head. For an instant, Mira was grateful for the smaller *Urbie*—the shot would've struck center mass on almost any other 'Mech.

Already she was circling, moving down the mountainside. Somewhere far away, she heard the staccato pop of LRM explosions. An ambush? Another lance making contact with the enemy? With her comms dead, it was impossible to tell. It didn't matter. Her strategy was the same either way: keep moving.

The enemy 'Mech emerged from the gloom, and Mira's heart leapt into her throat.

A long, ugly snout, olive-green and thick with armor plating. Two arm-mounted laser pods that swiveled to track her. Mechanical pincers that flexed and snapped, as if the 'Mech was a living thing. Her viewscreen flickered, and then confirmed the terrible truth.

It's a Crab. *By the Eight Hells, it's a godsdamned* Crab.

'Mechs like Mira's weren't designed for head-to-head fighting. The machine had a good twenty tons on the *Urbie*, with a weapons complement to match. When a light 'Mech engaged anything outside its weight class, the recommended strategy was to capitalize on your superior mobility, utilize hit-and-fade tactics, and keep your distance until you could be reinforced. Even so, it wasn't unheard of for a skilled enough pilot to overcome the tonnage gap through agile maneuvering and well-placed shots.

If it were a *Blackjack* or a *Cicada,* the odds would've been weighed in the enemy MechWarrior's favor, but something Mira could still overcome. With a *Crab*, she had no chance. If she tried to fight it head on, they would trade shots until her autocannons ran dry, and then those lasers would zap her and she would cook to death inside a metal coffin. Straight-up engagement was a long, drawn-out execution.

She sprayed another volley, and didn't wait to see where it landed. She swiveled her *UrbanMech*'s legs behind her, and ran.

Mira worked as she ran backward and serpentine through the blizzard. Carefully, she restricted her fusion engine's output, cutting power to everything but the systems necessary to keep her moving. There was no way she could outrun the *Crab*—her *UrbanMech*'s Leenex 60 engines made sure of that. The only way she'd survive is if the other MechWarrior couldn't see her. Heat, then, was the enemy. If her levels peaked too high, the *Crab* would know her exact location.

She called up her 'Mech's compass and surveyed the map of her terrain. The *Crab*'s projected position was displayed as a malign red circle across one area of the map, expanding with every second as the amount of potential locations it could occupy increased. Another burst of laser-fire lanced from the white and slashed a crescent across where her 'Mech's legs had been a second prior. Clouds of flash-evaporated steam whipped across the snow. The *Crab* was drawing closer.

The adrenaline pumping through Mira's body made her almost giddy. She imagined her death playing out, then again, then a dozen times, a hundred times on classroom monitors in military academies across Canopus.

An imagined query: *So, class, what did MechWarrior DuMont do wrong?*

A response: *Try to be a godsdamned hero, Professor.*

Sorry, Major. I'm going to die here.

She'd resigned herself to standing and dying with honor when something on the viewscreen caught her eye. A geological anomaly—a glacier spiderwebbed with vast crevasses, wide enough to permit a BattleMech. Preliminary scans marked it as "unstable." In another circumstance, she'd have steered clear, but now the prospect of falling ice seemed like the best of a pack of terrible options.

In a fair fight, I'm dead...
So I don't fight fair.
She wheeled her 'Mech around and made for the glacier.

All around Mira, glacial sheets of ice rose like the walls of a labyrinth. Carefully, she curved her 'Mech around one corner after another, desperate to shake off her pursuer. On mag-scan, the *Crab*'s signature was a ghost, bounced off the ice walls and reflected over and over again until it appeared as if it was everywhere at once. Mira could only hope it was providing the same cover for her machine.

Here, at least, the *Crab*'s engine provided less of an advantage. It didn't matter how well you could close the distance if you couldn't get a lock on your enemy's location.

As she gently urged her *Urbie* through the twisting fissures, she had time to think. She had to assume her lance believed she was dead, or were dead themselves. At the very least, whatever fighting occupied the rest of her comrades seemed to have distracted the *Crab*'s allies as well. No one was coming to save either of them.

She spun her *UrbanMech*'s upper torso in a slow circle as she moved, sweeping the barrel of her autocannon across the glistening sheets of the ice walls. One of the advantages of the *UrbanMech* was a 360-degree angle of rotation on the Urbie's arm-mounted weaponry, allowing her to cover her rear even while striding forward. Actually landing a shot would be difficult, but it was enough to give any pursuer pause.

Mira grimaced. *In theory.* Just because she had put the battle on more equitable footing didn't mean her base odds were much better. She was outgunned and outarmored in a machine she barely knew how to pilot. She wouldn't last long without a plan, and a good one.

Focus. Try to think. What did she know about the other pilot? How could she predict their behavior?

In her experience, most pirates were glory hounds. In pirate crews, reputation was everything, even more so than typical for MechWarriors. From a purely clinical standpoint, hunting her was a tactical error: the *Crab*'s value as a battlefield asset far outweighed the potential damage an *Urbie* could do.

It's not about the battlefield, then. It's about the kill.

Above her, movement. Something shifted, and a few fist-size chunks of ice spilled from the top of the wall and bounced harmlessly off her 'Mech's chassis. Her heart leaped into her throat, and she urged her 'Mech to a stop.

Mira flicked her view over to thermal. The world around her was a sea of cool blue. To her left, deep within the ice wall, a small, subtle bloom of heat slowly spread. For an instant, she watched, baffled, before she realized what it was and desperately spun her *UrbanMech* to run the other way.

The *Crab*'s shoulder smashed through the weakened glacier, its two massive arm-mounted lasers still steaming from flash-evaporated ice. It barreled toward her, spewing laser fire. Her console screamed as vast chunks of her armor was ablated off beneath the assault, exposing her 'Mech's structure to the frigid air. One alert after another popped up in the corner of her vision. One of the arm-mounted pods on the *Crab* glowed dimly, then sputtered and died.

Knocked the lenses out of alignment with that move. Risky.

As the *Crab* began to charge another burst, Mira spat another stream of autocannon rounds at it, then twisted her laser—not toward the enemy 'Mech, but toward the ground itself. When the laser kissed the ground, it sent up a bloom of steam between them, throwing off the *Crab*'s targeting for just long enough for Mira to turn another corner.

She urged the *Urbie* through one turn after another, weaving and twisting through the labyrinth. She could hear the *Crab* behind her, and she felt a slight satisfaction at hearing its loping, uneven gait—she'd managed to damage one of its legs.

The air was broken with the ozone hum of laser fire. In the brief moments when the *Crab*'s hull was visible between sheets of ice, she answered with her guns. It served to press the enemy 'Mech back, but barely, and she would not be able to keep it up for long. With every pull of the trigger, she watched her ammo readout tick lower, and lower, and lower.

Her 'Mech screeched an alert. Just in time, she wheeled her torso around to stop it from slamming into a sheer wall. She could hear the *Crab* approaching, preparing at any moment to turn the corner and cook her inside her cockpit.

Shit! Come on. There's got to be some way out of this.

She turned to face her attacker, and as she did, the solution appeared in a flash of desperate inspiration.

Mira DuMont squeezed the trigger on her autocannon and sprayed a volley of rounds into the walls of the ice around her. Another volley, and the grooves the rounds opened grew deeper, and deeper, and finally her gun clicked and would not fire. Empty.

One way or another, this ends here.

The *Crab* turned the corner, stalked a few steps forward on those strangely, gangly legs, and then, with machine indifference, fired the burst that killed Mira's 'Mech.

Her viewscreen exploded with laser light. Suddenly, the cockpit was unbearably hot—the laser burst had ablated off her armor and cut through to the sensitive internals of the *UrbanMech*'s engine. Another bolt lanced from the enemy machine and sliced her autocannon from her 'Mech's body and sent it crashing to the ground. Still another sliced through her legs, and she felt a terrible lightness in her stomach as her war machine sprawled back and slammed into the ground. She screamed as burning metal seared her hand. But she was not dead—not yet.

The *Crab* swung its great nose down, as if it were a wolf inspecting the recently dead. It stalked a few steps forward. Mira tasted blood, smelled smoke.

And all the while, she kept her hand on the controls.

I'm not dead yet, you bastard. Come on. Finish the job.

When the *Crab* did not move, she squeezed the trigger and lanced a burst of laser fire out at her opponent. It cut a shallow groove in her foe's torso—hardly a killing blow. And yet, the insult was felt. Slowly, certainly, with the callous stride of an executioner, the *Crab* stepped over her downed 'Mech and brought its weapons to bear on the *UrbanMech*'s cockpit.

Now.

She swung her laser toward where the autocannon salvo had made contact, and fired one last shot. It missed the *Crab* by mere centimeters, and instead tore through the glacial walls of ice, right where Mira had fired her autocannon.

The *Crab* swung its nose up toward where Mira had fired. For a few moments, there was nothing, and she believed with a deep certainty that the battle was over, that all her cleverness had been for nothing. She would die here, unremembered.

There was a deep groaning sound, as if Thraxa itself was waking up. She could almost see the enemy pilot's panic as—in a moment of desperate realization—the *Crab* began to backpedal. It was too late.

With a hideous, immense groan, a 5,000-ton slab of ice split off from the glacier and slammed into the *Crab*'s side. The machine staggered, flailed, finally collapsed as the weight of the ice buckled its armor. All that remained above the ice was one of the *Crab*'s arm pods, flailing, disarmed, and helpless.

Slowly, carefully, Mira DuMont released her hand from the controls and found with dim surprise it was red and blistered from the heat. Something sticky and wet rolled down her chin, and when she touched it, her fingers came back red and wet with blood. She looked back to the *Crab*, pinned like a butterfly in a specimen case, then darkness surged up to claim her and she quietly passed out.

Awake, under an anesthetic haze. By degrees, Mira returned to awareness of herself, and found she was no longer in her shattered *UrbanMech*. Her left arm was hooked up to a small battery of IVs that coiled and pressed into her arm like medicinal rope. Her right arm was gently restrained. From the wrist up, it was covered with a lattice of grafted skin, with raw and red flesh beneath. She lay back on the hospital bed, and lapsed into unconsciousness with a gentle professionalism.

She was looking out the window across the vast Thraxan tundra when Major Primm entered. Mira almost attempted a salute, but the dull ache in her arms made her think better of it.

The major's smile was almost sisterly. "I suppose it'd be foolish to ask how you're doing."

Mira eyed her injured arm. The grafts were beginning to spread, slowly returning the skin to something approaching human. "About as well as can be expected." She turned to face the Major, grunting with effort as she did so. "How's the lance?"

"Youta took some minor injuries—nothing major, less than you. Alvar and Jannic made it out okay. Jannic's beating herself up over what happened—says it's her fault the *Crab* went after you."

Mira nodded. "Good. Good." She leaned up and took a drag from a water tube the hospital staff had installed in her bed. "Jannic's a good pilot. I don't blame her—it was a worst-case scenario for everyone."

Primm walked to the other end of the room, staring out at the tundra. "It was. Those bandits were far better armed than they should've been. Old Star League tech. Someone was pushing hard for us to lose."

She turned back to Dumont. "But we didn't. We drove them back, preventing a lot of civilian casualties in the process. That *Crab* would've been a nightmare if it had supported their forces. A lot of people owe you, Mira."

She nodded soberly.

Primm continued, "The rest of the battalion is already talking about you, you know. You've earned something of a reputation for that little stunt you pulled. I can't deny its effectiveness—but for both of our sakes, I'd prefer if you tried to avoid things like that in the future."

She laughed. "Yes, Major. Of course, Major."

Primm stood up, adjusted her fatigues, and made for the door. "I've spoken to battalion command, and we all agree a bonus is in order for what you accomplished here. Right now, you should focus on bed rest and recovery. We'll have need of you soon, I'm sure."

The major brusquely stepped through the door and began to close it.

Mira croaked, "Wait."

Primm turned. "Yes, soldier?"

"My 'Mech—what happened to it?"

The major made a face. "The *UrbanMech*? Our techs were able to salvage it pretty much intact. We're refitting it now. Don't worry—this was a one-time arrangement. I'll see if we can't scrounge up a new *Commando* for you to pilot."

Something escaped from her then—a dry half-wheeze, half-chuckle. Primm frowned, a little uncertain.

"Don't bother," Mira said.

"Oh?"

Though her lips were cracked, and it pained her to do so, Mira managed a smile.

"Yeah," she said. "Keep the 'Mech. I think I'm becoming fond of it."

C.U.P.P.S. 2:
KOWALCZYK GETS AN UPGRADE

JAMES KIRTLEY

By the 3079 season, ratings for the FBS's surprise hit, *C.U.P.P.S.: Civilian UrbanMech Patrol and Protection Service*, were starting to flag. Approaching its eighth year, the show was starting to run out of good ideas, and the jokes were starting to fall a bit flat. Additionally, increased tensions and outright warfare between the Taurian Concordat and the Federated Suns made it more difficult, or more expensive, to smuggle trivids into the Concordat, which turned out to be the show's biggest market. The destruction of Samantha in what Taurians believed to be a Federated Suns' surprise attack, combined with the show's inexplicable decision to ignore the event and continue to set the show in the Taurian capital didn't help things, either.

At the end of the day, however, the ultimate issue was financial. The show's budget was getting out of hand, as it was estimated that an average of three *UrbanMech*s were wrecked filming each episode. While virtually all of them could be repaired, the cost of spare parts alone drove the ultimate cost above two million D-bills per episode.

Because of this and the increased need for BattleMechs during the Jihad, cost-cutting measures were introduced. Chief among these was significantly increased use of computer graphics to replace scenes originally filmed on location using actual *UrbanMech*s. While this significantly lowered the overall production value of the show (many viewers described the resulting sequences as "cheesy"), it also produced several new opportunities. One of these was the following episode from Season 8.

OVER BLACK
TITLE: C.U.P.P.S. s08e13: "Kowalczyk on the LAM"
TITLE: Samantha
      Taurus
      Taurian Concordat
      1 April 3079

INT. BRIEFING ROOM, CUPPS HEADQUARTERS - DAY

SUBTITLE:
BRIEFING ROOM, 09:00

We see the usual briefing room, with a series of small tables facing a podium. CAPTAIN BLOCK stands at the podium, preparing to address the assembled officers. KOWALCZYK, DIAZ, BECKETT, BUTTERFINGER, and HUTCHINSON all sit at their usual tables. Captain Block is chewing on a cigar and holding a coffee mug that says "NO" in big letters.

BLOCK
Listen up, jerkfaces! As you'd be aware if you were paying attention, last month a huge shipment of Spazz was somehow smuggled into the city.

Captain Block is obviously looking at Diaz, who simply rolls her eyes at him.

BLOCK
The mayor is becoming increasingly concerned, especially since Hutchinson arrested his son dealing at Calderon High last week. The good news for you screwups is that the mayor has secured us some additional funding, including a new, experimental 'Mech that we are to use to, and I quote, "Disrupt their operations, wherever they may be." I am to assign this 'Mech to my best officer.

Camera cuts to SGT. Hutchinson who beams, until:

                          BLOCK
    However, because he arrested the mayor's son
    last week, I'm assigning it to you instead,
    Kowalczyk. I'd say "Don't screw this up,"
    but I know you will somehow.

Camera cuts to Kowalczyk, who jumps to his feet
and gives a crisp salute.

                       KOWALCZYK
    Yes, sir! I mean no, sir! I won't let you
    down, sir!

                          BLOCK
    Kowalczyk! Shut up before I give it to
    Butterfinger. Your new ride is in the hangar
    in Bay Four. Wait!

Kowalczyk is already halfway out the door.

    There's a training manual on your desk. I
    don't want you touching a *single* control on
    that 'Mech until you've memorized the entire
    manual. Is that clear?

                       KOWALCZYK
    No, sir! I mean, yes, sir! That's clear, sir!

                  BLOCK (UNDER HIS BREATH)
    David Hume protect us. (To everyone): Well,
    what're you idiots waiting for? Don't you
    have work to do?

Everyone scatters.

                                            CUT TO:
INT. 'MECH BAY - DAY

In the background we can see the legs of an *UrbanMech*.
Unlike the usual 'Mechs of C.U.P.P.S., this one
appears pristine. Kowalczyk and Butterfinger can
be seen in the foreground. Kowalczyk is in his
C.U.P.P.S. cooling vest and shorts.

BUTTERFINGER
Wow, Jackson! This is really cool! A brand-new prototype 'Mech, and you're the first one to pilot it! I gotta ask, though--Did you memorize the whole manual like the captain asked?

KOWALCZYK (OBVIOUSLY DISTRACTED)
I read enough of it. I'll be fine. How hard can it be? I've been piloting UrbanMechs for years! This one can't be that different, can it?

BUTTERFINGER
I dunno, Jackson. You heard what the captain said. If you screw up one more time, he'll bust you so quick you'll--

KOWALCZYK
Then I won't screw up, will I? Tell you what, I'll bring the instruction manual with me. If something comes up I don't remember, then I can look it up. What could go wrong?

BUTTERFINGER
I don't know Jackson...

KOWALCZYK
It'll be fine! You worry too much, Sam. This is gonna be awesome, I promise!

With that, Kowalczyk starts climbing the ladder at the back of the 'Mech bay toward the gantry.

Camera cuts to the instruction manual, labeled "UM-L99"...still sitting on a workbench.

CUT TO:

INT: 'MECH COCKPIT

We can see the cockpit of Kowalczyk's new 'Mech. It has many more controls than the previous cockpit. Kowalczyk is fumbling to install his usual cup holder, but is having trouble finding a spot

where it would fit. He is holding a cup of coffee
between his legs.

> KOWALCZYK
> Of course, being the first in my squad chosen
> to test pilot the new -L99 is a huge honor.
> I know the captain said this should have
> gone to Hutch, but he was just trying to
> save his feelings. After all, I'm the one
> with the most arrests last quarter.

CUT TO:

EXT: STREETS OF SAMANTHA - DAY

We see Kowalczyk's new 'Mech, a UM-L99 *UrbanMech*
"running" down the street. It's a scene we've seen
many times before, except this time the 'Mech is
brand new and has two stubby little wings coming
out of its back. The 'Mech is computer rendered.

> KOWALCZYK (V.O.)
> The -L99 doesn't really pilot much
> differently from my old -60, you know. The
> left hip isn't sticking like before, that's
> nice. And they've replaced the autocannon
> with something new. The range profile
> looks pretty much the same, but there's
> this selector switch here I don't quite
> understand. No problem, I'll just look it
> up in the--

We hear the sounds of Kowalczyk fumbling about in
his cockpit. The *UrbanMech* lurches to the right,
coming dangerously close to a building on the side
of the street and crushing a mailbox underfoot.
The 'Mech stops before too much damage is done.

> KOWALCZYK (V.O.)
> Crap--I know I brought that manual.
> Where is it?

CUT TO:

INT: 'MECH BAY

Camera focuses on the workbench where we saw the manual before. It's still there.

> KOWALCZYK (V.O.)
> Uh oh.

CUT TO:

INT: C.U.P.P.S. DISPATCH

DOTTIE, the C.U.P.P.S. dispatch agent, sits behind a desk computer screen. She has a huge, bright orange perm and is wearing a tasteful, flowered blouse and a headset. She is painting her nails and chewing gum when her phone rings. She answers it.

> DOTTIE
> C.U.P.P.S. dispatch, this is Dottie speaking, how may I direct your call?

> BILLY
> Um. Yeah. Hi. Is this the Po-po?

BILLY is clearly young, most likely prepubescent, trying to hide it, but doing so poorly.

> DOTTIE
> This is C.U.P.P.S., sweetie. The police *wish* they were us. Now what can I do for you?

> BILLY
> Are you the ones offering a reward for information about Spazz?

> DOTTIE
> Oh, now honey, I hope you aren't mixed up with anything like that!

> BILLY
> No, not me! My compet--I mean, this kid Trent. He's got a shipm--I mean, I heard him talking about how he's got a shipment of Spazz coming in tonight at the docks.

> DOTTIE
Now, I don't think the docks are a safe place
for someone as young as you. Shouldn't you
be playing closer to home? Maybe a local
park, or arc--

> BILLY
I'm not young! I'm...thirty-four!

> DOTTIE
Sure you are, honey.

> BILLY
Look, lady. You want the info or not?

Dottie pulls a pen out of her enormous hair.

> DOTTIE
No need to get snippy, darlin'. What have you
got for me?

FADE TO:

COMMERCIAL

The traditional Crazy Eddie's Used UrbanMech
Emporium commercial is a sequence of quick
video clips interspersed with title screens.
Inspirational music is playing in the background.

TITLE SLIDE: DYNAMIC
An *UrbanMech* is running along a cliffside road,
sun glinting off its armor. At the end of the
clip, a solar flare glints off the cockpit glass.

TITLE SLIDE: EFFECTIVE
An *UrbanMech* is standing at an intersection of
city streets. Cars are driving by. A Taurian flag
is waving in the background.

TITLE SLIDE: DEPENDABLE
An *UrbanMech* is standing in heavy rain. The camera
pans around it, so we see it from every angle.

TITLE SLIDE: POWER

An *UrbanMech* is shooting its main autocannon with
grim determination at a target behind the camera.
Zoom in to brass shell casings getting ejected.

TITLE SLIDE: SERVICE
Dave, the Crazy Eddie™ tech, is wielding a welding
torch. He flips up his mask and gives a thumbs-up
to the camera.

TITLE SLIDE: INTEGRITY
Crazy Eddie is shaking hands with a person largely
obscured by the camera angle. Close-up to see lens
flare off Eddie's grinning teeth.

Crazy Eddie is directly talking to the camera.

                    CRAZY EDDIE
    I'm Crazy Eddie, and I've always been
    your *UrbanMech* dealer. You just didn't
    know it yet.

TITLE SLIDE: COMING IN 3079
A gorgeous scenic landscape at sundown. We see-
-almost entirely in silhouette--the form of an
UrbanMech with wings flying in past the camera.

TITLE SLIDE: UM-L99. TRANSFORMING THE FUTURE OF
URBAN SECURITY

                                        FADE OUT

                    KOWALCZYK (V.O.)
    You know, at the end of the day, it's not the
    UrbanMech that makes the C.U.P.P.S. pilot.

                                        FADE IN:
**INT: KOWALCZYK'S COCKPIT / EXT. STREETS OF
SAMANTHA - DAY**

                    KOWALCZYK
    I mean, *obviously* it's the *UrbanMechs* that
    give us our names--er, or at least the "U."
    But the *soul* of C.U.P.P.S, that's the people.

Our training. Our grit. Our determination
to keep the streets of Samantha safe for--

                DOTTIE (OVER RADIO)
Jackson, sweetie. You there?

        KOWALCZYK (FUMBLING WITH CONTROLS)
Dottie? Coming in loud and clear. What can
I do for you?

    DOTTIE (CLEARLY NOT HEARING KOWALCZYK)
Jackson? Are you there?

KOWALCZYK (FINALLY FINDING THE CORRECT SWITCH)
Dottie? Can you hear me now?

                DOTTIE
There you are, gorgeous. Look, it's probably
nothing, but we just got a call from a kid
claiming to know about a shipment of Spazz
coming in on the docks. Gave me the ship's
registry and everything.

                KOWALCZYK
Oh, Dottie, you're a lifesaver. How can I
ever repay you?

                DOTTIE
Just go get those drugs off our streets, hon!

The UM-L99 comically skids to a halt, then begins
running back the way it came. C.U.P.P.S. action
music plays, but ends quickly in a record scratch.

                DOTTIE (V.O.)
Jackson, are you *running* to the docks?

Cut back to Kowalczyk in his cockpit.

                KOWALCZYK
Of course. This is important!

                DOTTIE (V.O.)
But darlin', that new 'Mech of yours can *fly*!

> KOWALCZYK (UNDER HIS BREATH)
> Does *everyone* know more about this thing
> than I do?

> KOWALCZYK (NORMAL)
> Of course, Dottie! I'm just getting to a
> safe spot to take off.

Kowalczyk confidently flips a toggle on the console
to switch off his microphone. He then scans the
cockpit controls, looking for one control in
particular.

> KOWALCZYK
> Okay, which control was that again?

> DOTTIE (V.O. - SINGSONG)
> I can still hear you, Pumpkin.

> KOWALCZYK
> Heh. I knew that. Thanks, Dottie!

We see from Kowalczyk's perspective as he scans
the console looking for a particular control.
Eventually, he settles on a lever with three
positions. The lever is in the top position,
labeled "B." Below that is a label that originally
said "G," but that has been crossed out and replaced
with "A/M." Below that is "A." He pulls the lever
from the top position to the bottom position.

> KOWALCZYK
> Got it!

CUT TO:

EXT. STREETS OF SAMANTHA - DAY

We hear mechanical noises and then watch as the
UrbanMech transforms from BattleMech mode to
aerospace-fighter mode. There's a triumphant
crescendo of music that is suddenly cut off as the
now-aerospace fighter crashes to the ground with
a thud. We hear Kowalczyk swear, but it's mostly
bleeped out. It's clearly the F-word, however.

          KOWALCZYK (V.O.)
Dammit! Where's the throttle on this
thing? Aha!

The *UrbanMech* lies on the pavement. A revving
sound followed by a glow of light comes from the
engines at the back of the 'Mech. Suddenly, without
warning, the *UrbanMech* rockets off the opposite
side of the screen. We hear the 'Mech scraping along
the ground, then hear various vehicles crashing and
the obligatory cat screeching. The camera shakes.
Once again, we hear Kowalczyk swearing as a long
stream of bleeps.

                                  CUT TO:
INT. C.U.P.P.S. BARRACKS - DAY

Sam Butterfinger is sitting at a desk, reading
the UM-L99 instruction manual. The handset for his
phone is cradled between his head and shoulder.

          BUTTERFINGER
No... Yes... Okay, it says here you need
to "Engage the primary aerospace throttle
while in AeroMech mode before completing the
transformation process." Got it?

          KOWALCZYK (V.O.)
Thanks, Sam! I think I'm getting the hang
of it now.

          BUTTERFINGER
I hope you haven't damaged it too badly,
Jackson. Block will never forgive you if you
destroy that thing on your first patrol!

          KOWALCZYK (V.O.)
No, no, nothing like that.

          BUTTERFINGER
I hope for your sake you're right, Jackson.

Camera pulls back to show Diaz and Hutchinson at
another pair of desks nearby. Hutchinson is fuming.
Diaz catches Butterfinger's eye.

                    DIAZ
     Is that Kowalczyk?

Butterfinger nods.

                    DIAZ
     Is he <BLEEPED>ing up as usual?

Butterfinger nods.

                    DIAZ
     All right. Ten bulls says he's walking
     home. Who's in?

                                        CUT TO:
EXT: SKIES OVER SAMANTHA - DAY

The *UrbanMech* is flying in aerospace mode. It is
wobbling all over the place and is visibly damaged,
with dented panels and scratches all over the
cockpit screen. Plant matter is caught in several
places. A pigeon passes the 'Mech in flight.

                KOWALCZYK (V.O.)
     Coming up on the docks now.

                                        CUT TO:
INT. INSIDE KOWALCZYK'S COCKPIT.

It--and Kowalczyk--is visibly bouncing around.

                KOWALCZYK
     What ship was I looking for again?

                BUTTERFINGER (V.O.)
     According to Dottie's informant, you're
     looking for the...SS *Doru's Left Nostril*.
     It's listed as a 15,000-ton cargo hauler.
     Pier Three.

                         KOWALCZYK
          Got it! I see a bunch of activity. I'm gonna
          let 'em know I'm here.

                         BUTTERFINGER (V.O.)
          Careful, Jackson! You know the captain wants
          them alive, so we can find their supplier.

                         KOWALCZYK
          Relax! I got this.

Kowalczyk is scanning his console once more.

                         KOWALCZYK
          Autocannon Rate Selector? I wonder what
          that does. Well, clearly I want that all
          the way up.

Close-up on Kowalczyk spinning a dial labeled from
1 to 6. The 6 is printed in red with a big warning
icon next to it. Kowalczyk selects it anyway.

                         KOWALCZYK
          Okay. Where were those cop lights again?

                                              CUT TO:

EXT. DOCKS - DAY

As the *UrbanMech* flies through the port, the 'Mech
has various lights other than its police blues
coming on, followed by its flaps extending, then
its flares ejecting, then its windshield wipers
working, and finally its spinning blue lights and
police siren turning on.

                                              CUT TO:

Several people in stereotypical "Grizzled Dockhand"
outfits with black-knit beanies are carrying boxes
down the gangplank of the SS *Doru's Left Nostril*.
Parked at the dock end of the gangplank is a truck
with "DEFINITELY NOT FULL OF SPAZZ" painted on the
side. The dockhands point at the sky, then drop
their boxes and scatter.

> KOWALCZYK (VIA EXTERNAL 'MECH SPEAKERS)
Halt! Or I'll shoot!

They do not stop.

> KOWALCZYK (V.O.)
Okay, they asked for it!

CUT TO:

Exterior shot from above Kowalczyk's 'Mech in aerospace-fighter mode. We watch as the rotating barrels of the *UrbanMech*'s main cannon, now facing forward, start spinning.

> KOWALCZYK (V.O.)
Here goes!

The gun starts firing, spitting out a truly horrifying spray of bullets. The cartoonish recoil from the autocannon makes the *UrbanMech* start to slow. But the camera continues as if the *UrbanMech* has not lost any speed. Before the 'Mech disappears off the bottom end of the screen, it completely loses all forward momentum and starts to fall out of the sky. The camera jerks to a halt, and several seconds later, the *UrbanMech*, now in hybrid AeroMech mode, unsteadily reenters the frame from the bottom, wobbling as it goes.

CUT TO:

INT: BUTTERFINGER IN THE C.U.P.P.S. HQ

> BUTTERFINGER (READING MANUAL)
Huh. It says here "Firing the Primary Cannon in full-auto mode greatly increases the chances it will jam, and may interfere with regular piloting functions in aerospace mode."

> KOWALCZYK (V.O.)
What was that?

FADE OUT

Suddenly the sound of the autocannon cuts out. Kowalczyk shouts something that gets bleeped out. There is a horrifying crashing sound, and once again, we hear a long string of obscenities being censored.

FADE IN:

EXT: SAMANTHA DOCKS - DAY

The aftermath of Kowalczyk's assault at the docks. Apparently he has crashed, still in hybrid mode, into the side of the truck, which is completely destroyed. The gangplank has been completely riddled with bullets, and the remains fall off the side of the ship and plunge into the water. Several apparently dead dockhands are scattered around. Huddled, hands over his face in terror, in front of the burning remnants of a ground limo, is TRENT. He is roughly twelve years old. He is unhurt.

Kowalczyk recovers from his crash, and returning his 'Mech to BattleMech mode, he approaches the cowering child and points the 'Mech's autocannon in his direction.

> KOWALCZYK (OVER THE LOUDSPEAKER)
> This is Sergeant Jackson Kowalczyk of the Taurus branch of C.U.P.P.S. By the authority granted to me by Protector Boris Tharn, I'm placing you under arrest for the willful trafficking of Spazz on the fair streets of Samantha. If you resist, you will be dealt with extreme prejudice.

> TRENT (PUTTING HIS HANDS UP)
> By all the teachings of Immanuel Kant: I surrender, you psycho! Just point that <BLEEPED>ing thing somewhere else!

CUT TO:

INT: KOWALCZYK'S COCKPIT - DAY

As Kowalczyk is delivering his "end of episode sermon," he is flipping switches. We see through his various viewports as he begins leaving the port.

> KOWALCZYK
> At the end of the day, it's the knowledge that I've gotten a literal boatload of Spazz off the streets that really makes this job so fulfilling. And I gotta say, this new 'Mech has some amazing capabilities.

                                             CUT TO:

EXT. DOCK DISTRICT, NEW SAMANTHA, TAURUS - DAY

Kowalczyk heads back to the city.

> KOWALCZYK
> I mean, sure. There was some confusion early on, but I really think I've gotten the hang of it. The captain is going to have many more special missions for me and this new technological wonder for years to--

The voice of Dottie sounds over the radio.

> DOTTIE
> Jackson? Puddin'? You there?

                                             CUT TO:

INT. KOWALCZYK'S COCKPIT

> KOWALCZYK
> I'm hearing you, Dottie. What's up?

> DOTTIE
> Jackson, you'd better get back to HQ ASAP. I just heard Captain Block on the comm, saying something about "the mayor's *other* son" and "ten million bulls of damage."

> KOWALCZYK (SIGHING)
> Tell him I'll be right back.

The camera shifts to show Kowalczyk shifting the "Mode Selector."

                                        CUT TO:

Exterior following shot of the *UrbanMech*. The 'Mech transforms into aerospace-fighter mode, falling to the pavement once again. After a few seconds, we see the primary jets in the 'Mech's feet fire, sending it hurtling down the street, bouncing and scraping off the asphalt. It begins to shakily gain altitude. As it's approaching the height of the buildings, it suddenly veers into one, crashing through the corner, sending glass and concrete falling to the street below.

As the frame freezes with the *UrbanMech* flying into the sunset, we hear Captain Block:

                    BLOCK (V.O.)
        KOWALCZYK!!!

ICEBREAKER: A MECHWARRIOR: DESTINY MISSION BRIEFING

ERIC SALZMAN

LAPIZ
BLUE HOLE
HINTERLANDS
6 JUNE 3152

When the Jade Falcon Touman departed for Terra, Chingis Khan Malvina Hazen charged those left behind to hold her lands and await her triumphant return. As ranking officer, Star Commander Forster became the de facto ruler of Blue Hole, commanding her Watch detachment, paramilitary police units, and the *dezgra* or *solahma* forces comprising the planetary militia.

When the Lyran Commonwealth inserted Loki terrorists onto her world as part of Operation Black Ice, Forster lured them into an ambush using captured Heimdall recognition codes. Expecting a rendezvous with resistance fighters, the Loki team's mini-subs were torn apart by Leena's Undine militia, earning her the nickname "Icebreaker."

A fresh wave of hostile infiltrators has arrived on Blue Hole, and it will be up to Forster and her team to maintain control of Blue Hole in the name of the Chingis Khan.

COMMANDER'S CALL

"Security footage confirms the explosion at Napa Tidal Research was intentional sabotage. The infiltrators made off with at least a dozen Jonah mini-subs and disappeared. I have the crew of the *Rusalka* preparing for a rapid-response strike. We will eliminate these interlopers, just as we crushed the Lyrans. I need you to find out who they are, and track them to their lair."

Players will earn 5 XP for completing this mission.

OBJECTIVES

- Find the raiders and determine their intentions
- Identify their employer
- Defeat the threats to Blue Hole's independence

CUES

- For the Chingis Khan!
- Time to go for a swim.
- We found them!
- Where did those *surats* come from?
- It is a trap!

TAGS

- Jade Falcon Watch
- Spy Hunters
- Submarines
- Malthus Syndicate
- Mercenaries

SETTING

Blue Hole was annexed by Clan Jade Falcon in 3069, and its population is fully assimilated. The surface is covered by a lattice of broad rivers that empty into kilometers-deep lakes. A vast network of underwater channels (some natural, some manmade) large enough for submarines and BattleMechs to pass connects the lake bottoms. A few light monorails carry passengers along tunnels between major settlements, but Blue Hole's denizens primarily rely on submarines of all sizes.

Blue Hole's military command center lies deep within the underground network at Kitzeh. Thousands of other underwater habitats range from thriving aquaculture centers to flooded ruins. The labyrinthine passages offer innumerable hiding places.

Just as convoluted are the regional interstellar politics. Political shifts have left Blue Hole a single jump from the Vesper Marches, Alyina Mercantile League, and the Clan Hell's Horses Occupation Zone.

SCENES

Scene 1: Lapiz DropPort
Suggested NPCs: Sensor Analyst (Technician), Cargo Loader (Technician), Blue Narcissus DropShip Captain (Smuggler)

Icebreaker assigns the Watch team to determine how the infiltrators arrived. Lapiz DropPort technicians reveal that no unscheduled ships have entered the system. Laborer dockworkers tell investigators that a Free Guild merchant ship arrived a few weeks ago and refused to allow port laborers to help offload their cargo. Tips lead Watch investigators to a Blue Narcissus Free Guild crew, currently taking their shore leave at a dive bar. The Guild captain is willing to make a deal for information (demanding water-harvesting rights in perpetuity), but he and his crew will fight if threatened. Their information (whether bought or beaten out of them) is that they were well paid to bring Inner Sphere mercs from Almotacen to Blue Hole, no questions asked. They reveal the mercenaries brought crates carrying hundreds of tons of components.

Scene 2: Sigiriya
Suggested NPCs: Technician, Officer, Intelligence Agent

Security monitor footage tracked the mercenaries moving their gear toward disused tunnels under the Wide, Wide Sea. Watch analysts narrowed their final destination down to three sites. Icebreaker assigns the player team to investigate Sigiriya, an aquaculture habitat abandoned in the late 2900s.

The team can call in the Watch's main offensive asset, the Baleena IIC-class submarine *Rusalka,* and lead an Undine battlesuit raid. If they attempt a direct assault, they will be engaged by a platoon of parasubmersible infantry using Harpoons and backed by four Manta Fast Attack Craft. The *Rusalka* also has a Manta in its small-craft bay.

The Watch can also attempt a stealth incursion. Observation of the tunnels leading to Sigiriya will detect Seahorse-class cargo subs coming twice a day. If the players successfully board and seize control of a Seahorse, they can infiltrate the facility posing as Dark Caste laborers.

The Sigiriya facility is flooded, but the mercenaries have re-pressurized its docking port and are using it to assemble larger attack submarines on site. Technicians swarm over the hull of a half-completed Moray heavy attack submarine under the supervision of a mercenary officer and their employer's liaison officer, while several completed Manta Fast Attack Craft bob nearby. The Officer NPC is a former member of Kraken Unleashed, hired for his extensive blue-water naval experience, bringing equipment looted from Republic Armed Forces

naval depots as the Republic collapsed. The Intelligence Agent NPC is the operation's liaison with the Vesper Marches.

If alerted to the Watch's presence, the mercenaries will evacuate the facility and trigger pre-planted charges to destroy the evidence of what they were working on.

Scene 3: Kitezh

Suggested NPCs: Icebreaker (Officer), Blue Narcissus Captain (Smuggler)

With their base of operations discovered and their fleet understrength, the mercenaries nonetheless launch their mission—a decapitation strike aimed at the planetary-defense headquarters. As sensors in the tunnel networks reveal a hostile submarine fleet inbound toward Kitezh, the players must discuss options with their commander, Star Commander Forster. If the *Rusalka* survived the battle at Sigiriya, it can lead the defense.

Depending on how the encounter at the DropPort went, the Free Guild captain may offer assistance—if Icebreaker is willing to sign a planetary-defense contract with the Malthus Confederation. The players' input into the discussions can be determinative. If Blue Hole acts alone, it will have to contend with the mercenary assault force, which successfully assembled four Mantas and a Moray, backed by four Harpoon squadrons, for the strike. If it accepts Confederation assistance, the captain can call in a force of Neptunes the Guild had "just so happened" to have on standby, striking the mercenaries from the flank.

UNIT STATISTICS

BALEENA IIC
Tonnage: 200 tons
Move: 6/9
Armor: Front 22; Right/Left 16; Rear 16
Structure: 20 all sides
Weapons: Front: 2 LRT-20
Notes: Carries an Undine Binary

SEAHORSE
Tonnage: 250 tons
Move: 4/6
Armor: Front 25; Right/Left 21; Rear 20
Structure: 25 all sides
Weapons: Right/Left: LRT-10.

HARPOON
Tonnage: 20 tons
Move: 2/3
Armor: Front 0; Right/Left 0; Rear: 0
Structure: 2 all sides
Weapons: Front: 8 SRT-1 (2 shot)

MANTA
Tonnage: 50 tons
Move: 8/12
Armor: Front 52; Right/Left 39; Rear 31
Structure: 5 all sides
Weapons: Front: ER Large Laser and SRT-6

MORAY
Tonnage: 140 tons
Move: 3/5
Armor: Front 75; Right/Left 66; Rear 60; Turret 55
Structure: 14 all sides
Weapons: Turret: LRT-10, SRT-6, 2 ER Medium Lasers; Front: 2
    LRT-20; Rear: SRT-6

NEPTUNE
Tonnage: 100 tons
Move: 3/5
Armor: Front 78; Right/Left 58; Rear 38
Structure: 10 all sides
Weapons: Front: Large Laser, LRT-20, 2 SRT-6

JONAH
Tonnage: 1 ton
Move: 4/6
Armor: Front 2; Right/Left 1; Rear 1
Structure: 1 all sides
Weapons: None

THE SHADOW
OF THE MAD TEA MASTER

JAMES HAUSER

WESTERN SUBURBS OF SATSUMA
LUTHIEN
DRACONIS COMBINE
18 JUNE 3150

"It is said that his final gift made his executioner kill himself."

Shintaro Ichiyo stroked his graying goatee. His black hair was uncharacteristically long for a Combine noble, and he was often likened to a cat for his independent-mindedness.

"I'm sure you've heard the name Shoichi Harada," he said as he made eye contact with the other three seated in his neo-traditional living room. It combined the traditional samurai austerity with the twenty-ninth century "flow" style. In places, paintings and sculptures mocked the harmony of the style.

To his right was Julia Watanabe, dressed in normal business attire except for her silk blouse that sported several creatures of Combine folklore. Her long black hair was tied back, unintentionally emphasizing her glasses.

Across from Shintaro, Hiroshi Corso was dressed in a traditional kimono top and pants, as if to draw attention away from his Caucasian ancestry. His brown hair was neatly cut.

The fourth person was the red-headed Kameko Wexler. She was a master of high-form *origata*, the art of elaborate gift-giving. She was a senior instructor and occasional consultant of the noted Joyous Tears *origatadojo*. Her dress and appearance were letter-perfect.

"Ichiyo-*sama*," she said, "in my calling, everyone has heard of him: the Mad Tea Master. He is a legend, and perhaps a myth. Many have sought to study his techniques and psychology, but there is a question as to whether he even existed. We can find no records of him, which either means he is a fabrication, or all the official records of his existence were purged."

Shintaro smiled. "This is not surprising. He had a bad reputation. Watanabe-*san* and Corso-*san*, have you heard of this man?"

"In vague terms, Ichiyo-*sama*," replied Corso.

Watanabe replied negatively.

"*So ka.*" Shintaro nodded. "Shoichi Harada, according to legend, was born into a wealthy and well-connected family. All his needs were provided for, which left him a great deal of time to practice his favorite art, the tea ceremony. And he was very good at it, mastering its every intricacy. He made a name for himself at court in Imperial City by entertaining eminent guests at his tea house.

"After spending years perfecting the tea ceremony, his attention shifted to gift-giving protocols, and he excelled at that, too. Some say the blood of a fox flowed in his veins, and he became mischievous in his arts. It became a weapon of social status in his hands, and he competed fiercely but politely in a way only a member of the court could.

"Ultimately, his competitive nature, skill, and creativity led him to driving a rival into a nervous breakdown. This came to the attention of Coordinator Jinjiro, who had him questioned. A gift he sent to the Coordinator led to him being ordered to commit *seppuku*.

"There were four individuals present at the ceremony in which he killed himself. Three were friendly rivals, and the fourth was the one who would behead him. Each of them was given one of his high form *origata* gifts. He told the three rivals that each held clues to the recovery of a priceless treasure of House Kurita. As I said earlier, his executioner reportedly killed himself an hour after opening his gift at home. The gift and its wrappings were destroyed by his family. The other three did not speak of their gifts, but held onto them. So the story goes.

"Wexler-*san*, I understand that you are an expert in his work?"

She nodded. "Assuming he was real. There have been no small number of items claimed to be by his hand, but all but two have had inconsistencies or failed the isotope analysis. Only two haven't been disproven."

Shintaro nodded and reached under the table. His hands reappeared with a gift box and a series of large photographs, which he placed before Wexler. "You may recognize the one in the photographs: the famed Tokudaiji gift box."

"*Hai*, the *Yokai*-in-a-box." In Terran Japanese folklore, *yokai* were supernatural entities. Some were helpful, others harmful, and some just mischievous.

Wexler glanced at the pictures. "*Yokai* were his favorite subject. In fact, they were said to have been his third great passion. The gift this was wrapped around was a small chunk of granite."

Her eyes turned to the decorated parcel just taken from under the table. Delicately, she turned it a full circle, examining it in detail. "Tell me about this."

"I got it from an old Luthien family, recently fallen on hard times. According to family folklore, this was one of the three, like the one in the pictures. I paid a fortune for it."

Wexler gently lifted away the wrapping paper. Clearly it had been white at one time, but it had yellowed from decades of age. The bow implied a sense of completion. The box itself had been painted with oil pigments, mostly navy blue, turquoise with several green splotches. She removed the lid to uncover a jumble of folded paper. She took out her noteputer and photographed everything already opened. Studying the patterns for a few minutes, she gently tugged in a few spots. A flower popped up with a haiku.

The signs have been read
Through the valley's peace we walk
The cat's mew hearkens

She tugged on another spot, and much of the origami folds flipped out, revealing a small diorama. Flattened shapes with jagged edges stood up and surrounded a central scene. In the center was a wooden shrine marker housing a pair of jade *komainu*, "lion-dogs," that traditionally guarded shrines. The rearmost of the two guardians was standing on a metal box. Each newly revealed section was carefully photographed.

"I believe the third one resides on the grounds of the Plum Blossom *origatadojo* of Kagoshima," Shintaro stated.

Wexler froze. "Not them." She shook her head. "They guard it like a hideous family secret. No one outside of the dojo has been allowed to examine it in depth. There certainly are no pictures."

"I know. Which is why I want you and Corso-*san* to travel to Kagoshima and gain access to it. Photograph it. Learn its secrets. Corso-*san* will travel with you in case less delicate means are required. He served in a special forces role in my regiment.

"You see, I believe that this treasure of the Kurita family exists and that Shoichi Harada knew where it was. I intend to find it and present it to the Coordinator. It would be taken as a sign to reinforce her legitimacy."

"I'm honored that you would choose me for such an important mission, but I have responsibilities..."

"Take a leave of absence for company business." Shintaro politely slid an envelope to each of the others. "Upon completion of the mission, each of you will receive two times more the value on the paper that you now hold."

Eyebrows went up as the documents were examined.

"Wexler-*san* and Corso-*san*, you will note on the enclosed tickets that your ship will be lifting the day after tomorrow. Plan accordingly.

"Do we have any further questions?"

PLUM BLOSSOM ORIGATADOJO
KURODA
SAKURAJIMA
KAGOSHIMA
DRACONIS COMBINE
29 JULY 3150

Negotiations with the headmistress of the Plum Blossom *origatadojo* had not gone well. The secrets of their Harada were simply not to be shared. Without the mystery, one of the school's most prized possessions lost its mystique. They did not hide their treasure. In fact, it was displayed in a bulletproof ferroglass case in the executive conference room. But there was no mystique if no one knew it existed. They had to allow the occasional peek, and Wexler had been given that peek as a representative of the Joyous Tears *origatadogo*. She couldn't say why she really needed to see it, so Headmistress Chiyo LeMarka denied her anything more than a glimpse behind glass.

Plan B involved a nocturnal visit led by Corso-*san*. With luck, the skills acquired in service to the Dragon meant they could get in without being noticed.

They both dressed for the part: janitor's uniforms, a can on wheels, a mop, a broom, and a hidden *wakizashi* short sword apiece. He skillfully picked the lock on the service entrance. They wasted no time traveling to the conference room, and she slipped inside as he mopped the stone floor in front of the door.

Wexler carefully lifted the ferroglass case away from the Harada gift box and set it on the table. She froze when she heard muffled talking from the hall. Headmistress LeMarka demanded entry into the conference room, but Corso insisted it was unsafe until the fumes from the cleaning agents had dispersed. LeMarka seemed to see through the

ruse quickly and Corso refused to allow entry. Thumps on the door told Wexler he was physically blocking it. As quietly as she could, Wexler folded the gift back into place.

LeMarka changed tactics, and asked, "What would your mother say if she could see you now?"

As Wexler silently replaced the ferroglass case, she listened to LeMarka guilt-tripping Corso to wear down his resolve.

Clearly, the woman had raised children of her own.

Corso apologized profusely. The military had trained him to be ruthless in the face of the Dragon's enemies, and according to Shintaro, they had done it very well. But that training was now in conflict with maternal authority. It existed in all cultures, but the sense of guilt was cultivated to a high art in the Combine. Corso was being hammered heavily with the bludgeon of guilt in a way Combine mothers excelled in. Wexler knew there was no sneaking out of this situation. It had to be confronted directly.

Wexler opened the door. Corso was on his knees, bowed with his forehead just touching the floor, pleading for forgiveness. To his credit, he kept himself between LeMarka and the door.

"Headmistress LeMarka-*sama*, can we talk?"

LeMarka's eyes radiated stern iciness as she turned to Wexler.

"Wexler-*san*? You come as a representative of the Joyous Tears and then commit an act of burglary? Has your *origatadojo* put you up to this, or do you feel no compunction about dragging them down with you?"

"I assure you, LeMarka-*sama*, that this is not an act of burglary or espionage, and I do not represent the Joyous Tears in this manner. I can, however, make this right."

"Really?" Skepticism filled her voice.

"Please come in and sit down."

The two women sat at the table. Corso entered and stood off to the side, his eyes downcast. Clearly, he was still suffering from the effects of the guilt attack.

"Please let me assure you that nothing is any different than it was when you last left it. I needed to examine your Harada in detail for a client."

"Espionage?" The headmistress folded her arms.

"It was not done for competitive or prestige purposes. I am acting on behalf of a client who needs information on the three final Harada gifts."

"You did all of this in pursuit of rumors?"

"Why do you keep one of these rumors behind glass and clearly protected by an electronic security system? And how did you get here so fast anyway?"

"I was working late."

"An admirable work ethic." Wexler bowed to LeMarka.

"*Domo arigato*. I take it you've examined this one already?" LeMarka gestured to the case.

"I have. I have also studied the public images of the Tokudaiji gift box. My client has acquired the third one."

LeMarka's eyebrows shot up.

"It has been isotope-analyzed to the correct period and the style is consistent with the other two. My apology will be in the form of these holo-images."

Wexler took out her communication device and transferred the images to LeMarka's device. "My school has not seen these. You and I are the only two *origata* masters who now know the form all three have taken. Are these images a sufficient apology?"

LeMarka's eyes were locked on her screen. "Almost." She looked up and smiled. "I need to balance the scales with one of our competitors, and it seems that you two have the proper skill set to do it."

AUTUMN BREEZE ORIGATADOJO
KURODA
SAKURAJIMA
KAGOSHIMA
DRACONIS COMBINE
2 AUGUST 3150

Two nights later, Wexler was perched atop a slope overlooking their target. LeMarka wanted copies of the Autumn Breeze's origami, haiku, and witticism books, so Corso was sent in to get pictures. The structure of the *origatadojo* seemed to imply it was born a normal office building, but add-ons gave it the styling of an Edo-era castle. Corso had been inside for two hours.

A fire alarm sounded. From her vantage point among the bushes, she eyed a figure bursting through the door. It turned and began scaling the hill. She glanced back at the building, where the doors slid open and several human-sized cartoon characters stepped through with their arms outstretched in welcome.

They were on fire.

Corso pushed silently through the bushes and squatted beside Wexler. The wailing of an emergency vehicle grew closer.

"What happened? They weren't supposed to notice there was a break-in."

"It was their damn animatronic greeters." He nodded at the burning figures. "I guess someone left them in standby mode instead of shutting them completely off. They're activated by motion sensors, and they all tried to greet me with a hug after I left the vault."

Fire and police vehicles pulled up in front and their crews deployed quickly. A giant panda, a cat, and a bunny with ecstatically happy faces turned to the first responders in a fiery welcome.

"They had an eternal flame burning, and one thing led to another."

The cartoon robots stepped down the incline in front of the door and happily marched on the emergency responders. The police drew their weapons, and the firefighters grabbed their axes. The panda went face down in a hail of gunfire as the firefighters hacked away at the cat and the bunny, who cheerfully waved their burning arms.

"We have what we came for. We should leave while they're distracted."

They headed to their ground car a few blocks away and casually drove away. Wexler was puzzled. For a former DCMS commando, Corso wasn't doing so well. Her curiosity got the better of her. Rather than an outright confrontation, she asked, "How did you and Ichiyo-*san* meet?"

He cheered a little. "We both served in the First Amphigean. His company was assigned to escort my unit on a headhunting mission during the last battles of the Nova Cat rebellion. It was on this world, a few hours west of here. Our final victory in that conflict." His voice dropped. "But we both experienced personal downfalls."

He paused, as if unsure of how to go on. "The *tai-i* was a superb MechWarrior. He was in the air more than he was on the ground as he bounced around the Nova Cats and picked them off. The pilot of a *Nobori-nin* got in a lucky salvo that knocked him down, set off his ammo, and gave him a bad case of neurofeedback. The neural damage ended his military career. We met at a cafe while he was convalescing. When he heard I'd been invited to leave the service, he took me back to Luthien with him. We bonded because we'd both been forced out for circumstances beyond our control."

Wexler hesitated. "Forgive me if I'm prying, but why were you forced out?"

A set of headlights passed before he replied. "My superiors concluded that I'd done nothing wrong. But considering how our best plans unfolded, they decided I was dangerously unlucky. I think it all started when we ran afoul of that black-painted *Nova Cat* OmniMech."

PLUM BLOSSOM ORIGATADOJO
KURODA
SAKURAJIMA
KAGOSHIMA
DRACONIS COMBINE
3 AUGUST 3150

"I trust that all is in order." Wexler bowed and paused. "What have you learned about the Harada in your possession?"

LeMarka flipped through the last of the images. "All right, you have held up your part of the bargain. And the burning bots were a nice touch. The police recordings are all over social media."

She chuckled and gracefully strode over to the display case protecting the box. With great care, she removed the case and carefully placed the Harada on the table. The box itself was wrapped in white. Painted on the lid was a black horse with a brown dot beneath its tail and a blue man standing behind it with a broom. Within the box, an origami scene unfolded. The blue man with the broom grasped a red dragon. Another tab was pulled, and the blue man stabbed a black dragon. A third tab, and a black figure with the *kanji* for Harada held a box whose lid was partially up, revealing a pair of eyes. The black figure appeared to sneak the box away from the blue figure. In the center of the origami was the apparent gift: a peach seed.

"This is a box of stories. The symbol on the top, the blue figure with the black horse, represents a tragedy for the blessed Kurita family." LeMarka bowed as she spoke the family name. "It represents the first of the Von Rohrs."

The Von Rohrs were a shameful aberration to the Draconis Combine. Marika Kurita fell in love with her stablehand, Werner Von Rohrs, and bore his child. The child, Nihongi Von Rohrs, successfully executed a coup against the main Kurita line and took the throne in 2421. A cadet branch of the Kurita family took it back in 2510.

"Obviously, as a commoner, he was colored blue, whereas the lady is characterized by the aristocratic black. Inside the box, you see the first scene of the foul stablehand violating the sanctity of Marika Kurita's person with his lusts. In the next scene, one of Shoichi Harada's ancestors takes possession of the rumored long-lost Kurita family treasure during the misrule of that cursed line. Apparently, the family kept it hidden until Harada made his gift boxes."

"Then this box represents an explanation." Wexler nodded. "The Harada family took the treasure into protective custody so the Von Rohrs could not destroy it during their reign. Generations later, Harada decided to return it, but ran afoul of the Coordinator before he did. It was his way of saying 'I'll give it back, but I'm not going to make it easy.' Perhaps it was his revenge for ordering his execution."

LeMarka smiled. "Perhaps."

WESTERN SUBURBS OF SATSUMA
LUTHIEN
DRACONIS COMBINE
15 SEPTEMBER 3150

"And that is what the Plum Blossom's Harada seems to mean."

"Hmm," Shintaro acknowledged in his neutral manner.

"Watanabe-*san* and I have had time to examine the Tokudaiji gift box. As previously mentioned, the box was filled with *yokai*. A scarlet phoenix, a white tiger, a turtle and snake combination, a blue-green dragon, a rabbit in the moon, a three-legged crow, and a two-headed bird. A Terran would recognize all of these as constellations. Of course, on other worlds there are other constellations, so these are not readily recognizable to most people. There was also a fox, an old-fashioned wagon, a unicorn, and a badger.

"We assumed that these represented the constellations that could be seen from the world on which the treasure resides. The only world that has all these constellations is Soverzene, in its northern hemisphere.

"The Plum Blossom Harada told us how the Kurita family treasure got there, and I believe that the Harada now in our possession will give us the geographic location of the treasure. We all have a long trip ahead of us to Soverzene. That should give us time to work through the secrets of the box."

"But Ichiyo-*sama*, Soverzene is now a Rasalhague Dominion world," Corso politely pointed out.

"I know. Fortunately, I am proficient with the family *Panther.*"

Corso's brows knitted together in concern. "*Hai*, but it isn't fast enough to be a good raider. Will the Dragon lend us a regiment to aid us?"

Shintaro smiled. "Of course not. But you are correct, the raiding approach will not work. I have something else in mind."

VENDERELLE DROPPORT
VENDERELLE CITY OUTSKIRTS
SOVERZENE
RASALHAGUE DOMINION
5 NOVEMBER 3150

Shintaro Ichiyo watched the DropShip impatiently. It was parked just off the runway, and the cargo bay door was half raised. Due to a centuries-old modification, the doors would open no farther, so Shintaro's *Panther* BattleMech had been loaded into the DropShip on its back on rollers and now had to be unloaded the same way.

Upon arriving in orbit, he had hailed the senior military commander on-planet, Galaxy Commander Timon Hall, and explained why he had come. Not unexpectedly, the Galaxy Commander had denied him permission to land, so he issued a combat challenge for the right to conduct his search. Now at the spaceport, Galaxy Commander Hall was several hundred meters away with a small group of warriors sitting on the ground. Each warrior was either drawing or painting on paper, canvas, or a computer tablet.

Shintaro's curiosity got the better of him, so he and his three team members approached the Dominion warriors. "Good morning, Galaxy Commander."

"Good morning, *Tai-i* Ichiyo." Hall nodded back. He was of medium height, with brown hair that was graying at the temples.

"You may call me Ichiyo-*san*." He was reluctant to mention that he had retired from service. He gestured toward the drawing warriors. "What's going on here?"

The Galaxy Commander grinned. "They are competing for the right to face you in combat. There was a request to do the bidding a little differently, especially considering what you are bringing to the trial. So, it will be a test of their artistic skills instead. When I heard about the artistic trial, I was intrigued and decided to attend. They have one hour after the bay door opens to complete their work. The subject is their interpretation of the scene before us."

"Why this?"

"The absurdity of transporting a BattleMech in such a manner merited an artistic tribute. I am surprised the DCMS could not spare a more suitable DropShip for this mission."

"This was more of a personal mission. I chose not to get them involved."

"I see," Hall replied as he watched the unloading progress with his hands clasped behind his back. The chronometer on his wrist beeped. "The time is up."

The warrior artists turned their works to the Galaxy Commander. He made his way down the line regarding each one. The first was a realistic portrayal of the cargo bay with a red 'Mech on its back. There were a pair of others done in a realist style with lesser degrees of skill. Another portrayed the same scene in a Cubist style and another in an abstract style with exaggerated colors.

Hall paused in front of one in particular and grinned. It was also in the realist style, but in place of the BattleMech, a giant red tabby cat pushed angrily against the hull of the DropShip to free itself as bits of fur flew down to the ferrocrete. "Star Captain Evelyn Carrera, you have won the bidding."

"Thank you, sir." She stood up and her brown ponytail whipped around as she turned her head toward Shintaro. "How much combat experience have you had, *Tai-i*?"

"Well, it's been a few years, but—"

"I will pilot a *Bear Cub*." She turned back to the Galaxy Commander. "I choose the southwestern section of the Gingerwine Forest as the battlefield."

Two hours later, Shintaro stomped through a hilly landscape dominated by islands of trees. The neurofeedback injury that necessitated his retirement didn't seem to impede him significantly, but when the real shooting started, the vertigo could come into play again.

He was deeply worried this could be a fool's errand. It could be his *last* fool's errand. But since his injury had forced his retirement, his life lacked meaning. He would get up in the morning, search desperately for something to do all day, and then go to sleep. His wife insisted he get a hobby or a job to keep him busy, and his children had moved out long ago, leaving them with an empty nest. He found a hobby eventually, and it brought him to this awkward moment in time. He needed to find his mythical treasure. It would prove he still mattered.

The thought passed, and he considered the curious choice of terrain. His opponent had twice his speed, so she might prefer more open terrain. His jump jets would allow him to bounce in and out of forests, giving him some edge. He had a range advantage in weapons, so the trees may have been calculated to cancel that out. Mostly, he was hoping she had chosen this location so she had a scenic spot to fight in.

He paused his 'Mech and studied the seismic sensors for activity. Within moments, he had a contact vectoring on him. He pulled back within the edge of the trees in time to see her white *Bear Cub* running down an open corridor in the landscape. The left arm and right leg faded to gray while the other set was painted in blue flame.

A pair of red beams scorched the trees around him and took a chunk out of his torso armor. As she strafed by, he raised his ER large laser and fired, partially damaging her left leg. He triggered his jump jets to see where she was going, but she disappeared behind a stand of trees. As he landed, he recognized the uncomfortable tingle in his stomach that was the first sign of vertigo.

She went right, so he bore left, hoping to find a trail that would allow him to get right in front of her so he could unleash his full arsenal. She flashed across his path, and he turned around and ran the other direction. She seemed to be pursuing a similar strategy, except she was trying to come up behind him.

He scanned as he ran and suddenly caught her racing toward him in a gap to his left. He fired his large laser and medium pulse laser; both missed. She burned armor off his arm with her medium laser and hit his left torso with one of four short-range missiles, then stomped off through a gap in the trees.

He felt his gyro wobble through his neurohelmet, unbalancing his own brain. Closing his eyes briefly, he charged into a large open field so she couldn't flank him before he had a chance to turn. He waited.

Seconds agonizingly passed by before she crashed through the trees from another direction and charged across the field against his left. His Streak SRMs declined to fire, but his medium pulse laser hit her left arm. One of her medium lasers and three long-range missiles blasted more armor off his left torso armor as he swiveled to bring his large laser to bear. His targeting reticule flashed green, and he fired his large laser as both of her arms sliced the air with red light.

His world spun as his gyro lost the battle to keep his 'Mech upright. His head banged around in his helmet, and then he felt the moving stop. He opened his eyes against the nausea and looked at his damaged wireframe. His torso and arm were outlined in yellows and oranges. He closed his eyes as he struggled to stand his 'Mech up. The first thing he saw outside the view screen was a severed white leg with painted blue flames. Looking downward, he saw the rest of the *Bear Cub* on the ground in front of him.

He opened communications and ordered his opponent to yield, then closed his eyes and breathed deeply to clear the vertigo.

"Ichiyo-*sama*, the damage may be bad, but at least you are alive, and the mission is on track," Julia Watanabe offered helpfully.

Shintaro grunted.

He watched in dismay as the DropShip crew began loading his partially mangled *Panther* back into the cargo hold. He glanced at Corso and silently wondered if he should have taken the *Panther* into battle instead. Corso did have training as a MechWarrior. He dismissed the thought, knowing it would undermine his effort to be useful again.

Shintaro took a deep breath and decided to move on. "Now we will need a good map."

**IGA VALLEY
SOVERZENE
RASALHAGUE DOMINION
7 NOVEMBER 3150**

"We really should've camped by the truck or found lodging in the village," Julia Watanabe mentioned for the third time as they hiked across the valley.

After several mind-numbing hours of scrolling through the planetary net's civilian navigation program, Travel Soverzene, Shintaro knew the identity of the mountains they sought. The center of the Harada puzzle box matched a sparsely inhabited river valley, and even listed an old shrine, but the imagery showed a confusing jumble where the shrine should be. Shintaro had rented an all-terrain truck, and they'd spent the better part of the day driving through the mountains to the valley floor.

"Calling that a village is generous," Shintaro noted. "We have some time before sundown. Why not use that time to find our destination?"

"Sunrise and sunset are known as *omagatoki*," Julia replied. "They're when the boundary between our world and the world of the supernatural weakens. That's when *yokai* can be met."

"*Yokai*? Why worry?"

"Some are good, but many are mischievous or even malevolent."

Shintaro's eyebrow shot up. "Do you really believe in them?"

"I don't know. I can tell myself that they are not real and could not have hitched a ride aboard a JumpShip all the way from Terra...but since they're magical, why couldn't they? Anyhow, part of me says that they're only superstitions, another part says they could be real."

"This is like fear of the dark," Shintaro retorted. "At night, we imagine there are monsters hiding under the bed, but on a certain level the monsters are real. They go by the name lion, hyena, and leopard. For our ancestors on the African plains of Terra, these monsters were real, and stalked us at night when we couldn't see them. If you didn't fear the dark, you might wander off and never be seen again. Those who had an instinctive fear stayed by the fire and lived to have children. Consequently, we instinctively fear the dark and create predators in our minds to fill it."

Julia gave Shintaro a dirty look. "There are many things in the universe we don't understand. For all we know, there could be some truth behind them. I've heard stories of ghosts on JumpShips. And then there are the reports of some black 'Mech in the Periphery that sometimes acts without a pilot."

Shintaro took in the terrain. "As we walk, you can tell me more about them."

"*Kami*, or spirits, come in many forms. Some take the form of a small ball of fire that dances through the night, leading wanderers to their doom. Those are called *onibi* or demon fire. Then there are *reiki* or *onryo,* who are spirits or demons seeking revenge..."

The group continued through the wild fields and trees as Julia cataloged the many types of ghosts. Almost imperceptibly, the sun slid toward the horizon, the light yellowed, and the shadows lengthened. The winds began to whip the grasses and tree branches around.

"...and then there's the kind of *kami* known as a *teke teke*. They are always female and have no legs. They are often vengeful, and in many of the stories, you can't escape them. You can run, but they will be flying along right beside you. One was said to have kept pace with a train going 150 kilometers per hour."

"Oh, I heard about that one," Wexler chimed in.

They came to the remains of an old shrine marker silhouetted by the sky. Formerly a pair of poles with two crosspieces, one side had fallen to the ground. Part of one of the crosspieces was still attached, but its partner was broken up on the ground. Flecks of faded red paint were still visible.

"Oh, no." Julia froze. The other three paused. "I may have told a hundred supernatural tales. Has anyone been counting?"

"Why does it matter?" Shintaro was annoyed.

"It is said that if you tell one hundred supernatural tales in a single gathering, after you tell the hundredth tale, you summon a *kami*. And there are four of us. That is a very unlucky number."

The group started walking again, but Julia not as quickly.

"Watanabe-*san*," Shintaro said with a smile, "you've only told a few ghost stories."

"They don't need to have a plot. Just mentioning them counts as one story."

Shintaro nodded toward the horizon. "There it is."

In the distance, several structures loomed among a few old trees. A dead trunk ominously towered over the largest building. The grasses

seemed to wave them away as the wind cautiously whipped them around. The only sounds were the wind and their footsteps.

As they got close, Corso halted them. "Is there an animal in those grasses?"

Julia caught up as the others stared into the tall grasses. "It looks like a *komainu*." She stepped up to the stylized lion-dog and looked around. "There's the other one," she said as she gestured toward the largest of the structures. It was only barely standing, with chunks warped or fallen off.

"Be at ease," Shintaro reassured Julia. "As a shrine, this is sacred ground. The evil spirits should avoid this place."

"On the contrary. There are at least a dozen different types of *yokai* that inhabit abandoned shrines and temples."

The rest of the party glanced around. Corso stared cautiously at everything.

No one said anything.

"Let's make use of the light while we still have it." Shintaro walked up the stone steps to the door and took out his flashlight.

When he pointed the beam inside, two pairs of eyes lit up.

The party froze. A second glance revealed them to be a pair of Buddhist warrior demons staring down from the eaves with crystal eyes. Ornate pillars and carved wood decorated the walls and held up the roof. On the opposite wall, a Buddha statue smiled at the visitors.

Julia clapped her hands together twice, and the others followed suit. They all stepped inside.

Shintaro swung the light around and took in the room. "This is unusual," he remarked of a large, rectangular stone box at the statue's feet, covered with years of grime. "Does anyone see anything else unusual that was in the Harada box?"

They glanced around, and Julia nodded at the stone box. "That's the only oddity here. Maybe what we're looking for is in there."

"Corso-*san*, help me." Shintaro stepped beside the box.

Corso strode up, and together they grasped the lid and pulled. It hesitated briefly and popped off.

The flashlight illuminated a metal case. The *kanji* of the Harada family was painted across the top.

Shintaro lifted the case and carried it outside. He placed it on the ground in the clearing where the sun's rays still shone. He kneeled in front of it silently as the others gathered around him. He closed his eyes and took several deep breaths. When he opened his eyes, he smiled at each of his companions. They smiled and nodded back.

He turned back to the box and wrestled the corroded latches open. Reverently, he flipped the lid back and reached inside.

He lifted out a porcelain cat.

It was a *maneki-neko*, or a welcoming cat. It was white with a red collar and sat on a red cushion. Its eyes smiled as it raised its left paw in welcome. A golden coin was clutched in its right paw. Orange blotches seem to have been painted by hand in various places. The word *"Fuzzy"* was painted in black across its belly—in English.

"Seriously?!" Shintaro exclaimed with a hint of despair. "*This* is the treasure of House Kurita?"

FUCHIDA ORIGAMI AND STATIONERY SHOP
TOKYO
JAPAN
TERRA
5 JUNE 2027

Katherine Kurita watched her husband Takayoshi Fuchida help a masked, elderly customer leave the store. As an American, she was not as comfortable wearing masks, but now that she was living in Tokyo, she knew she had to get used to it.

Just a few years ago, they were both researchers at Stanford University in California, but Takayoshi and his research partner Thomas Kearny had published a series of papers that led to both men losing their academic credentials. Takayoshi found himself unemployable, but Katherine still had family connections back in Japan. Unfortunately, the best the family could do was to set them up in an origami and stationery shop.

Lacking any other customers, he sighed and joined Katherine behind the counter. Their son Mayabi was gurgling and flapping his limbs in his mini-crib. Their cat, white with orange blotches, was reclined on the counter and lay partially across his laptop.

"Faji, get off my computer," Takayoshi commanded.

The cat ignored him.

"Taka, he responds to 'Fuzzy,'" Katherine noted.

The cat raised his head at her voice.

Takayoshi slid the cat off his laptop, and the cat meowed in annoyance. He flipped the lid open and began poring through some data files. Fuzzy stood and stretched. With a great yawn, he returned to the laptop and walked on the keyboard. The computer beeped angrily, and Takayoshi picked him up and placed him near Katherine. "Go play with your mother."

Fuzzy walked across the counter to where Katherine had a ceramic cat. It was white with a red collar and sat on a red cushion. Its eyes smiled as it raised its left paw in welcome. A golden coin was clutched in its right paw.

Katherine had two small jars of paint, black and orange. The orange jar was already open, and her brush was covered in paint. She studied Fuzzy as she applied orange blotches to the *maneki-neko*.

He meowed, but Katherine remained focused on her painting. Fuzzy sniffed a small toy M-1 Abrams tank that was sitting on the counter. He meowed again, and when she refused to look, he batted it off the counter into Mayabi's crib.

"Bad kitty! Bad!" she scolded.

Mayabi grabbed the small toy tank and gleefully swung it around by the barrel.

"I wish your family could've gotten me a teaching job somewhere," Takayoshi said. "I would even have taken high school."

"It could've been worse. You could be a short-order cook like Thomas."

"That's not the point." Takayoshi scrolled through some pages. "It's possible for matter to exceed the speed of light. It's one of the most important things anyone has ever discovered. We could finally travel to other stars and find new homes for all the people on this planet."

"And screw them up like we did this one?" Katherine continued to paint.

"Opening up the universe could completely change humanity's perspective on everything. What will we have to fight over with countless worlds to explore and colonize?

"If I had a teaching job anywhere, I could show my students that we're not bound by the light barrier, and they could continue the work."

"Well, Taka, that's what happens when you pick fights with Einstein."

Katherine cleaned her brush and dipped it into the jar of black ink. On the belly, in her native English, she painted one word:

Fuzzy.

BREWER'S HOUSE OF CARDS

ERIC SALZMAN

The Vesper Marches are not a unified interstellar nation in any sense of the term. Duke Vedet Brewer is a master at telling everyone exactly what they want to hear, but when his people realize his assurances are no more than honeyed lies, what little goodwill he has secured will evaporate, forcing him to show his true colors.

—GRAFINA ANTJE KELSWA, 14 JUNE 3152

REPORT FROM THE NORNS: THE VESPER MARCHES

Lyran Intelligence Corps teams inserted onto worlds claimed by Vedet Brewer's Vesper Marches as part of Operation Black Ice have submitted comprehensive reports on local developments since Brewer declared the existence of his rogue state. Norn analysts have reviewed field reports and identified internal weaknesses, political fractures, and other stress points that could prove useful in efforts to undermine Brewer's rule.

MELISSIA

Since Brewer's intervention ended the civil war and eliminated the leader of the noble faction, the world has been governed by the Melissian Republic, with planetary affairs managed by a bicameral parliament. Brewer has elevated Graf Matthew Toliver to the rank of landgrave and made him the official representative of the Marches on Melissia. Toliver was aligned with the Republic during the civil war, but commands the respect of the nobility, helping to smooth over the recent violence. As his personal relationships and charisma are key factors in planetary stability, his removal may cripple the day-to-day operations of the Melissian government.

In an unanticipated development, on 13 June, a JàrnFòlk trading vessel appeared in-system, announcing itself as a trade delegation from the Klünder *sælgeflåde*. Brewer himself welcomed the *jarnskib* and its merchants to Melissia, though not all approved. Our agents reported at least one incident where operatives of the Malthus Confederation, which also trades with the Marches, assaulted a member of the JàrnFòlk delegation. The Klünder trader emerged unscathed, leaving five dead in his wake.

MACHIDA

A Lyran world conquered by Malvina Hazen's Golden Ordun, Machida saw its governing bodies and local elites massacred during the Falcons' occupation, which left a power vacuum once the Hesperus Guards drove the Falcon garrison into the wilderness. Duke Brewer dispatched former Melissian Grafina Cybele Ekonomos to rule in his name, naming her Landgrave von Machida. Her efforts to advance reconstruction efforts have been hampered by terrorist bombings, assassinations of local officials, and raids on supply depots. Our Black Ice teams on-world claim credit for only a fraction of those incidents, suggesting Clan paramilitaries and Watch cells remain an active threat.

CLERMONT

Landgrave Alban Dyhr has relied on expertise in communications and propaganda to manage the fallout from multiple public-relations crises. Though the Hesperus Guards successfully destroyed a Falcon redoubt by triggering a volcanic eruption, they underestimated the volatility of the magma pocket. Continued eruptions have forced the evacuation of the city of Ferrand in a major humanitarian crisis. Though Brewer's forces left the Clermontians with the initial impression they had been liberated by the Lyran Commonwealth, our agents quickly pierced that fiction with anonymous messaging on planetary info-nets. Between the spreading eruptions and pro-Lyran protests, Dyhr will have his hands full for the foreseeable future.

KIKUYU

Claimed by March forces, Kikuyu is more "conquered" than "liberated," having been under Clan rule for nearly a century. The mining-centric economy is based on work credits, and the civilians govern themselves through local, regional, and planetary caste councils, all of which subscribe to traditionalist Clan practices that require warrior leadership. Though the senior council leaders in the capital of Brandtfort Heights expressed willingness to report to the commanding officer of the Hesperus Guards' detachment that took the planet, they questioned

LEGEND

Spectral Class:
M K G F A B

Alyina Mercantile League
Arc-Royal Liberty Coalition
Clan Hell's Horses
Clan Jade Falcon
Lyran Commonwealth
Malthus Confederation
Tamar Pact
Vesper Marches

◇ National capital
● Region capital
◉ District capital

COREWARD
C
A — ⊠ — S
ANTI SPINWARD / SPINWARD
R
RIMWARD

Wotan (176) — 23.6 — Derf
Jump Route & Distance in Light Years

Wotan (176)
Jump Drive Charge Times in Hours (Standard)

(168) Erewhor

(187) Bone-Normar

(186) Barcelona

(190) Newtown Square

(17... Blac

(177) Mogyorod

(184) Kolovraty

(188) Kikuyu

(192) Roadsi

Hood IV

(183) Pangkalan

(205) Annunziata

Clermont
(191)

(198) Blue Ho

(188) Jesenice

(176) Chapultepec

(190) Melissia

(186) Machida

(181) Chahar

(197) Kwangchowwang

(206) Medellin

(195) Zhongshan

Adelaide
(208)

(187) Mahone

(186)

(172)

Blumenort

the right of an appointed landgrave to claim authority. They rejected Duke Brewer's representative as not only not being present for the Trial of Possession, but also holding no position within the castes' internal hierarchies. As a stopgap measure, Brewer appointed Hesperus Guards First Battalion CO, Hauptmann-Kommandant Helen Goreson, Military Governor, which appeared to mollify the civilian councils. Norn analysts have estimated the cost of fully "deprogramming" such a world at billions of kroner over the course of at least twenty years. It will prove instructive to identify Brewer's failure points going forward.

KOLOVRATY

Kolovraty is the most heavily garrisoned world in the Vesper Marches, lying a single jump from the Hell's Horses border world of Newtown Square. Following the clash with leading Horse elements on Mogyorod, the Hesperus Guards have been preparing for more fighting. The citizens of Kolovraty were far less assimilated than on neighboring Kikuyu, having fallen to Khan Ruel Chistu's broadly unsuccessful 3123 incursion. Most adults were born under Lyran rule and have been taking the lead in resurrecting a non-Clan government and teaching the youth about their heritage. Landgrave Xylo Lagana, a former Melissian baron, has nonetheless found it challenging to keep the Kolovratians in line while diverting significant amounts of their resources toward the Guards' efforts to fortify the planet.

ANNUNZIATA

A Roman Catholic theocracy headquartered in Efeso and traditionally ruled by the Annunziatan Religious Council, Annunziata had welcomed Duke Brewer's efforts to liberate them from the Falcons' Mongol-style occupation. They didn't protest the high civilian body count, attributing it to the will of God. However, they were far less receptive to the idea of submitting to the rule of Duke Brewer's appointed representative—Patriarch Anton, head of the Melissia Orthodox Church. Brewer apparently felt he was showing respect by sending a religious leader to rule the world. Faithful to mainstream Lyran Lutheranism, he was unaware of the intensity of the sectarian divide between Roman Catholic and Greek Orthodox traditions, dating back millennia. Black Ice teams stand ready to exacerbate these tensions.

PANGKALAN

The relatively brief Falcon occupation was centered on the capital of Langii, converting the city's food-processing industries to produce rations by the DropShip load. With no thought to sustainability, laborer work gangs ran Saturn harvesters day and night to process entire herds (including breeding stock) and fields of crops to supply the needs of Malvina's other holdings. Consequently, the once lush region around the capital has been stripped bare, forcing the populace to scavenge among crates of unshipped ration bars at Langii Spaceport or take *getek* boats out into the deltas in hopes of finding an area that isn't already overfished. The Falcons destroyed terrestrial shipping hubs to ensure no food left except aboard their DropShips. Landgrave Wilhelm Gette has requested support from Duke Brewer to deal with the looming famine, and the duke has relayed his logistical needs to his corporate benefactors on Medellin and to the Malthus Confederation, seeking to forestall mass starvation in outlying districts that have depended on shipments from Iskandar until new crops can be planted and harvested. Our operatives report the Confederation's Crimson Hellebore Guild has offered to supply the needed food, but has demanded workers for their forced-labor gangs in exchange.

CHAPULTEPEC

Landgrave Josette Kerr faces a difficult situation on Chapultepec, which had violently overthrown the Falcon garrison, then split into a five-sided civil war for control of the planet. Though the fighting died down when the Hesperus Guards arrived and the warring factions assumed Commonwealth laws would return, the rival warlords quickly realized Tharkad had nothing to do with the new contender for control. Black Ice teams have infiltrated the competing factions and concluded pro-Commonwealth agreements with these two: the Azcapotzalco Brigade and the Sons of Cuauhtemoc. Loki reports readiness to arm and train their cadres for an extended insurgency. The leaders of the two largest factions, Cocoliloc of Los Esquilados (the Shorn Ones) and Tecocoa of the Guerreros Aguila (Eagle Warriors), have boasted that Chapultepec freed itself from the Falcons without Brewer's help. Both faction leaders have demanded to be named Landgrave von Chapultepec in exchange for their faction's loyalty. The Comerciantes (Merchants) have rebuffed all outsiders' offers and demanded Chapultepec's independence on their terms. Landgrave Kerr has requested elements of the newly formed Vesper Marches Armed Forces be dispatched to support her authority, and she has sent recruiters to Arc-Royal and Kandersteg to hire mercenary auxiliaries.

JESENICE

This planet was conquered by the Golden Ordun and subjected to Mongol-style occupation. During the Falcon's occupation, the planet's mines were kept running around the clock with forced labor, feeding the Falcons' ravenous appetite for the raw materials to make endo steel, ferro-fibrous armor, and "Clan copper" memory metal. When insurgents turned the mining equipment on the Falcon garrison, the warriors destroyed it and forced surviving miners to continue with only hand tools. To maximize efficiency, the Falcons hastily constructed advanced foundries in the foothills of the Karawank mountains, blanketing the nearby city of Jelenkamen with toxic emissions. Though tens of thousands died in the mines, inflicting deep trauma on the surviving populace, Landgrave Oles Papandreouses has requested imports of new equipment so the mines can be returned to full production, giving the Vesper Marches a supply of strategic goods of a quality unmatched in the region. Talks of strikes by the miners' unions have increased in tempo, and labor riots have already disrupted the capital of Kosobrin.

PLANET DIGEST: LESKOVIK

ZAC SCHWARTZ

Star Type (Recharge Time): F5V (176 hours)
Position in System: 4 (of 12)
Time to Jump Point: 14.94 Days
Number of Satellites: 1 (Nasimi)
Surface Gravity: 0.95
Atm. Pressure: Standard (Breathable)
Equatorial Temperature: 33°C (Warm-Temperate)
Surface Water: 69 percent
Recharge Station: Nadir
HPG Class: B
Highest Native Life: Reptiles
Population: 347,000,000 (as of 3152)
Socio-Industrial Levels: B-C-B-C-A (3152)
Landmasses (Capital City): Dardania (Kosova), Kolonja, Tetova, Tirana

During the golden age of the Star League, humanity settled new worlds at a clip not seen since the days of the great Terran Exoduses. Revolutionary in this regard was the Jamerson-Ulikov purification process, making water potable on countless planets that had been previously deemed uninhabitable. One of the last worlds to be colonized prior to its 2622 debut was the muggy, blue-green orb of Leskovik. The first settlement, founded by a clan of Bektashi Sufis looking for a world on which to practice their beliefs in peace and seclusion, nearly met a premature end at the hands of its ecosystem.

With a moon nearly twice the size of Terra's, the planet's bodies of water had a tidal range significantly wider than they were accustomed

to: poor surveying failed to anticipate the near-daily flash floods from sudden tidal bores. Furthermore, Leskovik's native postsaurid fauna were considerably more aggressive than the highly managed ecologies of the colonists' native Hegemony—the expedition's leader and his entire retinue were eaten alive by a flock of sabertooth puffins shortly after debarking their DropShip. But the settlers were of hardy stock. They carved out a region in the northern highlands of the small continent of Dardania, safe from the worst of the flooding and the wildlife, dubbing their high-walled capital Kosova. The Bektashis were content to weather the elements and live a simple, sustainable lifestyle.

But soon after Kosova's establishment, they made a discovery that would change Leskovik forever. Oceans of shale gas, far vaster than on Terra, thrummed below the planet's surface, the residue of its ancient biosphere. The canny Bektashis quickly moved to exploit this resource before outsiders could intrude on their find, but the news could not be kept secret forever. Soon, waves of colonists from across the Tamar Pact began arriving to develop the planet with a glut of cheap energy. The period of Leskovik's history known as the Black Gold Rush had begun.

The next century saw rapid change come to Leskovik. Accessing the planet's natural wealth meant pushing back the more dangerous predators. Particularly fearsome was the massive whulk, an amphibious, armored carnosaur averaging twenty meters long and weighing up to fifteen tons, with a maw that could devour an armored personnel carrier whole. Thus, the first BattleMechs to set foot on Leskovik came not as invaders but as a form of aggressive pest control. Equipped with castoff *Ymir*s and *Commando*s, hand-me-downs from the Lyran Commonwealth Armed Forces, the militia fought what locals refer to as World War Whulk. Two decades of dedicated pruning of the global whulk population reduced the threat to a manageable level without driving the creatures into extinction, to the relief of xenobiologists across the Inner Sphere. With an environment as varied as that found on Terra, from parched desert to teeming jungle to windswept tundra, Leskovik offered many options for locating new settlements. Much of the wildlife was still quite dangerous, however, so most of the population remained concentrated on the island continent of Dardania.

The ever-present risk of flash floods over so much of the surface was dealt with much more creatively: raftlike networks of interconnected mobile structures, adapted for both land and sea, known as siphonopolises. These natatory platforms, collectively the size of small cities, centered around equipment for accessing the deep reservoirs of shale gas via hydraulic fracturing. Leveraging the plentiful resource into an industrial base specializing in the manufacture of advanced and exotic polymers, Leskovik's export economy boomed, and in short order, the resultant wealth accruing to the chief executives of each siphonopolis formed a class of powerful gas barons and their coteries. By the time First Lord Jonathan Cameron died in 2738, the gas barons, led by Sandro Qemali of House Qemali, had swept aside the anemic government in Kosova and shifted the planet to a system of confederated oligarchy. For his efforts, Qemali was elevated to dukedom by acclaim from his fellow oligarchs to represent them in the Lyran Commonwealth's Estates General.

For many worlds, the fall of the Star League was a catastrophe. For Leskovik, it proved to be good fortune...for its rulers. As the Succession Wars ground on and fusion power grew scarcer, the demand for a conveniently singular regional source of the polymers used to manufacture engine shielding and heat sinks exploded. By the outset of the Third Succession War, the only brake on the riches flowing into the gas barons' coffers was the shrinking number of JumpShips available to facilitate interstellar trade. Less fortunately, with those riches came raiders. The Second Succession War had brought the border with the Draconis Combine close enough for Leskovik to become a target for the Rasalhague Regulars. With the LCAF already stretched thin protecting worlds closer to the border, the local militia was often forced to fend for itself, sometimes acquitting themselves well against Kuritan regulars, but usually being swatted aside.

The aristocracy used the effectively permanent "state of military emergency" to further consolidate their power and justify increasingly harsh measures against the laboring masses as the Third Succession War dragged on. Using their vast wealth to attract various mercenaries of variable scruples, House Qemali and the gas barons tried to augment the militia with both their tutelage and their firepower, but the greatly denuded state of BattleMech infrastructure meant even they could only support a single 'Mech company. Both the militia and mercenaries, however, were accustomed to ending riots and uprisings by increasingly overtaxed, overworked laborers as the oligarchy pushed back against the Sphere-wide trend toward economic stagnation by squeezing every last C-bill out of them. In 3001, an armed uprising by the militant Roughnecks Union nearly succeeded in toppling the government. Fearing the regional economic disruption this might cause, Archon Alessandro Steiner dispatched a sizable contingent of Lohengrin and Loki to put down the rebels. Within a year, the rebellion was brutally and bloodily crushed, with tens of thousands of civilians dead or missing as collateral damage.

Much as with the Star League's demise, the Helm Renaissance and gradual upward curve of technology across the Inner Sphere were as devastating for Leskovik as they were felicitous for most others. Demand for a single source of polymer exports began to plummet as fusion engines and the ability to manufacture them became more and more commonplace. By the 3040s, the planet was in the grip of a global economic depression. The oligarchy, scrambling to retain their wealth and power, began to tighten the screws more than ever. Families of workers who spoke out were imprisoned to compel silence or compliance, rebellious villages were blockaded from food and medicine, and ex-Lohengrin private contractors committed calculated atrocities to terrorize the populace. The pitiless Baron Zogu, ruler of the siphonpolises of Kolonja, even took to feeding defiant subjects to his pair of captive whulks. By the decade's close, those Leskoviki who had not been cowed by the nobles were either in prison or dead.

Then the Clans arrived.

The Second Falcon Jaegers, also known as the Frost Falcons, landed on the Dardanian highlands on 17 September 3050, the day a new epoch dawned for Leskovik. Declaring a Trial of Possession for the world, the Frost Falcons bid down to their elite Alpha Trinary and then sallied forth to meet the Leskovik Militia in combat. Led by the canny Captain Beorn Von Kampen, the 'Mech company lured the Falcons deep into the labyrinthine complex of the planet's largest refinery before springing an ambush on them. As savage combat broke out between the two sides, an errant shot struck a huge tank of liquid natural gas. The colossal firestorm it ignited destroyed nearly the entire Trinary and consumed all of the militia save Von Kampen, who deserted his post and fled. After salvaging the few 'Mechs and extracting the few *giftakes* that remained, the Falcons declared victory. Then they acquired those nobles who had not already fled off-world and executed them by firing squad, declaring the time of neo-feudal lords was over. This engendered a sense of cautious optimism, not affection, from the people of Leskovik.

Nobody would ever accuse life under Clan Jade Falcon of being good. They were just as capable as the previous overlords of harshly punishing dissent. But they were not capricious or sadistic. All Leskoviki had food, shelter, and employment for the first time in the planet's history. While the Falcons certainly desired access to the cheap polymers critical to the manufacture of their advanced fusion engines and double-strength heat sinks, they were not monomaniacally focused on maximizing revenue, meaning they did not work the populace to the bone the way their old masters had. And unlike the mix of mercenaries and militia that had previously formed Leskovik's defense, the Jade Falcons regularly rotated entire Clusters through, providing a robust defense that shielded the civilian populace from both pirates and occasional probes from Clan Wolf.

That was not to say the century of Falcon rule was without incident. In October 3057, former ilKhan Ulric Kerensky led Clan Wolf's Tau Galaxy to Leskovik as part of his long march through the Jade Falcon Occupation Zone. Outnumbered, the Ninth Falcon Provisional Garrison Cluster withdrew into the walled industrial city of Belsen and dug in. The Wolves, poorly equipped for urban combat, took heavy casualties rooting them out, and in the process, damaged Belsen so badly much of the city had to be abandoned.

Far more consequential were the events of 3073. When Scientist-General Etienne's Society machinations shut down hyperpulse generators and merchant JumpShips across the occupation zone, many worlds that relied on trade for specialized goods experienced major disruptions. In Leskovik's case, the result was dire: an outbreak of highly lethal yimpisi fever, which the locals had no medicine for. Named for the Zulu word for "hyena" because its neurotoxic effects cause the victim to laugh uncontrollably, it ravaged the population. Nearly a third of Leskoviki civilians lay dead by the time shipments of the antidote serum arrived four months later.

Most recently, Clan Hell's Horses attempted to wrest away Leskovik as part of Operation Noyan. In June 3147, the Seventy-First Mechanized Cavalry jumped in and burned for the planet. Denied *safcon*, they lost a quarter of their force before coming to grips with the defending Eighteenth Falcon Regulars on the ground. Spreading their Trial of Possession to multiple battlefields across the globe, individual Trinaries fought each other. From the high desert of Tirana's Suleiman Dunes to the rolling emerald hills of Kolonja, battle was joined. The Horses met comprehensive defeat at every turn, fleeing with their tails between their legs.

When Malvina Hazen took the Falcon Touman to Terra, Leskovik was left to its own devices for the first time in its history. Their newly independent status has left them perched at the intersection of three neighboring powers in the Hinterlands region. Both agents of Syndic Marena and Khan Jiyi Chistu vie for the allegiance of Senior Laborer Ismail, the highest-ranking bureaucrat remaining on the planet after the Falcons left. A towering freeborn sired in a tryst between a merchant and an Elemental space marine, Ismail is currently undecided on which course to take, but with no one to defend Leskovik against the Horses' inevitable return save what miniscule mercenary forces can be marshaled from nearby Almotacen, time may be running out.

TERRAIN NOTES

Centuries of vigorous fracking have left Leskovik wracked with frequent earthquakes, some powerful enough to bring BattleMechs to their knees. For any scenario taking place on Leskovik, roll 1D6 every other turn. On a roll of 6, roll 1D6 again for a random-strength earthquake, per the rules on page 53 of *Tactical Operations: Advanced Rules*. Results of 1–5 correspond to the equivalent strength of an earthquake; a result of 6 is a reroll.

Leskovik encompasses nearly every form of biome, so players can roll on any extant mapsheet table to generate appropriate maps for a scenario. The low-slung and sturdy architectural style of Kosova and most other Leskoviki cities is designed to protect against earthquake damage: if players roll a map with buildings on it, all buildings are reduced to Level 1 height and increased one category of CF (from light to medium, medium to heavy, and heavy to hardened, to the minimum CF corresponding to that category). Likewise, any significant conurbation is surrounded by walls of a minimum Level 3 height; the exact dimensions are determined by the GM or players, as appropriate.

VIOLENT INCEPTION

RUSSELL ZIMMERMAN

PART 2 (OF 4)

TRIUMPH-CLASS DROPSHIP BONNEVILLE
IN TRANSIT
ENGADIN
FREE RASALHAGUE REPUBLIC
29 MARCH 3050

They fought, Hannah read.

The workouts when Hannah, Tomoko, and Shotaro took over the makeshift gym always went long, and the other two always kept it up the longest. Captain Munene had them burning at just over 1G toward a jump point, and they were meant to be making the jump just a few hours after docking with a JumpShip. Shotaro'd been insistent on getting in a good workout before his guts betrayed him, as they always did. Since leaving Solaris for the first time, the big MechWarrior had been accosted by jump sickness with every interstellar hop. Jump sickness was the least of his worries once he and Oga faced off, though. He was bigger, she was faster. They were both good.

Hannah...wasn't. She'd done...*fine-ish*...in her hand-to-hand competency/qualifications back at Buena. She'd maintained fine-ish with the militia back on Vendrell. She'd worked out since then. But fine-ish wasn't good enough to match hands, feet, elbows, and knees with Oga or Kanezaka.

So they fought, Hannah read.

That was how she'd made it through the War College of Buena. Books. Reading. She'd prided herself on *knowing* things, while other cadets had been better at *doing* things. Here and now, aboard the *Bonnie*, compared to these two? Hannah had the same position, the same value, the same mindset. Whether sparring on the mats or duking it out in the simulator bays, those two were talented, Hannah was smart. They worked out their bodies, she worked out her mind. Tackling Auburn's *The Star League and the Commonwealth* really *was* a workout, too. He'd been mandatory reading back on Buena, and she'd recently circled back around to some of his later works to see if they might grant her a better understanding of—

"What'cha doin'?" Tomoko Oga, fresh from their workout, had magically appeared on Hannah's bench and slung a sweat-slick arm around her, squeezing her water bottle to spritz Hannah with it.

"Hey! Watch it!" Hannah scrambled to keep her dataslate dry. Sure, the manufacturers *said* they were water resistant, but why risk it? At the blotchy mark left on her workout clothes, she just scowled and shook her head. "You're in a good mood. Let me guess, spinning ba—"

"Spinning backfiiiiist! Ha-*ha*!" Tomoko hollered, half-pulling Hannah into a headlock and shaking her, excited and exuberant. "Even Shote can't stop me!"

Sure enough, the big MechWarrior was leaving the gym at that moment, broad shoulders slumped, posture slouching in that way that showed he wanted a good solo brood instead of being grouchy around others. The jump sickness meant he'd have a date with the head soon, his simulator pod scores were still garbage, and another loss to Tomoko meant his day was thoroughly shot, so off he went to sulk. Hannah felt sorry for him, but then her eyes widened slightly. That left just the two of them in the makeshift workout room!

Suddenly in a hormone-flooded panic due to their closeness, she tried to ignore the other girl's smell and did her half-assed best to shrug off her grabbing, shaking arm.

"Ugh, what's got you in such a mood?" Tomoko let her loose, only to laugh and shove her playfully. "Sorry, did I interrupt you reading another boring book on ancient history?"

"It's not boring! It's about how the Lyran Commonwealth inter—"

"Boring!" Oga booed.

Hannah made a face. "—racted with the Star League, and esp—"

"Booooring!" Tomoko slung an arm over her shoulders again.

"Get offa me!" Hannah scowled and tried to twist free.

"Hannah-*kun*, tell me some history that's not gonna bore me to death," Oga said, breath hot in her ear. So hot Hannah felt a flush spread across her face.

She shrugged Tomoko off and gave her a long look, searching her face for sincerity. Tomoko loved winning at anything, and the only way to win was to play games.

"Really?" she asked, eyebrows up.

"Yeah. Not some dusty old stuff. Tell me about…" Tomoko gave her a long up and down look, then a catlike smile.

Oh, no. Hannah knew what was coming.

"Tell me about *you*, Miss Fancy Pants Leftenant Hannah Rippon-Hart."

ROSEWOOD
VENDRELL
LYRAN COMMONWEALTH
10 AUGUST 3049

Hannah's grandmother had taught her, long ago, that one must not only pick their battles, but choose their battlegrounds, their weapons, the lot of it. She had always paid rapt attention to Grandmother's lessons, and not just to earn a little extra dessert or avoid a tongue lashing. Grandma Olivia knew more than most people about this sort of thing, having served honorably in the Arcturan Guards before injuries forced her out of the cockpit.

And yet, despite knowing and trying to follow that advice, here the young MechWarrior was, trapped in an elevator, on her way to a fight where she knew full well her opponent had already decided the time, the weapons, the battlefield, and even the stakes. Everything. None of this was of her choosing, but she had no choice but to fight it, regardless, just as she had every two months since her return to Vendrell.

Every sixty days, or damned close to it. She felt her stomach lurch in time with the elevator as it shuddered to a stop.

It's that time again. Might as well get it over with. She set her face in a no-nonsense grimace, trying to channel Grandma Olivia or at least Aunt Fatima, trying to look serious, professional, stern. Fearless.

The elevator doors opened, and she strode down the hallway, doing her best to ignore the plush red carpet underfoot, the rows of portraits artfully hung just so in polished wooden frames, and the ornate chairs and gleaming tables that lined the hallway.

All the splendor and luxury did was make her feel out of place; mostly because she was. The antique finery of the capitol building clashed with her outfit—*also* of her opponent's choosing, as he'd summoned her quite suddenly—of sweat-stained coveralls and scuffed combat boots. She was in the drab black of a Vendrellian Militia MechWarrior, one of four on the planet, and had just finished a weekend exercise. Cold TastePaste, hot cockpit, field work. She'd been called to this new battlefield while elbow deep in the ankle actuators of her family *BattleMaster*, and hadn't had time to change. The War College of Buena had trained her in how to be a 'Mech tech almost as much as a MechWarrior, but hadn't, sadly, taught her how to magically clean up in the blink of an eye after the work was done.

Just another way he's ambushing me today, Hannah thought as she approached the end of the hallway. *Oh well, nothing I can do about it. Here we go.*

She strode through the double doors at the end of the hallway, flanked by Vendrellian Guardsmen in their fancy uniforms, slapped her heels together, and snapped off the sharpest salute of her life.

"Leutnant Hannah Rippon-Hart, reporting as ordered, sir." She held her chin up high. The Lyran Commonwealth and Federated Suns might have integrated their massive interstellar militaries and normalized their ranks, but, by God, Allah, and pigheadedness, the Vendrellian Militia still used the old Steiner rank model.

"At ease, MechWarrior." The Duke of Vendrell gave a flippant, half-hearted salute without making eye contact, just enough of a token gesture to count, but not enough to return any respect. He had a small gavel near at hand, an old enemy of hers, ready to use. Hannah adjusted her stance appropriately, hands at the small of her back, keeping every movement crisp and professional.

The office was far from empty. A pair of kommandants sat off to Hannah's right, and the duke's personal assistant, a pinch-faced woman who must have looked forty-five since the day she was born, served as a courtroom stenographer. After all these summons and tribunals, they still went through the official motions.

It's cute how they try to make it look legitimate, instead of acknowledging it's just a long-running grudge. No lowly hauptmanns invited, of course. That would have let Aunt Fatima in the room, and oh, how she'd chew them up!

Lastly, standing to Hannah's left, draped head to toe in his most formal and decorated of uniforms, stood Hauptmann-Kommandant Archibald Frederick Uwe von Humboldt, who'd been second in command of the Vendrellian Militia for as long as Hannah'd been alive. Archibald was a tank commander, and always had been. Hannah, meanwhile, served with her Aunt Fatima in the planet's only lance of BattleMechs, which gave her glamour and prestige that belied her low rank. Archie seemed determined to make up for it by wearing every medal and ribbon he owned, and his crisp, white, high-collared uniform stood in stark contrast to her grubby, greasy coveralls.

His skin and hair were far lighter than Hannah's, wisps of white fringe around the sides and back of his head, also in stark contrast to her tight black curls; if he'd been a MechWarrior, he could have claimed his prominent bald spot was for better neurohelmet connectivity, but he wasn't, so he opted for a sad little combover instead. The bulk of his hair was on his face, a pair of bushy muttonchops that met in a drooping, walrus-like mustache over his bare chin and thin lips.

The two couldn't have been more opposites; Hannah was tall and lean, dark, young, dirty. Archie was shorter, rounder, paler, white-haired, white-uniformed, spotless. By contrast, he looked far more professional. Officer material. Mature. Reasonable. Serious.

All by design. All to salt whatever new wound was coming.

Also, he was able to be here on time.

"It was good of you to join us, MechWarrior. Eventually." The duke gave a smile that wasn't a smile. Constantly referring to Hannah's position, rather than her rank, was a way to remind her she wasn't *fully* commissioned, yet. She was just a junior officer, a mere leutnant, as she'd been since the day she'd graduated the academy.

"My apologies, I arrived as close to thirteen hundred as I was able." Hannah's tone was a bit more curt than it should have been. *Since I was informed of this meeting at 1245*, she thought, sparing the slightest glance off to one side. The gilded clock on the wall showed 1302.

"Your Grace," the hauptmann-kommandant corrected her, one alarmingly bushy eyebrow lifting archly.

"My apologies, *Your Grace*." Hannah gritted her teeth, but managed the honorific. "I arrived as close to thirtee—"

"Von Humboldt, you may begin," the duke cut her off with a negligent little wave. He was a few decades older than Hannah's near-twenty years, and even more darkly skinned, with his head a clean-shaven, deep mahogany orb. He hadn't worn his dress white uniform for today's meeting, though he could have. He'd spent some time in the cockpit of a 'Mech in his younger days, and was nominally the leader of the planetary militia. He'd opted instead to stay in his usual day-to-day civilian garb—respectable, conservative, bespoke. He could wear whatever he wanted; it was his planet.

"Your Grace, may it please the tribunal." Archibald gave a little bow to the gathered officers. "Please allow me to begin today's proceedings with an apology. It would seem that yet again one MechWarrior, out of the many in the proud ranks of the Vendrellian Militia, demands the bulk of our time, and never, I fear, for a *good* reason."

I am literally one fourth of the MechWarriors in the Militia, you dung heap. Hannah kept herself rigidly at ease, chin up, eyes forward, mouth a grim line that matched the duke's own grimace. *And we all know the no-good reason I keep demanding your attention.*

"Alas, protocol demands that, once again, this MechWarrior stand before us, facing a grave charge, indeed," he continued mournfully. "And consuming yet more of this august tribunal's time, attention, and perhaps most of all, concern."

Spit it out, you lump. What trumped-up nonsense are you laying on me today?

Hannah had done well at the War College of Buena. Very well. She'd finished second in her class; she'd been first across the board in every *academic* endeavor, but her field scores had held her back enough to keep her from quite topping the rankings. Despite her high ranking, though, strings had been pulled to get her a posting back here, to the humble Vendrellian Militia.

In the two years since? She'd been attacked with tribunal after tribunal, summons after summons, and one slipshod accusation after another, until her record had been spotted by citations as though they'd been taking potshots at her file with a machine gun. Hannah hadn't yet formally won her commission, stellar academy performance be damned, as instead they'd hurled obstacle after obstacle in her way. Considerable leverage had been applied to steal Hannah back to Vendrell after the War College, and once they'd gotten her, the very same lever had then been turned into a rod to beat her with.

"Though I don't doubt, senior officers one and all, that the pertinent details of the report are already quite clear to you, let the tribunal please look to the paperwork prepared for them today to refresh their memories," von Humboldt continued after his dramatic pause. Paperwork Hannah certainly hadn't been allowed to see in advance. "And let us recall January's Monte Lupus exercises, which the MechWarrior, unfortunately, took part in. Some of you, I am certain, remember the unfortunate incident, horrible as it was to see in person."

Hah! In person? Not likely. None of them have been to the mountain in ages. Hannah couldn't help but give Archie side-eye, glaring. *I can't believe they're bringing up the winter exercise, though. That was ages ago. How many more of these reports do they have typed up and ready to go?*

Like clockwork since her return to Vendrell, Rippon-Hart had faced report atop report atop report for bad behavior, poor field scores, poor marksmanship, insubordination, conduct prejudicial to good order and discipline, minor infraction after minor infraction. The last one had been for drinking on duty, because she'd been photographed lifting a glass of wine in a toast at the Winter Holiday formal while decked out in her militia whites. Charged with drinking! By Lyrans! And when half the world *knew* her Muslim faith wouldn't allow her more than a polite sip as part of the toast!

Again and again, they had erected roadblocks to her commission. Every infraction carried with it a sixty-day suspension of possibility for promotion. They'd strung them out meticulously, sixty days apart, like carefully cycled volleys of fire to keep a 'Mech from overheating. If infractions overlapped, you could get discharged. If infractions were spaced apart, though? They could toy with you, keep you at whatever rank they wanted for as long as they wanted to do so. Never giving you a chance to advance. Never giving you a chance to breathe.

Hannah bit her lip. *I can't believe it's already time again. It feels like the last one was just...*

"As the report shows, during this winter's Vendrellian Militia mountain-fighting exercise, there was a grievous incident of negligence," Archibald continued with melodramatic deliberation. "Wherein a BattleMech, supposedly one the finest and certainly one of the most expensive defenders of Vendrell and the royal family—"

Hannah bit her lip harder, fuming.

"—attacked a tank crew! During what was meant to be a *routine* advance-and-fire drill, the lives of a loyal, hard-working crew were put at risk by the ineptitude, the jealousy, the wrath—or perhaps all three, I do not claim to have every answer!—of the MechWarrior that faces the court today."

"Your Grace, permission to spea—" Hannah tried to cut in during von Humboldt's next dramatic pause...or maybe the old windbag just had to catch his breath every so often.

"Denied." The duke lifted two fingers as though waving her request away. Hannah fumed. Archie trundled on.

"Alas, tribunal, here I must once again apologize, as I am but a humble provincial militiaman, a tank commander grown long in the tooth, and not a graduate of the esteemed War College of Buena. Tell me, MechWarrior, what armor does a Scorpion armored combat vehicle bear?"

Chastised when last she spoke, Hannah stood still as a statue, mouth a straight line.

"Answer, MechWarrior," the duke grimaced right back at her.

"ProtecTech Light," she said, words clipped. "Four tons."

"*Sir.*" Von Humboldt lifted one bushy eyebrow.

You want a sir? I'll give you a sir.

"Hauptmann-Kommandant von Humboldt, *sir,* as per the most recent specification sheets and recognition guides for the Scorpion armored combat vehicle, sir, and according to this MechWarrior's best recollection, *sir,* the Scorpion armored combat vehicle bears four tons of Pr—"

"*MechWarrior.*" The duke raised his voice and an eyebrow, rather than his gavel. His sharp tone was enough to cut her off. Despite herself, she flinched at the sound. "That is enough."

Archibald gave his friend, the duke, a fawning little bow.

"My! That isn't very much protection against the likes of an assault 'Mech, is it? And where, please, MechWarrior, is that armor the thinnest? Hmm? Were one to graduate, with honors, from the War College of Buena, say, where would one have been taught to attack a Scorpion armored combat vehicle, to disable it in the most efficient manner possible?"

It's a malfing Scorpion. I can attack it anywhere I want to, you son of a... Hannah wanted to say.

Instead, she sighed. "In the rear, sir,"

"Mm-hmm. And tell me, MechWarrior, to your 'best recollection,' at the time of the incident in question, where were you, in relation to this friendly, loyal Scorpion armored vehicle? Were you in front of it? To the left, perhaps? To the right?"

"I was behind it, sir. Duke, please may I—"

"No." The duke didn't even shake his head. "You may not."

They're really out to have their fun, Hannah fumed. *They backstab me every chance they get, and they still have to twist the knife each time.*

"I see. And tell me, MechWarrior, according to standard combat protocols, what is the pilot of, say, an assault-class machine like a *BattleMaster* instructed to do in the very closest of close-combat scenarios against a combat vehicle like a Scorpion? Something to do with the bipedal nature of a BattleMech, I believe, isn't it? A rather unique maneuver, something combat vehicles can't mana—"

"Step on it. We're trained to step on it. Like a bug." Hannah, MechWarrior, turned her head ever so slightly, looking von Humboldt, tanker, square in the eye. She didn't quite threaten him. "*Sir.*"

They're blaming me for this?! Hannah fumed internally. *They know why it happened!*

"And you did just that, didn't you, MechWarrior? Stepped on it? Tell me, was the Scorpion's turret pointed to the rear during all this? Was it firing on you? Were you, perhaps, defending yourself? Please, there must be some reason why you attacked it!"

"I didn't attack the Scorpion, sir. I touched it with my foot. Your tankies were gunning it, hot-rodding, pushing their specs and trying to speed up the mountain. She didn't let them get away with—"

"'She'?" Archibald asked.

"Monte Lupus, sir. You can't race up her, not in a rig like that. You've got to go at a steady pace, especially in something put together by Quikscell." The Quikscell Company was notorious throughout the Inner Sphere for their lack of quality control, their cheap designs, and their unreliability. Planetary militias that didn't want to pay for better equipment loved Quikscell. So did piggish officers like Von Humboldt, who liked to spend as little as possible while getting as many shiny tanks as possible to brag about commanding. "You've got to drop into a lower gear, take your time with it, make sure your treads are getting good traction on the ice and—"

"Oh! Oh, goodness me!" Archibald huffed and puffed and made a big show of turning back to his desk and sifting through the papers there. "I seem to have, oh my, Your Grace, esteemed tribunal members, I am so terribly sorry, perhaps my understanding of the *MechWarrior's* academic credentials are incomplete, but for the life of me, I can't seem to find anything in these transcripts that speak to the MechWarrior's qualifications and certifications as a combat armor driver, and yet here we are, being lectured by—"

"I practically *grew up* on Monte Lupus, von Humboldt. I've been driving around up there for as long as I can remember! Come on! When I was a kid, I used to drive a Sherpa Canteen around with my grandfather, *feeding* the Vendrellian Militia during these winter training exercises. Remember?"

"We remember you before the Academy quite well, indeed," the duke cut in again, making his displeasure at the break of etiquette clear. And more. Hannah did her best not to wince.

"My point, sir, Your Grace—" She dipped her head ever so slightly to the duke, acknowledging that he'd spoken. "—was simply to remind the tribunal that I know the terrain, and how vehicles of approximately a Scorpion's size respond to it. Our old Sherpa's only just a little bigger, and you all know I've driven that up there. You can't trust the traction control on a Quikscell product, and your crew starting to skid proved that. They risked a tumble off the mountain on one side, and the disruption of our exercise's formation on the other. Our live-fire exercise included particle projection cannons, Hauptmann-Kommandant, and large lasers, the autocannons of its fellow Scorpions, and the large-bore autocannons of our Pattons as well."

"So your claim, then, is that you attacked them..." Archie coaxed laughter from the kommandants. "...to protect them?"

"Yes," Hannah said, absolutely straight-faced and honest. If the gathered officers wanted to claim that a little tap of an assault 'Mech's foot was worse than a PPC blast up the tailpipe, let the duke's little stenographer write that dumb malfing opinion down. "If you call it an attack, then, yes, that's why I did it. I worried about them falling off the mountain or surging into the line of fire, and when they failed to respond to radio commands, I thought—"

"That stomping on it was the only possible way to arrest their movement?"

"I *touched* it with my *foot*, sir. Because your tank crew was slipping on the incline and backsliding. I knew that them losing traction and sliding down off the side of Lupus would be the *best*-case scenario, and the worst would be them crashing into the rest of the formation or getting blown up. If your other green tankies panicked, it would be even worse, start a chain reaction. So I stopped them with the best tool I had at the time, the foot of my *BattleMaster*."

Hannah looked, exasperated, from the hauptmann-general to the kommandants to the duke. She wished they'd just *listen*. The tankers themselves had listened, and understood after the fact, and been grateful! But none of these men, none of these senior officers, had been there. Not in the cold, the snow, and the stone. None of them had been to Monte Lupus in a decade or more, while Hannah'd practically grown up there. They didn't care about the truth, though, because the truth didn't matter to them. Only another slip of paper in her file.

"Tell me, MechWarrior." Von Humboldt continued to use the title as though it were an insult; Hannah supposed, when it was used instead of one's proper rank, it kind of *was*. "Can you show me where, in any of the combined-arms manuals you so recently studied on Buena, it recommends stomping on a friendly armored combat vehicle in such a way?"

"You know I can't." Hannah let a bit more exasperation out than she meant to. She sighed to maintain her composure. "Sir, I had to make a decision, in a split second, to try and save lives, and I *did*. I did what came naturally."

"Stepping on it, to…arrest its movement?"

"Touching it with my 'Mech's foot, sir."

Silence filled the room for a moment. Archie looked to the high table, seeing if he should proceed or not.

The duke narrowed his eyes thoughtfully, waited until he knew every eye was on him, and then reached and—suddenly, almost catlike—threw a bauble off his desk. It was a globe-shaped paperweight, a gift from the Magestrix herself, a glass ball laser-etched with Vendrell's continents on it, a frosted, icy-looking thing. It rolled with the force of his push, bouncing heavily, careening across the carpet, unerringly, toward the door.

Reflexively, Rippon-Hart broke her at-ease stance and flicked a foot out, sideways, catching the tumbling orb with her midfoot. Childlike. Instinctual. Stopping a runaway ball. The paperweight Vendrell ricocheted off her rubber-soled boot, then came to a stop in the plush carpet.

The tribunal tittered and gasped dramatically.

Hannah looked puzzled for a split second, then saw the game. She hadn't blocked the backsliding Scorpion that way, not with a quick, harmless deflection. Not with the instinctive, smooth shift in stance. The duke knew Hannah was lighter on her own two feet than she'd ever be in a *BattleMaster*, or any other 'Mech. She'd been top of her academy class in academics…not in piloting.

Pick your weapons. Pick your battles. She'd done neither.

"Let the record show how easily, and some might say naturally, the MechWarrior deflected that paperweight, and that said paperweight, a mere glass bauble rather than high-quality, recently purchased combat vehicle, is entirely unscathed! Tell me MechWarrior, did you similarly, harmlessly, use the inside of your *BattleMaster*'s foot to stop the descent of the supposedly runaway tank?" Archie asked.

"No, sir, I—"

"You stepped on it, did you not?"

"I *touched* it with my *foo*—"

"Stepped on it, some might say, like a bug? That *was* the phrase you used, wasn't it? I don't recall, was it 'stepped,' or 'stomped?' Stenographer, do we need to check the records?"

Instead of answering, Hannah gave him the coldest side-eye she'd ever given anyone. She tried to channel her aunt, her grandmother, the Fox women of Mountain Wolf BattleMech fame, every mythological Valkyrie and Amazon to ever live, and the legendary Medusa, all at once.

No luck. He didn't die. The senior officer allowed himself a smirk before continuing.

"You're right, I suppose the distinction between 'step' and 'stomp' doesn't matter. It certainly didn't matter to the Scorpion, did it? It was a total loss, and apparently, only through dumb luck—your dumb, their luck, perhaps?—the crew survived! According to the report, it looks as though you caused damage to the turret, destroyed the engine, and caused a deformation of the engine compartment itself. You shattered the rear armor, cracked the drive sprocket—" The kommandant-hauptmann raised his voice to trundle on, himself a tank, unstoppable.

"Sir, I made a quick decision to try a—"

"Warped the turret ring, disabled the main gun's hydraulics entirely, and very nearl—"

Enough! Fine!

"Can we just get this over with?" Hannah raised her voice now, too. Sometimes a teenager needs to talk like a teenager, academy training and rank be damned.

Her impatience earned her gasps from the sidelines again. An indignant sputter from von Humboldt. A frown from the duke. She pressed on.

"Look, *sir*, I understand. We all understand. I kept your little Quikscell special from running into your other little Quikscell specials and falling off Monte Lupus, so I'm in trouble. Fine. Can you just formally assign me the infraction, and we all get back to our lives? I've got an ankle actuator—same leg, actually, same foot as the one you're writing me up for, small world, huh?—that I need to fix after a rough time at *this* weekend's exercises. I'd like to get back to the repair work. That's why I was late to the hearing, and I'm *sure* you've all got more important things to do, too."

Like go play golf together after this is done.

In true Lyran tradition, the crème de la crème of the Vendrellian Militia were cronies, a gentleman's club, bosom buddies for longer than Hannah'd been alive. They'd be chortling to themselves about the tribunal over snifters of brandy and planning their tee time before the elevator even carried her down the stairs, she was sure.

Why are they wasting so much time?

Scandalized, the kommandants looked at each other, at Archibald, at the duke. Impassive, the stenographer squinted and waited.

The duke broke the silence, voice deep and powerful. "We *do* have more important things to do."

Hannah breathed a sigh of relief. At least the tooth would be yanked, the sham over with. She'd get sent back to her unit without a commission and with her tail tucked between her legs for another sixty days. She was used to it.

"Which is why we won't allow you to waste any more of our time, MechWarrior. *Ever.*" It was the duke's turn to pause dramatically. The stenographer readied herself before he continued, then typed furiously.

I'm...not crazy about how he said that.

"Given the MechWarrior's lackluster performance since their return to Vendrell—"

"'*Their*'?" she interrupted.

"—despite the planet's investment in seeing to their education at the War College of Buena, and given the frankly record-breaking number of infractions accrued by the MechWarrior in so brief a period of time, given their casual admission of guilt in the Scorpion affair that nearly claimed the lives of loyal Vendrellians, and furthermore, given their blatant disregard for protocol, disrespect for rank, and disdain for tradition, it is the unanimous judgment of this assembly—" The duke's voice, as dark and smooth as the wood of his desk, rang out as though he were pronouncing a death sentence. "—that nothing in the career of this MechWarrior gives us any reason to believe further investment, such as a full commission, *into* that career will in any way benefit the good people of the planet."

Hannah stood frozen, heart pounding in her chest, lip curling in disgust.

"Protocol." "Tradition." Just say it. Hannah glared at the duke, daring him, silently, taking everything he was saying more personally than professionally. *Just say why you're really mad at me.*

"No humble leutnant with a record so riddled with failure and disappointment, accordingly deemed by this tribunal to be a danger to the soldiers serving around them, shall—"

"Danger?!" Hannah sputtered incredulously.

"—continue to serve the people of Vendrell in such a capacity, as doing so, they weaken, not strengthen, the curtain of steel the Vendrellian Militia represents—"

"Are you *kidding* me right now?!" Hannah's composure broke with her voice.

"—and furthermore, no longer should this MechWarrior be entrusted with so valuable a weapon of war, negligent and dangerous as they have been with it, as a proud *BattleMaster*, and—"

"My 'Mech?!" Hannah hated how plaintive her voice was in that moment. She knew she sounded like a child losing a toy, not a MechWarrior being Dispossessed. Her stomach churned. Her head spun. It all felt unreal. "You can't!"

But he was the one person in the world who could.

"—so it is the decision of this assembly that the MechWarrior's accident-, incident-, demerit-, and failure-riddled career with the planetary militia is at an *end*."

Nothing left to lose, then. Hannah's eyes narrowed.

"Listen to yourself! 'The MechWarrior.' You won't even say my name, will you? 'The MechWarrior,' even now?!"

She snarled and made the mistake of taking a half step forward.

The pair of Vendrellian Guard—she'd honestly forgotten they were there; the house soldiers were like furniture or decorative suits of armor around the ducal estates—were on her in an instant, one on each of her arms. The kommandants murmured in shock and dismay. Archie held a handkerchief over his mouth as though he might faint. The duke was, entirely, unrattled by what would no doubt go down in the logbook as an "attempted attack."

"Let the record show the leutnant's...conduct...in these chambers today does nothing but reinforce the opinion of this assembly." The Duke of Vendrell stood up, unnecessarily, to project his voice even more clearly. "This other-than-honorable discharge is complete as of this moment. I will call them 'leutnant' no more. Their time of service is at an end."

"Say it!" Hannah taunted him. Begged him.

Archibald von Humboldt hadn't been Hannah's opponent at all; he'd just been one of the chosen weapons, like the glass globe, the report, the tribunal. Her enemy had been the duke, and he had just beaten her, soundly. Absolutely. Crushingly. He had finally decided to simply pull the trigger, to show he could. He was disgusted, ashamed, and angry, so now *she* was Dispossessed.

The duke raised his gavel and looked her in the eyes.

"Coward! Say my name!" Hannah lifted her head, half-begging, half-furious.

The duke lowered the gavel like an executioner, cutting off her sentence and her career, both, with a report like a gun.

With that swing and that *crack*, Hannah's father, Duke Alexander Rippon-Hart, took from her the *BattleMaster* that was her birthright, and the Vendrellian MechWarrior career that had been her only dream.

MOUNTAIN WOLF BATTLEMECHS HQ
MONTE LUPUS
VENDRELL
LYRAN COMMONWEALTH
11 AUGUST 3049

"Mint?" Brandon O'Leary asked expectantly. The Chief Executive Officer of Mountain Wolf BattleMechs used his polished wooden pipe to scoot a little glass bowl across his desk toward Hannah. Everyone who stepped into his office risked diabetes and fresh, minty breath all at once, but especially his beloved granddaughter.

"Um...no, thank you, sir." Hannah stood before him at ease, though she didn't need to any longer. He was a civilian, after all, and, well, so was she, right? But military academies get their claws in deep, and a great many cadets never quite stood or spoke the same.

Brandon made a bit of a face at her reacting to him so stiffly and formally. He was older and balder than Archie von Humboldt, but softer, and his voice was deeper, kinder. His voice, and the top of his head, were both as smooth as the perpetually empty pipe he kept on hand.

"Hmm, a drink, then, perhaps?" He raised his bushy white eyebrows, hopeful to offer *some* sort of civility and generosity. Like any good Lyran with an office, his had a small but well-stocked bar. O'Leary had married into the Rippon-Hart family, and while he respected their Muslim faith, he had long since stopped pretending to share it. Hannah had snuck a sip and risked a stained soul a time or two, but she had never wanted to be *drunk* until very recently. Because of that want, she didn't dare take him up on it.

If I start drinking right now, I might never stop, she thought. She wouldn't be the first Dispossessed MechWarrior to go down that road. She shook her head. "No thank you, sir."

At the second "sir," O'Leary let out a little *harrumph* that had to fight hard to make it through his fantastic mustache.

"Well then, at least have a seat, won't you?" He pointed with his pipe. People from here to Alpheratz knew how comfortable O'Leary's chairs were.

"Thank you, sir. I prefer to stand," she said, trying to sound professional, but worried she sounded rude instead.

He made a face again. "Well, then, I give up. I'm not good for much, and if you don't want a mint, some Loeches Reserve, or a seat..." He spoke slowly and measuredly as always, and perpetually with just a hint of amusement to his tone, like a late-night show host.

"Then what the hell are you doing in my office?" He smiled and shrugged. The heartfelt care and curiosity in his voice kept it from sounding genuinely exasperated.

"I..." Hannah swallowed, suddenly not just nervous about what she was about to ask, but ashamed anew that she had to ask for it. Ashamed, furious, helpless.

I'm here to beg, she wanted to say. *I'm here to beg to be worth something again. To be able to do something, anything, in a 'Mech.*

Hannah hadn't spoken to anyone about what had happened yesterday. She hadn't had to speak the words. She hadn't had anyone to speak them *to*. She hadn't been allowed back to the militia base, even, to tell her lancemates or her aunt goodbye. Now she had to tell someone.

"I would like, sir—I mean, I know this facility is a long way from operational, but I'd like to work site security, if you'll have me." Her voice came out sounding little-girl smaller than she meant it to. "Or, or maybe I could work as a test pilot, sir, even if you've only an opening at the Alpheratz plant? I'm willing to trav—"

"Ab*surd*!"

A sharp and scornful voice blasted Hannah from behind, an ambush through Grandpa Bran's open door. She knew who it was immediately. Hannah's grandmother, the Dowager Duchess Olivia Rippon-Hart.

"And stop stooping to '*sir*' him, girl. You'll be Duchess of Vendrell someday! He's only just a *graf*, and only even *that* because I made him one so the marriage wouldn't embarrass me," Grandmother scolded her as she rolled into the room. Her wheelchair was a fine thing, polished wood and aged leather hiding electronics, as beautiful and dark as she was, and it fit in with the finery of the Mountain Wolf CEO's furniture; it ought to, made as it was by the same woodworkers.

Pushing Olivia's chair was the head of the Mountain Wolf Vendrellian security team Hannah had just asked—begged—to join, and one of the fierce warrior-women she'd tried to channel during her tribunal. Captain Rachel "Red" Fox. Hannah's senior by nearly two decades, Captain Fox had taken over as Brandon O'Leary's bodyguard years ago, handling the responsibility of keeping the CEO and his Lyran holdings safe.

Meanwhile Rachel's mother—Cassandra "Scarlet" Fox, another native of Vendrell and a Mountain Wolf legend—still led the company's security team at their active facility in far-off Alpheratz. There, 800 light years away in the Outworlds Alliance, Hannah's uncle Cameron ran the day-to-day of MWB's primary factory. Here, in Lyran space, her grandfather Brandon saw to the political dealings of the company among the nobility while preparing for a Vendrellian plant he meant to open in just a few years. At both ends of the Inner Sphere, Fox women kept O'Leary men safe.

But looming above all of them, Fox women and O'Leary men alike, was a scathing, sarcastic titan seated on a wheeled, wooden throne. Olivia Rippon-Hart, former MechWarrior, former Duchess of Vendrell, had long since taken on the role of hen-pecking matriarch. She was mother to three, but only Hannah called her...

"Grandmother!" Hannah's face split in a bright smile, and she lunged to give the ferocious dowager duchess a hug.

Olivia gave her the briefest of return hugs before warding her off with a swat from a little fan and made a fussy face. "Enough, girl. I can tell you've been on a field exercise. You reek of axle grease and TastePaste." She sniffed disdainfully, which Hannah knew meant *Hello, my girl.*

"And compose yourself! You're a Rippon-Hart of Vendrell. Don't carry on so in front of the peasants," she scolded, which sounded just like *I love you, too.*

Hannah sniffled, then straightened and turned to the other newcomer to the office. "Hello, Captain." She gave Captain Fox a watery smile and a nod. The Fox women were both MechWarriors, as Grandmother Olivia had been in her prime, along with Hannah's aunt, Fatima. When Hannah was a child, she believed the four of them— Cassandra and Rachel Fox, Fatima and Olivia Rippon-Hart—had veritably held up the sky. She had thought of them every day while struggling through the academy. She had done her best to make them proud.

And now...

"Good afternoon, Leutnant." Fox reached to shake her hand with a crisp nod and a smile.

Hannah wilted. "Err, no, I'm not actually a leut—"

"Shh." Fox shot her a wink, gave CEO O'Leary a polite nod, and took a few steps back and to the side.

Hannah didn't understand that, any more than she did the rest of just what was happening.

"Pfft! Listen to you." Olivia took over the room, as she always did, in whatever room she was in. Her tongue was the sharpest thing on Vendrell, and the most lethal. Everything she said was scathing by default, lashing out at everyone in earshot. With her days in the cockpit behind her and her title abdicated to her son, Duke Alexander, her mind and her tongue were her only remaining weapons. She honed and wielded them unrelentingly. "Carrying on and begging to be some silly test pilot or an overgrown security guard. *Hmph!* What nonsense! Lowborn work."

Brandon O'Leary snorted, and Rachel Fox shook her head with a wry smile. Rachel's mother had been a dear friend to a much younger Brandon O'Leary, but also a veteran MechWarrior of the Third Lyran Regulars, a talented 'Mech tech, and a brilliant engineer. Together, the two had dreamed up the *Merlin*, the first new BattleMech the Inner Sphere had seen in generations. Fox and O'Leary had both test-piloted it, and in the decades since, *both* Foxes had worked Mountain Wolf Security. They were security staff and test pilots, all. Olivia had unerringly blasted the entire lot of them and their lives' work with verbal broadsides carelessly, teasingly, just carrying on to show she could.

It's when Olivia Rippon-Hart *wasn't* being casually cruel that she was up to something.

"And you!" She clucked and pointed her fan at her husband. "I settled you down and civilized you here on Vendrell ages ago, and you've still no proper Lyran manners? You've *guests* in your office, Brandon. Pretend you weren't raised in a DropShip and offer them drinks!"

"Oh, at once, Lady Archon!" Bowing and scraping on his way, smiling wryly the whole time, O'Leary scrambled over to his small bar to prepare the former duchess her favorite with his own two hands. Apricot nectar, orange juice, a splash of lemon, a bit of sparkling water. His age-spotted hands moved with practiced precision, showing it was a drink he'd made for her dozens, if not hundreds, of times.

"And don't make it too sweet this time!" Olivia said, making a face.

"Oh, of course not, Lady Archon. You're already sweet enough, Lady Archon!" Brandon chuckled and got back to work. There wasn't a drop of alcohol in her "cocktail." A long-dead Hart had been an officer with the long-dead Twentieth Lyran Guards on Dar-es-Salaam, centuries ago. He had left the world with a new bride and a new faith. Since then, some Harts, now Rippon-Harts, had been more devoutly Muslim than others, but all had at least respected the faith. Olivia had never been a big drinker, but as she'd aged, she'd become even less interested in alcohol and grown more into her faith. Perhaps because it was haram, or perhaps simply because she'd lost her taste for it, she had long since weaned herself entirely from the harder stuff. Brandon knew what to put into her drink, and what not to.

"Can I fetch anything else for you, Lady Archon?"

"Unlikely." She waved at him airily. "I still half expect you to mess this one up. I'm not eager to ask you to try and learn something new."

Hannah couldn't help but smile and shake her head at the pair of them, Grandmother making a show of being fussy and intolerable, Grandfather making a show of fawning sarcastically as he served her. They hadn't started out in love. Hannah'd grown up on stories of how Mountain Wolf BattleMechs had resettled here on Vendrell. The ducal family had needed money after her grandfather—her *biological* grandfather, Sebastian Rippon—had died, and at nearly the same time, Grandpa Brandon's father had passed away and left him with a corporation and a pile of anxiously hoarded C-bills, but no direction.

They had both lost, been left alone, and been left in need of a partner. Brandon O'Leary had come to Vendrell and solved both family's problems. He had offered the young Vendrellian widow enough money to change both their fates; she'd had little choice but to make him a *graf*-consort and put some respect on the O'Leary name by taking him as a husband. They had found one another out of necessity. Their stars had aligned, and an alliance had been formed.

No, they hadn't started out in love, but they'd grown into it over time. They'd grown comfortable with one another, grown warm, grown close, mellowed into love until one day they'd looked around and realized their marriage of convenience had become more real than most. In many ways, they were the cleverest and luckiest pair of people on Vendrell.

Still, Olivia made a face at her first sip of the drink Brandon had prepared, as though she expected him to have botched it. He returned to his desk without waiting to watch her reaction; he knew he'd done fine. He always did.

Hannah sniffled and smiled a little at the familiar warmth of their absurdity.

"So." Her grandmother's disdainful snort dragged her back to the here and now after she enjoyed a sip. "*Really*, Hannah? This was the best you could think of? To grovel to this peasant-born oaf and beg for a few kroner in exchange for stumbling around Vendrell in his horrid machines, or exiling yourself to Alpheratz to get shot at by pirates? Are you truly so desperate for money?"

Brandon shrugged good-naturedly instead of taking offense.

"I—Grandmother, it's not about money, I just, I need to do *something*, I..." Hannah faltered, looking from her grandmother to Captain Fox, one of her childhood heroes to another. She didn't want to say the words. She had to, though. Hannah forced herself to admit what had happened. "I'm not a leutnant anymore. I'm not part of the—"

"Oh! So, you and *That Man* had your little talk." Olivia snorted disdainfully and took another sip.

Brandon frowned. Captain Fox kept a carefully, professionally, neutral face.

"You...know?" Hannah blinked like an idiot.

Her grandmother looked offended. "Of course I *know*! It happened on Vendrell, didn't it?"

"But how can you... Grandmother, how can you call it a 'little talk'?"

"Because he is a little man," Olivia said coldly, certainly, finally, about her only son. "And he talked."

She hadn't called the duke by title, or name, in years. Hannah knew why, and she blamed herself.

"You know he..." Hannah felt her voice crack again, saw the room go blurry as tears rushed unbidden to her eyes. "You know he took my 'Mech?"

Hannah had wanted to use her family's *BattleMaster* to protect her family's world for as long as she could remember. She'd never felt so proud in her life as when she'd been accepted into the academy and the duke had formally given her the 'Mech. Her stomach roiled at the loss. Her grandmother's apparently didn't.

"Oh, that. Well, I didn't think you were here, hat in hand, begging for work, because I'd missed the silly thing parked out front!" Olivia Rippon-Hart said dismissively, as though the *BattleMaster* hadn't been in her dead husband's family for centuries. As though she hadn't handed it down to her son. As though her son hadn't handed it down, in turn. "I married cleverly, if low. As it turns out, your grandfather here, toiling yeoman that he is, runs a BattleMech *manufacturer*, silly girl. There's a *Merlin* out there with your name on it, so you don't much need That Man's fussy, ancient 'Mech, do you?"

It was Olivia's way. It was how she tried not to show her true feelings. It was how she said *It's not the end of the world*, and *I'm sorry he hurt you*, and *There, there*. A *Merlin* was a fine heavy 'Mech, and she loved her Grandpa Bran dearly, but it lacked the prestige of an assault 'Mech like a *BattleMaster*. Most of all, though, it wasn't *that one*, the family 'Mech, the pride of House Rippon. That had been taken from her. Grandmother knew that.

And so Hannah was terrified the usual rough teasing wasn't enough this time. She felt it in her belly. Her shame welled up and threatened to escape her. She knew, here, in this room, that speaking of her failure to these three people out of all the galaxy, she'd need...more. More than her grandmother's teasing jabs.

A sob tightened her chest as she did her best to bite it down alongside her shame. Her shoulders rocked and her nails bit into her palms, hands in tight-clutched fists at her sides.

Seeing her struggle, her grandmother's resolve and façade broke before Hannah's did. She wheeled herself closer and leaned out to take her granddaughter's hand in her own wrinkled, age-spotted one. When she spoke again, her voice was as soft and sincere as anyone on Vendrell had ever heard it. Low and close and private as could be, Olivia Rippon-Hart turned warm.

"Come child, enough. *Shh*, sweetling, *shh*. He doesn't think he took the *BattleMaster* from you, because he doesn't think he ever gave it to you! He gave it to that silly boy we all *thought* you were for so long. And then when the boy didn't return from Buena, and beautiful Hannah did, That Man felt he'd lost a son and gotten some stranger in return. He's wrong, but he's consistent, as the pigheaded so often are. It's only natural he should decide to take back his 'Mech eventually, if you didn't relent. It's only natural he should try to shame you, pressure you, choke you, into pretending to be a boy again."

Olivia clutched Hannah's hand tightly with one of her own and reached up to softly cup her cheek with the other. "But you didn't, sweetling. You didn't. You didn't let him turn you back into who you're not, no matter how he huffed and puffed! I know it doesn't feel like it, dear girl, but *this* is you *winning*! And I am so very proud of you."

Hannah let out a sob, sides tight, heart pounding, but the one sob—the one, good sob—was all she'd needed, once she'd had some support. Staring into her grandmother's eyes, feeling that soft hand on her cheek, the warm squeeze of her other hand, hearing the comfort, pride, and sincerity in her grandmother's voice, all helped her recover herself. It helped her, as much as the words, to gather her composu—

Abruptly, the moment was over. Olivia's soft touch on her face turned into a grandmotherly scrub, roughly rubbing one of Hannah's own tears into her cheekbone harshly, wiping at some imagined spot with her thumb.

"So, enough of that! Look at you, grease on your face still, and carrying on so in front of the help." Olivia Rippon-Hart composed herself, tut-tutting, shaking her head. "Stop all these hysterics at once. You'll make the peasants think we're soft."

"And you!" The former duchess pointed at her husband. Again. "Enough of your cruel toying with the girl. Can't you see she's hysterical? Go on and tell her!"

Brandon gave his faux-shrewish wife a flat look that made it clear—as though there were any question—whose idea it had been to "toy with" Hannah in the first place, then he bent over to recover something from a desk drawer.

"Of course, dear. Oh, and Captain Fox?" he said, barely glancing up as he rummaged in his desk.

"Sir?" The redhaired MechWarrior snapped to attention.

"You're fired," he said off-handedly.

"Sir." She nodded, smiled, and immediately strode over to the office bar. She was *not* pouring herself merely a mixture of fruit juices.

Hannah blinked. "Wh...what just—"

Her grandfather slapped a folder onto his polished old desk and nodded matter-of-factly. "Here we are!" Brandon shoved the folder across the desk to her, hand lingering for a moment to nudge the bowl of mints her way again, not-so-subtly.

"Go on, read up," he said, but nodded at the mints, her, and the mints again.

She gave him a confused smile, but reached for the papers instead of the candy. She cast a glance around the room as she opened the folder: Grandmother busied herself swirling her drink and *certainly not* dabbing at her own eyes after their moment of tenderness; Rachel Fox drank down an amber-colored shot of something potent and carelessly poured herself a second; and Grandfather Brandon snuck himself a mint with a pickpocket's nimble fingers. No one explained anything to her, they just left her to read.

Hannah flipped to the first page.

...does hereby state that the sponsored unit (further referred to as "the unit") shall remain available to Mountain Wolf BattleMechs (further referred to as "the sponsor") at all times, inasmuch as the size of the galaxy and the nature of interstellar travel permits. The unit shall attach an emergency release clause to any contracts agreed on with third parties (further referred to as "other employers"), making it clear that the unit must be allowed to withdraw from any non-emergency contract with other employers and endeavor within all reasonable measures to transport itself with all due haste to the site of any sponsor emergency, with neither the unit nor the sponsor being held liable for...

"What, uh..." Hannah looked up, from one face to another, then back down, flipping a few pages away. Then a few more. Then a few more.

...whenever available, the unit will travel along standard sponsor trade routes and use up to one-half (50%) of their available cargo space for the transport of trade goods on behalf of the sponsor and the sponsor's affiliates. When made available for hire, the unit will first pick from among contracts offered by the sponsor, then the sponsor's affiliates, and if no suitable work is found (as agreed on by the unit's senior officers, see 3:2b–d), they will search for work in accordance with standard Mercenary Review Board (further referred to as the MRB) protocols and practices. A percentage of the unit's profits shall be sent to the sponsor dependent on how long it has been since the unit worked directly for the sponsor or a sponsor-affiliated company (laid out in 5:1a–c), until such time as the unit has paid back a sum of...

"We drew the documents up and registered the unit last year." Grandpa Brandon smiled as she read. "It's been in the works for quite a while. Things are all in place, the company already exists on paper! Truthfully, the duke's timing wasn't far off from what we predicted!"

...the unit shall be provided at a fair price with sufficient basic necessities as decided by the sponsor so as to function efficiently in the field, including all necessary repair parts, repair and maintenance tools, missiles (short-range and long-range), autocannon and machine-gun ammunition (of appropriate calibers, as needed), small arms, sidearms, survival gear, first aid supplies, uniforms, basic commissary goods (with profits going to the sponsor, rather than the unit), sufficient food and water to stock the galley...

"What *is* all this?" Hannah's voice cracked again.

"Don't be dim." Olivia rolled her eyes. "It's just what it looks like. Mountain Wolf's so-called next big thing. It's the paperwork for a mercenary company. Mountain Wolf BattleMechs' *own* mercenary company, grubby little coin-hoarder that my husband is, to make sure everyone sees all the ugly toys he makes. A bunch of stomping, shooting advertisements. The 'Mountain Wolves,' silly as the name is, seems to be the best he could come up with! Hmph!"

She pointed at her husband with her fan. "He gets to show off Mountain Wolf hardware to the Inner Sphere as his sponsored band of miscreants run and fetch and do errands for him, his business associates, and for anyone else rubbing two coins together. It's all part of his lead up to finally cutting through That Man's bureaucracy and getting his silly little factory up and running here on Vendrell. Mountain Wolf is offering up nearly a company of their ugly *Merlin*s, several of them already filled with security MechWarriors, to get things started and to make sure everyone knows who they'll be working for."

Brandon O'Leary nodded eagerly. "Most are in mint condition! Fresh from Cameron's lines! The *Bonneville*'s due here any day, 'Mech bays full. We've everything we need to get things started, and announcements have gone out to all our partners!"

Olivia rolled her eyes at the fiduciary details, then flicked her fan at Rachel Fox. "Meanwhile, the junior Fox, finding herself no longer constrained by her position with Mountain Wolf BattleMechs proper, will take to the stars and go on a grand, semi-independent adventure. As a major, she'll see proper military action, tour the stars as the commanding officer of her own quaint little outfit, and I presume, finally earn her mother's respect, or whatever it is that drives the lowborns to such wild acts of desperation and bravado."

Fox smirked crookedly, shrugged, and lifted her glass to toast the idea.

"When it comes to MechWarrior recruitment, on top of the dusty Periphery rabble already wedged into cockpits, I've taken it on myself to speak with Gilda and Melissa a bit," Olivia said, as though she were flicking off a bit of dust or lint from her sleeve—lightly, airily, sounding like she was discussing knitting-circle friends, not Hauptmann General Gilda Felra of the Twenty-Fifth Arcturan Guards and Leftenant General Melissa Waverly, the fiery Kommandant of the War College of Buena. Being a military officer was a terribly political affair in the Lyran half of the Federated Commonwealth, and the dowager duchess had long had powerful friends. A budding unit could do a lot worse for recruitment than reaching out to contacts like those.

"Between all of us, we've a few ideas for rounding out the merry little band of for-hire peasants. My husband already has a few delivery jobs lined up that will take the unruly lot deucedly close to that miserable den of sin and iniquity, Solaris, and Major Fox will no doubt find a last few suitably dangerous MechWarrior ruffians there. Then, off the murderous rabble will go and shoot people for money, one supposes, sometimes while accompanying some sort of Mountain Wolf cargo from place to place."

Olivia slapped her fan into her palm. Then, she snapped her fingers to get Hannah's attention, and pointed straight at her with the collapsed fan; a holovid officer pointing with a swagger stick, flexing absolute power over her subjects.

"There's one last, crucial piece to this machine, though! Because *you*, bright-eyed War College graduate that you are, are joining them. Recently discarded, you find yourself free from your militia duties and with no current prospects or direction of your own, so off you'll go to the Mountain Wolves, to serve as Major Fox's executive officer." Olivia glared up at Hannah from her chair, daring her to disagree. "Use that fancy degree of yours, and that big head, hmm? Do something with all that training our money paid for! If That Man shan't make use of you, then by Allah, we shall."

Hannah reeled, eyes wide. She'd been ambushed all over again. This time wonderfully, but...still, it was quite a surprise. Olivia gave her a moment, then her grandmother's cutting tone grew softer again, and warmer. She was only kind in low, private, tones.

"This way, you'll be out from under That Man's thumb, sweetling. You'll be Major Fox's good right hand. You'll see the stars. You'll lead troops. You'll make us all so very proud." The old woman's voice nearly cracked, and her eyes were visibly wet. "That Man would have smothered you here, girl. He would have ground you under his heel until he was certain your fire was all the way out. He'd have killed you, or you him, and we, all of us who care, saw it coming. This way he won't. He and that silly Archie think they've beaten you, and no doubt expect you to come crawling back. To change for him. To beg *them* for work. This way, as a Mountain Wolf, you shan't."

"Instead, my dear, you and the Wolves?" Grandpa Brandon smiled, rapped the stem of his old pipe twice on the table, and then pointed it skyward. "You'll just fly away, where that horrid little tanker, and even your father, can't reach you!"

Olivia squeezed her hand again and watched Hannah's face as her husband continued.

"I know more than most about the difference a father can make, for good or ill," Brandon said, his perpetual good cheer fading just a bit. His business persona—doddering, lovable old Brandon—slipped and he showed someone realer. Someone more true. "Mine, Michael O'Leary, was...not a kind man. He may have not even been a good one, though it hurts to say. All he could focus on was loss. He blamed the rest of the universe aloud, and me most of all, but in private, oh, when he was at the bottom of a bottle, or lying awake at night in his bunk, I know he blamed himself. Only himself. He couldn't see any brightness in the future. He could only see distant, lost light in the past. I know he thought he was a failure, that he was the one who would finally kill the company, to shame every O'Leary who'd come before him, to let slip through his fingers everything our family had ever made. A history going back to the Star League, and he thought he and his parenting were ending it. You see? Your father, sweet girl, I don't doubt he feels the same. I did what I could with Alex, Lord knows, but I was never Sebastian. The noble peers and the council would never let me fill those highborn shoes. I was never..."

As a lowborn merchant, little more than a traveling salesman, Brandon O'Leary had never gotten the respect of the Vendrellian nobles. Alexander Rippon-Hart, Hannah's father, had been raised on stories of the noble blood of his birth-father, Sebastian Rippon, while trying to be *parented* by Brandon. Trying to be a father to such a proud young man couldn't have been easy for O'Leary.

He cleared his throat. "Never mind all that! This is about you, not me, my dear. All I mean is I know Alexander's not really cross with you, no matter how it might look, he's not cross at all. He's not angry, he's *afraid.* Afraid he did something wrong, afraid he hurt you, he broke you somehow, afraid he'll be the downfall—through you, somehow through his parenting—of *two* ancient houses, all at once. Rippons and Harts, both, all dead-ending with you, simply because you're Hannah now, and he can't wrap his head around that. Can't wrap his heart around that. Alex thought, after all their troubles and all their tries, he thought he and your mother had finally given Vendrell an heir, another Duke Rippon-Hart, a son who could carry all that responsibility. He was so proud, so relieved, and, oh, he had such plans for betrothals, alliances, trade partnerships, and..."

There was something far-off in Brandon's gaze as he petered off for a moment. Hannah could only imagine that, perhaps just after she had been born, the highborn Alexander may have finally bonded, just a bit, with his lowborn stepfather. Hannah knew she wasn't the only one that proud Duke Alexander was hurting with this new rejection and distance.

"But he was wrong. Just as my father was wrong, and the *Merlin* is proof of that, though he never lived to see it! And the *Night Hawk* coming back will be yet more proof, eh? And your father, too, will be proven wrong some day! It will take him time, Hannah, to see he's not wrong about what you'll do, only about how you'll do it. You'll be a duchess instead of a duke, but, oh, sweet girl, we all know you'll do such great things for Vendrell! But for now, do them for me, for Mountain Wolf, instead, will you? For a few years? In time, he'll have no choice but to take all of this back. No choice but to someday see he was wrong, and eventually, Rippon-Hart stubbornness be damned, to even admit it."

Hannah had never seen Grandpa Bran so sincere, so earnest, so vulnerable before. The old man had been handling clever negotiations and cunning deals all over the Inner Sphere for almost fifty years, and she now saw a hunger in him for this one last, good deal. How much of Mountain Wolf BattleMechs was riding on this harebrained idea's success? And how much of the gamble was for her benefit, more than the company's?

Brandon held his pipe tightly in his wrinkled hands, white-knuckled as he waited for her to answer. Hannah looked from her grandfather to her grandmother to Rachel Fox and saw all of them waiting. Waiting on her.

She nodded weakly.

"Hah! That's my girl! Show them!" her grandmother exclaimed with as warm a smile as any she'd ever smiled, and with eyes shining like lasers. She raised her glass, and the toast was returned by Fox's stiff drink and Brandon's gleaming pipe.

"Let's show 'em what Mountain Wolf BattleMechs can do," Fox drawled with a crooked smile, "and a few Vendrellian women with their blood up!"

TRIUMPH-CLASS DROPSHIP *BONNEVILLE*
IN TRANSIT
ENGADIN
FREE RASALHAGUE REPUBLIC
29 MARCH 3050

As Hannah finished her story, Shotaro clapped and smiled, and Tomoko whooped and cheered something in Japanese, but finished with a hoot of "Girl power!"

Hannah was mortified to realize she'd struck Major Fox's pose as she told the part of the Mountain Wolves' founding. A terrified part of her wondered how much she'd play-acted the rest of it as well. She was bothered by how bothered she felt, wanting Tomoko and Shotaro to like her. She knew an executive officer shouldn't worry about that, but worry she did.

Oh, Allah. Was I doing the voices? I bet I was doing the voices. She waited for them to make fun of her. She waited for it to feel like her classmates at the Buena War College all over again. Instead, as the cheering subsided, the pair gave her bright smiles.

"So we've got *you* to thank for the job, huh?" Tomi laughed. "Some folks around the stable said my old man was hard on me, and others said my family spoiled me, but *whew*, Hannah! I never got in trouble so hard I got a whole merc outfit as extra chores!"

Hannah giggle-snorted. "It's not *my* outfit, it's Major Fox's, and it's not extra chores, it's—"

"It's them trusting you to do it right," Shotaro said, giving her a reassuring nod. "Trusting you more than your father trusted you. Trusting you to use *us* to prove him wrong."

"Or..." Hannah smiled ruefully, teasing. "Or Grandpa Bran's the penny-pincher Gran-Gran likes to say he is, and he was just finding a leftenant desperate enough to take a lowball offer."

"Nah." Tomi scrunched up her nose and made a face. "I'm pretty sure Shote got it right on this one. They think you won't frag it up. Imagine the bad PR!"

Tomoko's hands danced as she framed imaginary headlines. "'Brandon O'Leary sends granddaughter to fiery death in worthless *Merlin*, she takes a whole company with her, news at eleven!'" She laughed. "'And this just in, *Merlin*s are fat *Vindicator*s anyway, what's anyone like about these thi—*ow!*'"

Shotaro silenced her with an elbow and a glare. Tomoko drew back like she might respond in kind and their sparring matches might continue, but Hannah cut them off with a sharp clap and an impersonation of her own.

"Hey, now!" She turned her voice low and lazy, rich with a Deep Periphery twang, and paused slightly to cartoon-spit an imaginary mouthful of Joshua Leaf juice. She put her hands on her hips and twisted her lips in what she hoped was a mockery of a mustache. "There ain't no fightin' on the *Bonnie!*"

Sergeant Brownpants, through and through. Spot on. Her impersonation had hit the senior NCO dead center, and the laughter from the other two as they all left the makeshift gym proved it.

Maybe doing the voices wasn't so bad, after all. And...and maybe leaving wasn't either, Hannah thought as Tomoko threw a sweaty arm over her shoulder while they walked.

The trio were boisterous, roughhousing as they went, filling the DropShip halls with laughter, acting their age as they rode out the long travel time before their first missions. Hannah was acting more like a rowdy cadet than when she'd *been* a cadet, and she knew it, and she let herself. *Gran-Gran, Grandpa Bran, Aunt Fatima, even my father...I left my family behind. But...maybe I found a new one. Maybe the Mountain Wolves are the family I was supposed to have, all along.*

But she couldn't help but remember it *was* a job, and a dangerous one. And they hadn't truly even started that dangerous work yet. She knew the worst was yet to come...

TO BE CONTINUED IN SHRAPNEL #19!

ALL'S FAIR IN LOVE AND INDUSTRIAL ESPIONAGE

MATT LARSON

How can we expect another to keep our secret if we cannot keep it ourselves?

—François de La Rochefoucauld, *Maxims*

WOLF'S DRAGOONS COMPOUND
SPACEPORT XB2
CARVER V
CAPELLAN CONFEDERATION
27 FEBRUARY 3014

Begin Transcript

[*Captain Marcus Way, head of Wolf's Dragoons technical services corps, takes the podium in front of the smoke-filled conference room.*]

Marcus Way: Okay, okay, everyone, settle down and take a seat. I know you all have a significant task with coordinating equipment inspections before we pack up for New Delos, so let's get through this.

[*His nostrils flare, and he coughs hard twice.*]

These local cigarettes are putrid. Your inner corruption will have you all quoting Amaris within the month.

[*Scattered laughter washes over the room as Way flips on the large wall screen and turns toward two armed men in the corner.*]

Way: All clear?

Wolfnet Sergeant: *Aff.* All in attendance are confirmed to have come from the Homeworlds.

Way: Right. Today is part technical briefing and part history lesson. We'll leave the real technical nuts and bolts for after lunch, but for now we are going to focus on the development of the Bandit and Badger. As Homeworlders, you all are familiar with the ubiquitous, more capable version of the Bandit. Everyone has them, and they are produced by no fewer than five Clans. But the Badger probably didn't come up in training. There is a reason for that. A careless, shameful one, and the critical lesson of this story. If you were one of the select personnel at the Blackwell plant back in 3008, this will mostly be old hat. For the rest of you, listen carefully. A century and a half ago, fraternization outside of the organization cost Clan Wolf a technological edge and a great deal of prestige. We cannot allow a repeat. The stakes for secrecy are much higher this time. You will not go down as the reason we were compromised.

[*The screen image changes to a schematic of a Star League* Mercury *featuring its interchangeable weapon mounts.*]

After Clan Coyote bridged the Star League *Mercury* into genuine OmniMech technology, other Clans eagerly awaited their own similar breakthroughs. Technological progress on military gear had ramped up to a near-exponential rate, and it was only logical that tankers and fighter jocks would get their own iterations in short order. But as you know, once the MechWarriors have their fill, they have little interest in other pursuits.

[*The next slide appears, showing a chubby wolf lying on its back. Laughter again.*]

Priority immediately shifted to producing as many OmniMechs as possible in both quantity and variety. It would seem everyone else would, as always, have to wait their turn. As years turned into a decade, it seemed the wait would be indefinite. We have records of Steel Viper scientists in 2858 briefly experimenting on vehicle hulls with modular slots that would slide in and out of the chassis, but the lack of flexibility, and the tendency for the slotted equipment to spontaneously eject, caused them to abandon the project within six months.

Fortunately for those craving their own Omni equipment, necessity provided relief.

[*The transition to the next slide reveals a blueprint schematic of the Elemental battle armor.*]

After our scientists developed the Elemental in 2868, OmniMechs were adapted to act as carriers in the subsequent design generation, beginning with the *Nova*. Unfortunately, there were never enough in all places to move the suits where they needed to go. Further compounding transport bottlenecks, the vintage Turhan was the only extant vehicle capable of moving a Point of battle armor and simultaneously possessing adequate protection for the cargo. Heavy APCs had, and still have, a nasty tendency to explode at the first provocation. The rapid proliferation of pulse lasers led to an unacceptable number of barbecued Elementals.

[*Captain Way takes a sip of water and transitions to a portrait of Hell's Horses Khan Eric Amirault.*]

No sooner had our Clan revealed to the others the tremendous potential of battle armor, than the Hell's Horses bid to trial for our innovation, seemingly before anyone fully understood we possessed it. They offered us the opportunity to trial for their infantry-breeding protocols to sweeten the deal. Our rivals quickly rolled out a variant of the Svantovit in 2870 to accommodate a full Point of battlesuits. That vehicle became the standard for battle armor transports at the time, and it spread quickly to all corners of Clan space.

[*The next slide features Amirault's Clan Wolf contemporary, Alexis Ward.*]

Still seething from the loss of Elemental preeminence, Alexis Ward searched for an opportunity to save face. Her late-night dive into WeaponMaster communications uncovered a research funding request from not long after Clan Wolf's acquisition of OmniMech technology a generation before, ordering a move forward with a similar program for vehicles. By March of 2871, a team had been assembled, and work began. To avoid direct competition with the new Svantovit, the

WeaponMasters pitched and received the go-ahead to develop a lighter, tracked vehicle that might prove less vulnerable to immobilization and operate in wooded areas.

[*The presentation cuts to a candid photo of a Clan Wolf technician and a Clan Hell's Horses scientist, embracing and laughing in a public park.*]

Meet Technician Lilia and Scientist Carlos. Strana Mechty, the most cosmopolitan of Clan worlds, offers many temptations, even if considered modest by Inner Sphere standards. Lilia was a rising star in the technician caste—she possessed a brilliant mind with an obvious talent for design. A mutual indiscretion by our two protagonists would lead to Clan Wolf forfeiting a substantial battlefield advantage and personal prestige that would have cemented her as a luminary among our people. Some of you are of the age and talent to have participated in the annual Strana Mechty Interclan Robotics and Theoretical Physics Competition before departing the Homeworlds. While both the technician and scientist castes agree this event promotes competitiveness and innovation that benefits all levels of Clan society, the warriors often grumble about the risks of sharing secrets with what are ostensibly the enemy. In this case, the fears of Clan Wolf's leadership were realized when a very specific romance turned into a rare case of espionage. Clans Wolf and Hell's Horses met in the consolation final that winter of 2872. Clan Wolf won the day, and the stage was set for our drama when the teams shook hands. When Carlos and Lilia met to congratulate each other, there was more than a feeling of collegial respect. She sought him out later that day, and they began spending most of their time together. This culminated in the acquisition of a room at a residence away from both Clans' dorms. There are plenty of holovids you can watch to get the general idea of what happened next, but this particular cohabitation ended up being coincidentally disastrous.

[*Way moves to the next slide, displaying the schematics for the Badger's interchangeable turret.*]

As young lovers do, Lilia and Carlos were eager to share secrets with each other. Lilia's divulging happened to be far more detrimental. Their common interest in applied engineering was an immediate point of connection, and their discussions on design philosophy quickly transitioned to theory crafting about Omni technology. Lilia's team had struggled to make significant headway as they attempted to succeed where the Vipers had previously failed. The pair quickly worked up schematics for an innovative design concept that called for an almost completely empty hull, save the critical components such as suspension, transmission, engine, controls, and crew compartment. They further worked out a system of flexible armor panels that could be shifted to take advantage of several hull points accommodating pods and turrets. This achieved the primary goal of designing an APC/IFV that could balance troop-carrying capacity and weaponry to match the mission at hand. After three sleepless nights working out schematics and simulations on Carlos' noteputer, they spent an evening out together. At this point, each Clan had taken an interest in their missing personnel's activities.

[*A montage of two dozen or so pictures of the couple taking in the relatively spartan sights of Katyusha City cycles in the background.*]

They knew they were being watched. The lovers agreed to separate the next day and take copies of their findings back to their superiors. But love is a fickle thing, isn't it? When young Lilia awoke, Carlos was gone. Security footage had him returning to his group in the middle of the night. And with him? All the work they had done together. Lilia returned to her superiors in shame. All that prevented her banishment to the laborer caste was a small bit of leverage: the only knowledge of the vehicle schematics, apart from what was stored on Carlos' noteputer, was in her brain. So the race was on.

[*Way moves in front of the podium.*]

Re-creating Lilia's previous work took precious time. Without Carlos to provide the engineering expertise, she had to walk our own WeaponMasters through the math. This was no easy task. She often raged at their inability to make the leaps in logic she found so natural. Meanwhile, the Horses quickly put their own prototype together. It took a year of trial and error, but by early 2875, both Clans had working prototypes that showed promise.

On 5 February of that year, a Star of unidentified Horses hovercraft and a Star of OmniMechs challenged our forces on Tiber to a Trial of Possession for an ammunition plant. Both the plant and the outcome of the trial itself were inconsequential. The main objective was to rub Khan Ward's nose in the completion of the Bandit. The Badger was approved for deployment a few weeks later and participated in a reprisal, but its reduced speed and armor caused it to fare much worse. The final analysis was that the Badger was an inferior platform, and Ward ordered the project shelved before full production could even be arranged.

[*Way spreads his arms in a conciliatory gesture.*]

Perhaps we did get the last laugh, though. An incensed Ward went before the Grand Council and accused the Horses of espionage, a most dishonorable charge, and demanded a Trial of Possession for the Horses' Bandit plant. In a reversal of fortune, our Clan won the day and seized the plant. In a fit of pique, Khan Ward then ordered a series of technology swaps that dispersed the Bandit's design to multiple Clans, guaranteeing mass proliferation.

[*Way turns off the projector.*]

I again urge you to recommend to your personnel that they take interest in each other rather than strangers who can disseminate our secrets.

Such actions have personal consequences as well. Carlos would find great rewards for his duplicity, and his actions earned him great notoriety. The loss of the Bandit created the necessity to produce another Omni tank. Carlos led the team that produced the Epona. But Lilia? She spent the rest of her life servicing tractors.

May you all heed this warning. Any questions?

[*A number of hands shoot up from the audience.*]

End Transcript

CHAOS CAMPAIGN SCENARIO: RAID ON TOMANS

LUKE ROBERTSON

In the aftermath of the collapse of the Jade Falcon Occupation Zone, the Lyran Commonwealth conspicuously failed to attempt to recover the star systems it had lost to the Falcons a century before. Faced with this reluctance, Hauptmann-General Sarah Regis occupied Arcturus with the Twenty-Sixth Arcturan Guards. In defiance of her superiors, she declared the re-creation of the Tamar Pact and set about enticing regional worlds to her banner.

In January 3152, Tomans joined the Pact. A century of indoctrination left this planet culturally Jade Falcon, and the lower-caste council's ruling in the absence of the warriors feared being absorbed by the neighboring Rasalhague Dominion. The Tamar Pact offered them a chance to maintain their independence.

In the Rasalhague Dominion, the rise of the ilClan led to a simmering civil war as society tried to resolve how it would respond to this momentous change. This prevented the Dominion from exploiting the neighboring Jade Falcon Occupation Zone for over a year. By the time the Rasalhagians felt confident enough to respond, the military situation in the Occupation Zone had become unclear, requiring reconnaissance in force. The foundries of Arcturus and Pandora were the ultimate targets, but to get there, Tomans was the first step.

Arriving on Tomans, the Rasalhague Dominion discovered the Tamar Pact as a new factor in the region—with a battalion on-world to contest the matter.

—Contemplating the ilClan,
John Onubogu, Hesperus Publishing, 3152

This scenario can be played as a stand-alone game or incorporated into a longer campaign using the *Chaos Campaign* rules (available as a free download from https://store.catalystgamelabs.com/products/battletech-chaos-campaign-succession-wars).

For flexibility of play, this track contains rules for *Total Warfare* (*TW*), with *Alpha Strike: Commander's Edition* (*AS* or *AS:CE*) rules noted in parenthesis, allowing the battle to be played with either rule set.

TOUCHPOINT: A SIMPLE OCCUPATION

Point Commander Tan's Odin crawled silently through the streets of Grant's Station. Between the soft rubber tires and fuel-cell engine, the 20-ton reconnaissance vehicle barely made a sound in the haze before dawn. A few late-night revelers and early morning sanitation workers were the only ones awake to see the military vehicle head toward the docks. Advanced electronics both hid the tiny tank and reached out beyond the multistory buildings. A few kilometers outside the city, two Stars were forming up in the woods, ready to move in. With the defeat of Clan Jade Falcon on Terra, there should have been no military here. But long experience had shown the value of reconnaissance.

That experience paid off as the Odin's active probe detected a hard contact behind a building. Tan gulped as the computers identified a 100-ton Demolisher II. He tapped his driver, Monica, who immediately stopped. Keeping their eyes on the Demolisher, the pair tried to flank the interloper tank to discover whether it had any support. A block farther on, the probe picked up a 'Mech moving toward them. The probe detected encrypted radio chatter, and the 'Mech stopped behind a building.

Monica glanced at Tan. "She knows we are here."

As she started backing the Odin up, infantry fire erupted from the buildings ahead of them.

Tan answered with a spray of Gauss rifles while Monica drove their Odin behind a building. With more and more contacts being detected, it was time to go.

Even as he reported heavy contacts back to Star Colonel Lena, Tan realized this wasn't some scraped-together militia. This was a serious military unit.

This trip to Tomans was not going to be a simple occupation.

SITUATION

GRANT'S STATION
TOMANS
TAMAR PACT
20 JUNE 3152

Keen to discover just what has happened in the Clan Jade Falcon Occupation Zone over the last year, the Rasalhague Dominion deployed elements of the First Tyr Assault Cluster to reconnoiter and possibly seize Tomans. Instead of an undefended world, they stumbled into a battalion of the First Tamar Jaegers garrisoning the planet in the name of the Tamar Pact. Not looking for a fight, the First Tyr pulled back from Grant's Station. But the Jaegers, seeking to make a statement of the strength of the Tamar Pact to their larger neighbors, moved forward to engage.

GAME SETUP

Recommended Terrain: Open Terrain #2 (*Map Pack: Grasslands*), Open Terrain #3 (*Map Pack: Grasslands*)

The Defender arranges two maps with the long edges touching. The Defender's home edge is the unconnected long edge of Open Terrain #3 map. The Attacker's home edge is the opposite, on the unconnected long edge of Open Terrain #2 map.

Attacker

Recommended Forces: First Tamar Jaegers "Pride of Arcturus"

The Attacker is a Regular-rated force consisting of a company of heavy 'Mechs, a lance of heavy vehicles, and a platoon of battle armor. The Attacker's forces are drawn from the Lyran Commonwealth Random Assignment Tables (see pp. 117, 118, and 120, *Tamar Rising*). One 'Mech of every four may roll on the Jade Falcon assignment tables (see p. 122, *Tamar Rising*). The First Jaegers favor mobility and have access to Clan technology. The Attacker enters the battlefield from their home edge during the Movement Phase of Turn 1.

Special Command Abilities: Esprit de Corps (see p. 84, *CO* and p. 104, *AS:CE*)

Defender

Recommended Forces: First Tyr Assault Cluster, Rasalhague Galaxy "Through sacrifice the beast is bound"

The Defender is an Elite-rated force consisting of a Star of assault 'Mechs, a Star of light and medium vehicles, and a Star of battle armor.

The Defender's forces are drawn from the Rasalhague Dominion Front Line and Vehicle Random Assignment Tables (see pp. 142, 145, and 147, *Dominions Divided*). To reflect the First Tyr's preference for Assault 'Mechs, add an additional +1 to the standard Dominion +1 modifier when rolling on the random weight-class table. The First Tyr favors assault 'Mechs, but relies on their vehicles to protect their flanks. The Defender may position their units anywhere within ten hexes (*AS*: 20") of their home edge before the start of Turn 1.

Special Command Abilities: Esprit de Corps (see p. 84, *CO* and p. 104, *AS:CE*), Family (see p. 22, *Turning Points: Tokasha*) Tactical Specialization/Defense (see p. 87, *CO* and p. 108, *AS:CE*), Zone of Control (see p. 87, *CO* and p. 109, *AS:CE*)

WARCHEST
Track Cost: 400

OBJECTIVES
We Need the Intel (Defender Only): For every immobilized attacking unit at the end of the game. **[90]**

We Need the Metal (Attacker Only): For every immobilized defending unit at the end of the game. **[65]**

SPECIAL RULES

Forced Withdrawal
All units adhere to the *Forced Withdrawal* rules (see p. 258, *TW* or pp. 126–127, *AS:CE*).

AFTERMATH
As the last Jaegers 'Mech retreated over the hillside, the First Tyr were at a loss. Who was the mysterious force defending Grant's Station, and why did they engage so aggressively? Deniers in the expeditionary force were already muttering about the Dominion's Joiner leadership sending them on a fool's errand. Discussions with the leadership in Grant's Station revealed the existence of the Tamar Pact and its secession from the Lyran Commonwealth. For Star Colonel Lena, steeped in the history of the Free Rasalhague Republic, the scrappy little secessionist state appealed to both her romanticism and knowledge of the practical benefits the Rasalhague buffer state provided the Draconis Combine a century before. Lena's offer to the Jaegers was simple. The First Tyr would stand down, and both sides would report to their superiors for direction. While the Dominion dangled the carrot of a secure border for both realms, the stick remained very much in play.

METACHROSIS

GILES GAMMAGE

WEST OF NEW MONACO
DUSTBALL
MALTHUS CONFEDERATION
6 NOVEMBER 3151

Some things never change.

The dunes shifted and stirred against the side of the land yacht as the setting sun drowned itself in the sand sea. Over many sunrises and sunsets, Dustball had changed hands many times, from the Lyran Commonwealth to the Arc-Royal Defense Cordon to the Lyran Alliance and, finally, to Clan Jade Falcon. But through much of its history, some things had remained the same: the gambling, the nightclubs, the underworld business those vices attracted, the family that ran the business.

And how they ran it.

The land yacht was a toy of the elite, of the Malthus family that had effectively ruled the planet through their criminal syndicate for centuries. The behemoth machine was over 100 meters long, twenty meters wide, and ten meters high, resting on four sets of massive double treads; its domed upper deck featured a swimming pool, a helipad, even a dance floor. A dance floor which ran red—and not because of the sunset. The bullet holes, laser burns, and scattered bodies were entirely the work of people. The name *"KILLER KRAKEN"* was painted on the stern in big, bold letters. It was a monster's name, but those on board were all too human.

The man standing near the stern was, he liked to think, not a monster. He bore the name of a legendary killer—a ruthless bandit and marauder—but told himself he was no more a monster than the yacht was. He was a hard man, he admitted, maybe even a cold one, but then, it was a hard, cold galaxy. But he was not a monster.

"Valasek, you monster," said the man pinned to the deck.

Balor Valasek sighed and scratched his temple with the barrel of his needler pistol. He was misunderstood, he felt, on account of his name. The name of his ancestor, to be more precise: Helmar Valasek, bandit king of Santander V, leader of Santander's Killers, one of the most infamous raiders and assassins in the history of the Inner Sphere.

Four figures stood (or lay face down, in the other man's case) by the railing at the stern. Balor's two surviving associates, Rathbone and Xosha Bloodgood, pressed a third man against the deck: Ezekiel Malthus, currently a minor scion in the ruling Malthus family and very shortly to become a minor collection of bones in the middle of the desert.

"We came to talk, and you tried to murder us," Balor pointed out. Mildly, reasonably, his voice even and level. "You *did* murder poor Kilgore. I don't think you get to call anyone a monster."

"I know what you're planning," Ezekiel said. "It's insane."

"I just offered to lead your people against Sudeten."

"You'll bring the Jade Falcons down on us all."

"I'm sure we can deal with them." Oh, a few might die, but that was a constant in the galaxy. It would be necessary though. The liberation of Sudeten with himself in the lead would be the first step to reclaiming the glory that was his birthright.

"We? Hah." Ezekiel spat without much success, the spittle hanging on his chin for a moment before oozing onto the deck. "You'd get us all killed, and for what? Petty pride, an old name, and a planet that wouldn't want you even if it knew you existed."

"You have a strange way of begging for mercy."

"I know better than to beg for the mercy of monsters." Ezekiel struggled, but it was futile. Rathbone was pale and bald and big, Elemental big, while Bloodgood's thinner frame was wrapped in muscles like corded steel and her mouth was grimly set. Together, they kept Ezekiel immobile.

"You mistake me for my ancestor," Balor said. He crouched down, jammed the barrel of his needler under Ezekiel's chin and forced his head up. "You know, much like this planet, Santander V was also a dry world. I heard Helmar Valasek had a way of dealing with traitors. If someone betrayed him, he had them thrown from a VTOL into the desert to die."

A civilian helicopter waited patiently on the pad behind them. The sand clawed greedily against the hull of the land yacht. The desert stretched unbroken from horizon to horizon in every direction.

"You animal."

If Balor was upset by the demotion from monster to mere beast, he did not show it. "I told you, I am not my ancestor. I won't throw you into the desert from a VTOL." He gave Ezekiel a reassuring smile. "You can go over the railing right here."

Ezekiel *did* beg then, as Rathbone and Bloodgood hoisted him into the air and tossed him, screaming, over the railing, where he bounced off the side of the hull before crashing into the sand, evidently breaking a leg in the process. He lay in the dunes, thrashing and screaming threats and insults at them.

"There will be trouble," Bloodgood said as the yacht rumbled back toward New Monaco and she watched the vultures circle above the dwindling figure in their wake. "That kind of intimidation might have worked for your supposed great-to-the-whatever granddaddy, but the Malthus family won't be scared of your name. We'll have to run."

Rathbone shrugged, which was a minor miracle, given his wealth of muscle and poverty of neck. "That was fun," was all he said.

Balor took no pleasure in the process. He wasn't a monster. He did what he must, because a cold, hard galaxy demanded that he be hard and cold, and some things never change.

NEWTON
BUTLER
ALYINA MERCANTILE LEAGUE
22 JANUARY 3152

"Evening, sir." The night security guard touched two fingers to the brim of his cap as Bertrand stepped out of the BattleMech warehouse and into the night air. Bertrand nodded absently. He had already forgotten the man's name. He had seen marvels: BattleMechs! The planet had only a few of them now, but there were more to come, and he—Bertie, the merchant-caste negotiator—was responsible for hiring them. *Him.* Once a no-name nothing and nobody under Clan Jade Falcon, soon a name to be reckoned with. The thought made him giddy.

It had rained while he was inside, and the ferrocrete apron around the warehouse was mirror-slick and treacherous as a crusting of black ice. The security guard escorted him through the layer cake of security gates, with their steel bars and key cards and punch codes, past the icing-white outer wall and its frosting of razor wire, out into the street.

Bertrand tottered carefully out to the curb, where his taxi waited in the shadow of the walls, wreathed in the wispy fumes of its own exhalations. As a member of the Alyina Mercantile League's new elite, a taxi—one of the first in a new crop of private vehicles that had sprouted since the end of Clan public transport regulations—was a rare and precious thing, but he promised himself even this was just a start. One day, when his name carried more weight, there would be limousines and luxury yachts, he promised himself. He was meant for greater things.

The security guard waited patiently by the passenger door. "Impressive, aren't they sir?"

"Hm? Ah. Oh. Yes." Mentally, he was still back inside. Due diligence, inspecting the goods before he signed any contracts.

"Reckon they'll make the Commonwealth or Hell's Horses think twice about poking their noses around here." Butler was the home to valuable shipyards, and the Alyina Mercantile League was already threatened by larger, more powerful neighboring realms. Some things never change.

The security guard opened the rear door for Bertrand.

"That is the general idea," Bertrand agreed and dropped himself into the rear seat with a sigh. He nodded again to the security guard, who closed the door with a thump.

"Where to, sir?" asked the cabbie. He was remarkably short, eyes barely above the steering wheel, and alarmingly old. The face was deeply carved as though by chisels, the hair white and wispy, the eyes bionic, the teeth steel-clad in primitive dentistry. Bertrand guessed he was over seventy, and was off by a decade. He read the license displayed on the back of the driver's seat, and gave a short bark of laughter.

"'Short Change'?" he read. "What a curious name. Nothing to do with the quality of service, I hope."

"A nickname. On account of my height." That was a lie. Short Change was a code name, one given to him by the Word of Blake. As a child-soldier inserted onto the planet as a sleeper agent, he had driven a bus for the Clans for decades, waiting for orders that had never come. "Where to, sir?"

"Independence Avenue," Bertrand replied. He did not acknowledge the security guard's salute as they pulled away from the curb.

There was a rear-seat entertainment unit that hinged down from the ceiling. A news program was playing, and the churn of history had brought old names bubbling back up to the surface again: Kell and Carlyle, Ward and Hazen, Redburn and Ricol. *The Inner Sphere is incapable of changing,* Bertrand mused. *What humanity needs is new faces, new names. Names like "Bertrand."*

Short Change mistook his introspection for worry. "Everything all right, sir?"

"Oh, a good start, I suppose," he replied, mistaking the intent of the question. "But we'll need to hire more."

"Mercenaries, sir?"

"The more, the merrier."

"Just as you say, sir." There was a long pause. "Only, you never know what kind of MechWarrior becomes a mercenary. Not the best sort."

"Oh come now, they're hardly monsters."

JEBE HIGHLANDS
ROADSIDE
INDEPENDENT SYSTEM
3 FEBRUARY 3152

Winter Curzon waited for the target to appear.

Winter was a bounty hunter, and she had discovered that bounty hunting involved little hunting and plenty of waiting. Waiting for bounties to be posted, waiting for information on the target, waiting for the target to appear, waiting for the client to confirm delivery of whatever body bits or pieces they'd accept as evidence, waiting for payment.

Winter was patient, though. She had plans. She needed the money to tread the well-worn path to mercenary independence. Money, and a name. A reputation. Money would buy warriors, but the name and reputation that went with it would ensure they stayed bought.

Her red-and-black *Scourge* sat astride the mountain road, ankle-deep in snow, a splatter of scarlet color amid the white, like a bloodstain. She yawned and stretched. It was snowing with soporific slowness, making it hard to stay alert.

Bounty hunting would be easier out of her 'Mech. It was a little-known secret of bounty hunting that people were much easier to capture or kill when not encased in 100 tons of fusion-powered armor, titanium, and tera-wattage weaponry. Easier, but much less impressive. And you needed to be impressive if you wanted to make a name for yourself. To mangle an ancient saying, fame and fortune flowed from the barrel of a gun, as they had for centuries, as they always would.

"Who is he?" her partner Venn asked, more out of boredom than curiosity, judging by the tone of his voice. His 'Mech lay deep in the trees off to the left.

"A Pryde," she said. "At least, that's the theory."

It was a big galaxy, and it could be hard to be sure that people were who they claimed. The target might very well belong to the famous Jade Falcon Bloodname lineage, or might have been named for their behavior, or their favorite Jane Austen novel. Renegade, martinet, or literature aficionado—in the end, it was all the same to her. Their target was a bounty, and the hunting merely a well-trodden path to something more.

The sensors pinged as an unknown BattleMech approached. It was a monster, a 65-ton *Hellbringer*, bristling with particle cannons, lasers, and a short-range missile launcher. It advanced down the middle of the road, scorning stealth, *so perhaps the pilot is named for their personality after all,* Winter thought.

She sat upright, rolled her neck, flexed her fingers, and gripped the controls. The *Scourge* raised its right arm slightly in salute. The target slowed, seemed to hesitate, then picked up speed again, coming straight for her.

Challenge accepted.

On cue, Venn triggered the quartet of command-detonated mines buried beneath the road. The explosion was a volcanic geyser, a vertical pillar of flame that blew off one of the huge war machine's legs. It came to rest on its back and did not move, seemingly content to watch the roiling, flame-flecked charcoal pillar of smoke climb farther and farther into the sky. A Gauss round to the immobile BattleMech's cockpit made sure it stayed down.

Winter nodded in satisfaction. The old-fashioned might say boobytraps were underhanded, but you had to change with the times.

She was delighted to find a notification from the Malthus Confederation about a new bounty waiting for her when she returned with the remains of the putative Pryde in tow. No waiting required this time.

**NEWTON
BUTLER
ALYINA MERCANTILE LEAGUE
26 MARCH 3152**

Balor and his two companions sat around a u-shaped couch at the back corner of the bar. After their failure to win friends and success in feeding the vultures outside of New Monaco, they were in town to meet a man named Bertrand, who was offering employment with the Alyina Mercantile League to support the Light of Heaven aerospace mercenary unit currently garrisoning the planet. A detour, to be sure, but Balor still harbored hopes of using it to make a name for himself. He would lead a daring strike to annihilate the remnants of Clan Jade Falcon, just as the Inner Sphere had done with Clan Smoke Jaguar during Operation Bulldog. History would repeat itself.

The back wall behind them was entirely taken up by the floor-to-ceiling glass of an enormous aquarium tank. There were no fish inside, but rather spearhead swarms of a local species of squid. These ones entertained the patrons by changing the color of skin cells into a dazzling array of colors. An ability called metachrosis. To the religiously inclined, they were evidence of the wondrous imagination of the Creator; to the scientifically inclined, they were evidence that all the squids that never learned the skin-changing trick had died out.

A woman appeared at their table, athletic, coolly professional, every centimeter a MechWarrior. Her smile was as wide as it was insincere. She extended a hand. "Balor Valasek? Curzon. Winter Curzon."

Balor did not take the hand. He regarded its owner for long enough for it to become uncomfortable. The woman's smile and hand did not waver. "Never heard of you," he said at last.

"I'm a bounty hunter."

"Well, double-barreled PPCs for you."

Winter withdrew the hand, but only to reach inside her jacket and retrieve a folded paper printout. This was a bit of showmanship; the printout was unnecessary as anything other than a prop. She held it up, wedged between index and middle fingers. "Fact is, I've got a bond right here. And you're never going to guess whose name is on it."

Rathbone growled and was about to stand, when Xosha clicked her tongue and shook her head, freezing him. "Man by the door. Doesn't look happy to see us, so I'm guessing that's a gun in his pocket."

Balor squinted through the hazy, lazy smoke and saw a reddish-haired man with a suspiciously long coat leaning with deliberate casualness against the wall. His gaze was fixed on their table and anything but casual, he arched an eyebrow when their eyes met. Balor raised his glass in a silent toast.

"There a point to this?" he asked Winter.

"Look, if it was just about the money, I'd be waiting outside right now, ready to shine a Sunbeam into your eyes the moment you walked out. But it isn't just the money, is it?"

A slow smile of understanding spread across Balor's face. "No," he agreed. "There's the matter of...publicity. So, a Clan-style trial then? 'Mech on 'Mech? Autocannons at dawn?"

"My thoughts exactly. Just pick when and where."

Balor nodded and leaned back against the couch with deliberate ease, his legs stretched out underneath the table. "Well..." He made a show of considering it. "How about—" He threw Xosha a wink. "—right *now*?"

On "now" his boot kicked the underside edge of the table, violently flipping it and their drinks up and toward Winter, letting his momentum carry him tumbling over the back of the couch and behind it for cover, reaching for a hold-out needler he kept in a shoulder holster.

As he somersaulted backward, Balor had a snapshot glance of the man by the door, just enough to see him throw back his coat and draw a Clan-made Avenger CCW semiautomatic shotgun, just enough to realize that was bad news, just enough to catch the bright muzzle flash as the man opened fire. The solid slugs whistled over his head, then the glass in the squid tank shattered.

A roaring wall of water and bewildered cephalopods hammered into his back, knocked him flat, and blasted the couch, table, and bounty hunter off the floor and into the sea of humanity behind them.

The squids flashed red, black, red, black, in distress.

Lights flashed red, black, red, black as the militia patrol cruiser streaked past the alleyway, wailing off into the night.

Balor leaned against concrete, bent nearly double, panting hard. The hold-out needler dangled from one hand. It still had one volley left in the magazine. He didn't think he had killed anyone, but there had been an awful lot of people in the place, and he had fired an awful lot of skin-shredding polymer needles without an awful lot of aim, so you never knew.

"Was that *really* necessary?" Xosha asked from where she slumped near his feet, knees drawn up against her chest.

"An honorable duel?" Balor scoffed between breaths. "A fair fight? Be serious."

"First rule of combat: never fight fair," Rathbone advised. He stood facing the mouth of the alleyway, a magnum revolver tiny in his giant fist. He hadn't had the gun when they had walked into the bar. Balor was fairly sure Rathbone *had* killed someone back there, possibly more than one.

They were interrupted by the scuff of boots on gravel and a sudden shadow at the mouth of the alleyway. Balor's head jerked around, eyes squinting, trying to see who it was, when Rathbone's hand and the incongruously dainty revolver came up.

"Followed!" the big man growled.

"Wait, that's Ber—" Balor had time to say before the rest of his words were drowned out by the thunder crack of the gun.

Balor could only watch Bertrand, merchant-caste recruiter, man on the rise, fall as he was kicked backward by the impact and flopped out the alley and into the street, minus a large section of his neck.

Bertrand frowned, his mouth moving once or twice as though to protest he was destined for greater things. He wasn't even destined to make the evening news. The death of a minor official would soon be overshadowed by what was about to happen.

This, Balor thought, *is bad news.*

It was bad news for several reasons. First, Rathbone had just fired a revolver in an enclosed space without any ear protection. In medical terms, this was known as "a bad idea." Second, he had just shot the man intending to hire them. In business terms, this was known as "less than ideal." Third, the militia would be on their way and would not be in a conversational mood on arrival. This was known as "the icing on the cake."

Balor was strongly tempted to join in the fun and use his last volley of needles to tear Rathbone a new mouth somewhere below his chin. In the end, he didn't. Shooting Bertrand had been rash, but it was a hard universe, cruel to those who hesitate, and that would never change.

"Come on," he said instead. Loud, too loud, barely hearing his own voice. "We've got to get to the 'Mechs."

It took Balor three steps to realize Xosha wasn't following them. He turned to find her still sitting in the alley, unmoving, slowly shaking her head.

"I won't tell them where you've gone," she said.

Balor hung his head for a moment, drew a deep breath and looked up.

"I know you won't," he agreed.

The needler was in his hand, and in the narrow alleyway it was very hard to miss.

Winter wrung out the towel, watching the water puddle and run in the narrow crack between the militia patrol cruiser and the curb. She sat on the hood, Venn leaning against it beside her. They were watched by Point Commander Hutomo of the law enforcement wing of the planet's militia. He was slightly short, with the solid build of a wrestler, and chewed gum with the determined ferocity of a man who chose the wrong week to give up smoking.

"What a mess," Hutomo muttered around the now-flavorless wad of rubber. His hand rested heavily on the butt of the service pistol holstered at his side as he debated whether to try to arrest these two. Things were confused. The Jade Falcon *touman* was gone, the planet was run by the merchants now, the old certainties had crumbled. Change was frightening.

The bar was on fire. It hadn't been when Hutomo's men had arrived, merely a bit watery and filled with a surprising number of camouflaged squid. Sullen flames licked the roof now, as if someone had read a firefighting manual back-to-front and decided to put out the water with fire. A roomful of disoriented mercenaries had reacted to the militia with what was, in hindsight, sadly predictable violence.

A shrouded corpse was wheeled away on a gurney. Hutomo considered it as he chewed and turned back to the pair by the cruiser. "Who were they?"

"Criminals with a price on their heads," said Winter. "Wanted for murder."

"Oh yeah? By who?"

Winter's tight smile teetered on the edge of condescension. "Client confidentiality." It was, she knew, far more convincing than saying "the Malthus crime syndicate."

"The heck is that supposed to mean?"

"I'm a bounty hunter." She flashed the bond with Valasek's name, too fast to read, but she needn't have bothered. Hutomo barely glanced at it.

"Oh yeah? You anybody famous?"

Venn chuckled softly as Winter stiffened, then forced herself to smile. "Not yet."

Hutomo shrugged. The day had already been long, the night longer, and he had enough to worry about without trying to wind up dead like the body on the gurney. "Well, good luck with that," he said, waving them away. "You won't catch them—they'll be on the other side of the planet by now."

Venn pushed himself upright. Winter was sliding down from the hood when she heard gunfire for the second time that night. She and Venn froze and exchanged a look, then turned in sync toward the Point Commander.

Hutomo's shoulders slumped as he offered his heartfelt opinion: "Shit."

The night security guard hadn't heard anything. He was inside, staring up at the things he was supposed to be watching over: BattleMechs. Three of the titanic war machines were lined up, as imperious and aloof as ancient statuary, as unstoppable as history, as unbending as fate. He admired. He daydreamed. He was so engrossed he did not hear the door open, nor the footsteps approach until they were close behind.

He whirled, bringing up his gun, to find two men facing him. One was well-built, bald, bearded, and grim-faced. The other was nearly albino white, bald, and as massive as a BattleMech.

"H-h-halt," the security guard squawked.

Balor flashed the warehouse code key at the man without breaking his stride. "Don't you know who I am?"

"Nope." The security guard shrugged. "Now halt."

"I'm the owner of these 'Mechs and I'm in a hurry. So stand aside."

"You are?" the security guard perked up, his smile briefly the brightest thing in the room as an idea occurred to him. "I challenge you!"

Balor was in the process of striding past the man, but halted in mid-step. "What?"

"A Trial of Possession." The recent upending of caste hierarchies in the Alyina Mercantile League had emboldened some in the civilian caste to attempt things previously reserved for warriors alone. "For the BattleMechs."

Balor rolled his eyes and nodded to Rathbone. "Sure. Here are the terms: here, now, I nominate Rathbone as my champion."

The security guard's smile had just enough time to slip before the battering ram of Rathbone's fist collided with the fragile surface of his face, then his face collided with the ferrocrete floor. The concussion caused enough damage to his short-term memory that he didn't remember being punched, and enough to his long-term memory that he forgot his own name.

Winter and Venn were riding in the back of the militia cruiser, Hutomo at the wheel. The lights glittered, the siren blared its war cry. Hutomo swerved in and out of traffic as the radio crackled with the guerrilla staccato of incoming reports: bodies found, a disturbance in the warehouse district. Hutomo spun the wheel, ignoring the clamor of angry horns, and rocketed away in a new direction.

"Thought they'd head for the spaceport," he said over his shoulder.

Winter grunted and straightened herself, having been flattened against the window during the latest hairpin turn. She wished Hutomo wouldn't take his eyes off the road. "Probably looking for something."

Beside her, Venn drew a sharp breath. "You think he—"

"Might have," she agreed. To Hutomo, she said: "Better slow down in case—"

The wall of the building to their right erupted outward in a spray of shattered steel girders and boulders of concrete. A gargantuan foot slammed down into the asphalt directly in front of the cruiser, creating a wall of titanium and steel perfectly positioned for them to slam into at full speed. There was no time to brake, only time for a startled yelp before the car impacted the side of the foot, mashing its nose into a tangled accordion. The rear tires were briefly airborne as the cruiser did a half pirouette before bouncing to a halt.

In the accident, Winter received a few bruises and a gash along the left thigh. This would shortly prove far less lucky than it seemed. Venn lost an eye to a shard of flying glass and would remain in hospital for several months. Point Commander Hutomo was killed instantly, crushed when inertia attempted to drive his chest cavity through the steering column, and would remain dead for the foreseeable future.

Winter kicked open the passenger side door and staggered out on uncooperative legs. The road beneath her trembled under the pounding footfalls of a pair of BattleMechs, now striding away, heading for the spaceport.

Her own BattleMech was nearby, if she could get to it in time. *Not on foot, though.* A backlog of cars, taxis, buses, and trucks had collected in front of the wreckage. A few shadows stood in headlight beams, looking anxiously at one another, hoping someone would do something so they didn't have to. *Help is not on its way. Guess it's up to me.*

Winter staggered back to the cruiser and retrieved Hutomo's service pistol from the wet ruin of the front seat. She held it outthrust in one hand as she lurched toward the nearest vehicle—a taxicab with the withered hunk of an old man behind the wheel. She fought down a twinge of guilt. *Poor little guy.* But it was a cold and hard galaxy, and she was in need and in a hurry.

"Get out," she barked. "I'm commandeering this car. Clan business."

The old man took his hands off the wheel, strangely clear-bright eyes never leaving hers, levered open the door with geriatric deliberation, and shuffled out of the car.

"Come on, come on, *come on*," Winter urged impatiently, waving him away from the vehicle with her gun. "Move, move, *move*."

The cabbie moved with all the speed and grace of a bag of gravel.

Winter opened her mouth, but her words were lost as a deafening boom shattered the sky. She turned to see a black-tarred fireball rise into the sky. Winter had a moment of shock, then one of elation. A gleeful smile spread across her face. *The idiots, in their desperation to escape, are attacking the city.* Now if she brought Valasek down, she'd be doing more than collecting a bounty; she'd be a hero.

She only looked away for a moment. When she looked back, the cabbie was holding a small, chunky pistol leveled at her chest.

Rathbone listened to Valasek attempt to convince the DropShip captain that she needed to prep for immediate launch. Valasek's BattleMech strode in front of him, cratering the road with each footfall, ripples of panic spreading out from each impact, scattering traffic, sending pedestrians scurrying. Valasek's 'Mech was a *BattleMaster*, in conscious imitation of his supposed ancestor Helmar Valasek's ride. Rathbone's own BNC-3S *Banshee* was also an ancient design, its death's-head profile unchanging through the ages, though it had been upgraded with more modern weaponry.

"This is an emergency," Valasek was explaining.

"What emergency?" The voice was suspicious. The DropShip captain who had brought them to Butler, Lesedi Kurita (no relation), was a mercenary too, with no particular loyalty to Valasek or anyone else. More interested in protecting her ship than the ambitions of a would-be hero.

Rathbone grinned at the silence that followed. He reckoned he could hear the gears grinding desperately in Valasek's head. He twisted the *Banshee*'s torso to the right and settled its crosshairs over the largest building in sight. It was a commercial office tower, scaled in polished glass from roof to foundation. The corporate logo said "Welltek." A pair of blinding lances of white-blue light pierced the building just below the logo. Two floors abruptly ceased to exist as anything above the atomic level. The top third of the building was transformed into a column of flame-flecked smoke, boiling into the air.

"It's a revolt!" Rathbone shouted into the comm. "The Free Guilds are attacking the city!" It sounded plausible enough. Tensions with the Guilds had already erupted into fighting on the planet once before. All he and Valasek needed to do was provide a little evidence to back up the claim.

There was a beat, in which Rathbone guessed Valasek was processing what had just happened, trying to catch up mentally. Valasek then twisted his 'Mech the other way, and his quad lasers leveled a grocery store. "They're firing on everyone, they've already massacred a dozen people!" he added.

"What?"

The two MechWarriors began to fire indiscriminately left and right, annihilating a post office, a few more corporate offices, a pharmacy, a barber shop.

"They're out of control!" said Rathbone.

"They're massacring people!" Valasek shouted. "They're headed for the spaceport!"

"My god, yes, I see the explosions," said Captain Kurita and cut the channel.

Rathbone could hear Valasek laughing, giddy, exhilarated as their BattleMechs brushed through the fencing surrounding the spaceport and out onto the sprawl of the landing pads. They stopped. The laughter died.

A bright torch was flaring in the sky. A spike of flame blasted from the engines of the DropShip as it climbed higher and higher and higher. They had succeeded. They had indeed convinced Captain Lesedi Kurita that the Free Guilds were attacking, and her DropShip was in imminent danger. They had completely convinced her of the need to escape. And she, assuming their approaching BattleMechs were the very threat they claimed was terrorizing the city, had ordered a liftoff without waiting for them.

The two BattleMechs tilted upward, watching the DropShip's trajectory in silence. Behind them, the city burned. Valasek was swearing over the channel, but Rathbone was philosophical. The DropShip was but one possible route out of the situation. There were others, if one was willing to adapt.

Rathbone took the primary and secondary fire controls in hand, and centered his targeting crosshairs on the middle of the *BattleMaster*'s back.

The woman looked away. She'd said it was "Clan business," so Short Change naturally assumed she was a member of the Clan Jade Falcon warrior caste. Her arm holding the pistol was bloodied to the elbow. It drifted to one side as she turned to face the detonations puncturing the night sky.

Short Change's cringing, fearful face instantly steeled into an expressionless mask. The raised hands drooped slightly. He flexed his wrist and a spring-loaded holster on the inside of his forearm dropped a laser pistol into his palm. It was a cut-down version of the Mark XXI "Nova" laser pistol and carried only enough power for two shots, but at point-blank range that was plenty. Indeed, it was overkill.

He was calm as she swung back. He had waited his whole life for a moment such as this, when his long, long decades of hiding would present him with a chance to strike. He had worn many labels over the years—orphan, acolyte, spy, driver, cabbie—without ever changing who he was. Assassin was just one more label.

He saw the electric jolt of recognition as she registered what he was holding.

"Wait, I'm—"

He was sure he knew what she was. He fired twice. The gun itself was silent, but the air hissed and recoiled from the corona-hot light. The first shot went through her heart, the second a few centimeters below it. She frowned and stiffened for an instant, as though to scold him. Then seemed to lose her train of thought. Her eyes rolled upward, and she slipped to the ground.

Short Change waited, expecting retribution and death, welcoming it even.

Instead, there was applause.

The crowd applauded. Slowly at first, scattered, then gaining confidence with ever-growing volume. The locals knew what they had seen: one of their own, the oldest, smallest and weakest among them, standing up to one of the warrior caste and emerging the winner. It was a vicarious victory in a city that seemed suddenly under siege.

They cheered and whistled and clapped.

Okay, Balor Valasek thought while his only way off-planet vanished into a wavering firefly of light somewhere in the stratosphere. *Okay, not great, not the end of the world. We still have the whole city as hostages. We can work a deal.*

He remained firm in this belief right up until the moment twin PPCs blasted into the rear of his *BattleMaster*. The ground lurched, as though pulled from under his BattleMech's feet, and the heads-up display voiced concern over damage to the gyro.

The fight was effectively over before it began. Balor was no Black Widow, no Morgan Kell or Kai Allard-Liao. Not even a Helmar Valasek. He managed a staggering, drunken sailor's half turn, fanning wild laser fire across the spaceport, before Rathbone's second fusillade took the *BattleMaster* full in the head and chest. The 'Mech, already off-balance, tipped over onto its back with a titanic crash.

Unlike Ezekiel, Balor did not beg at the end. He watched the *Banshee*'s arm hurtle down toward the cockpit without fear or regret. He had done what he had to do, there was nothing he would change.

He closed his eyes the moment before impact.

Rathbone would be hailed a hero, his own role in causing the disaster lost in confusion. His name would be on everybody's lips. It would come as a shock to many when he was killed a few weeks later in a dispute over an unpaid cab fare.

Until then, the stars swam by in the midnight sky above.

There would be no great consequences to the night's tragedy; it was a minor incident in a slice of the Inner Sphere already energetically tearing itself apart at the seams. The Malthus family would remain forever frustrated in their thirst for revenge. The name Valasek was gone and would remain so, buried forever beneath the sands of history.

More heroes would rise and fall, more bandits and pirates would come and go, more bounty hunters, more mercenaries, more sunsets, more blood on the sand.

The stars swam by, cloaked in the night like a school of squid.

PLANET DIGEST: ANTARES

TOM STANLEY

Star Type (Recharge Time): F5V (176 hours)
Position in system: 1 (of 1)
Time to Jump Point: 14.94 days
Number of Satellites: 1 (Scorpius)
Surface Gravity: 0.91
Atm. Pressure: Standard (Breathable)
Equatorial Temperature: 20°C (Cool)
Surface Water: 70 percent
Highest Native Life: Amphibians
Recharge Station: Nadir
HPG Class: B
Population: 220,100,000
Socio-Industrial Levels: C-D-C-C-C
Landmasses (Capital): Koch, Westmacott (Antares City), Tibullus

Antares' F-class star, named for the famous nearby Antares red supergiant, glows white, providing enough warmth to create a "Goldilocks" zone for the only rocky terrestrial body orbiting it.

The singular planet contains three landmasses: Koch, Westmacott, and the Tibullus archipelago. The planet is visually pleasing, with its pink dust and orange sands for beaches; but visitors have to contend with bone-white thorn spikes, clumps of dark blue brush with tough, swordlike leaves, and the sea life.

Koch is the second largest landmass, sitting at the equator and having the largest population density due to its climate. West of the city of Alba lie the Rakusian Hills, where massive iron-ore concentrations were found and used locally, but weren't of sufficient quality to export.

Westmacott, the largest landmass, is situated farther south, and is famous for the Westmacott Plains. The plains are a result of shale plates from a former ocean bed that dried up a millennia ago. During the height of the Star League, it was home to massive solar-panel collectors that powered local observatories on the nearby plateaus.

Antares City sits on Westmacott's western most coastline, offering a safe haven for boats and explorers. It remained the planet's capital, even though Koch had more land to cultivate for farms compared to the salty holdings on Westmacott. The colonists relied on fishing and undersea resource harvesting originally as they explored deeper.

Northeast of Koch is the Tibullus archipelago, once a landmass that sank into the ocean. The remains of a vast, underwater mountain range are the only parts that dot the ocean today, providing affluent citizenry small, cozy hiding spots during their visits.

Scorpius, the moon's name honoring the constellation, is very similar to Terra's moon in size and composition. Underground ice has been discovered in greater pockets, allowing refueling and mining stations to be built on the surface. The only functional colony, Base Ishara, was lost in 2850 due to a lack of critical components.

In 2237, a collection of protesters and pacifists assembled against the Expansionist political faction in Terra, condemning the military action against the rebellious colonial worlds. Defectors from the defeated

Terran Marines also joined, lending their voices and firsthand knowledge of the events. The Liberals won elections and swept the Expansionist influence out quickly, along with granting independence to all worlds beyond the small border established for the Terran Alliance.

Within a few years, various conglomerates pooled money together for the Wayfinder Warrior Project. The WWP provided ship passage, supplies, and all means of support for veterans wishing to colonize these newly "liberated" worlds. One of the destinations was the Antares system: initial surveys spoke of a habitable world with water, but mediocre UV light. While many would balk at leaving Terra, a paradise compared to Antares, a collection of Terran veterans relished the challenge, with their speaker, Lieutenant Salman Masood, quipping, "We're done with politicians on Terra giving us no choices as we face dangers they make. At least now it's our choice to embrace the dangers of space, as we sail to Antares' light."

Early in 2245, the colony was founded, and it sent a message to Terrans: "Vote with your feet and suitcases along with your ballots." Antares offered a peaceful haven from the push and pull of Alliance politics and corruption. When some couldn't make the trip, the WWP lent them support until the project was shuttered in 2251. Antares and similar independent systems expanded human space through the decades that followed, despite Terra's failures.

During the early years of Antares, life was quiet as people survived and charted the stars on their new home. Eventually the colonists sold this information to the Alliance, Hegemony, and the growing Tamar Pact, as the system was situated far past "civilized" space. Most of their efforts also went into undersea exploration as well, cataloging various xenofauna and flora for study. Their one weakness as a colony was manufacturing: the ore on Antares was of a poor quality for any sophisticated industry; thus, they imported supplies from the nascent nations around them as the Terran Alliance withdrew any form of official support due to politics.

The Tamar Pact approached Antares with an offer to join in 2400, both benefiting from each other's trade and the latter's position in space. With the Draconis Combine on the Pact's border, expansion needed to happen elsewhere. The Planetary Science Chair, an early technocratic government of Antares, took pride in the star charts they could offer and whatever trade data they had for Tamar's foodstuffs and mineral wealth of the Pact. Now officially in the Tamar Domains, the Antareans were nestled in the far end of it, but were happy to contribute to the Lyran Commonwealth.

The Good Years, which fell between 2600–2650, saw the development of various sciences and communications on Antares, and gave the populace more choices in their government as they prospered and considered their lives when dealing with their Planetary Science Chair.

The Planetary Science Chair fared well during the early years, but the slow pace of advancing technologies and demands caused a political upheaval and gave way to the Scorpius Collective, an oligarchy that included heads of the various industries, one representative Star League officer, and a civilian voted by the populace. Though shaky, it lasted well until Operation Revival and the coming of Clan Jade Falcon.

Antares' greatest development came during the Good Years; Alba, a city mostly known for food production and industry before the Star League, now became a repair depot for the Star League Defense Force. The system was two or three jumps away from the Rim Worlds Republic, had connections within the Lyran Commonwealth if the SLDF needed to keep an eye on any House activities, and still maintained various satellites from its early stellar exploration years. Combined with the surplus farms and Antares City's beach scenery, it offered a little "slice of home" for soldiers still on active duty.

Kerensky's Exodus and the First Succession War caused infrastructure to be lost, however, making Antares lose most of its ability to grow surplus food. Volcanic activity also threw more dust into the air; thus, the sun started to glow redder during certain times of the day; a bitter irony, given the supergiant they lived near. Commonwealth scientists and engineers couldn't replicate some Star League technology to clean up the world, since the endeavor grew costly as the years passed.

The loss of Base Ishara during the Second Succession War showed Antareans how hard life would be in the coming years. Ishara's fusion power reactors faced repair problems, along with shortages in critical foodstuffs. The planetside population was taking more food shipments from the lunar colony each year for their own numbers. Talk of rebellion was few and far between as more people left for better places. Parts of the old colony can still be seen from planetariums, a sad reminder of how far the planet's prosperity has fallen.

Antares wasn't always left behind, however. ComStar's Primus Waterly enacted a policy called Bread Before Books, appealing to poorer worlds like Antares. The populace enjoyed not only the protection provided by the 222nd Division, but also food kitchens and research grants sponsored by ComStar. Because of this generosity, Antareans proposed the military voice of the Scorpius Collective be a ComStar officer instead of a Lyran one. The citizens didn't know of ComStar's desire for the contents of a Star League depot literally kilometers under the city of Alba. But ComStar would not be able to reap either benefit when Jade Falcon claimed them both.

The irony of Jade Falcon's invasion was this: for the first time in decades, the system was highly prized, but the populace was unaware of the planet's secret. The Star League supply depot hidden on the world was one the Falcons knew of, given their records of the planet's history; also, the city contained a sophisticated water-purification system. Though the planet's defenders put up a strong battle, they were crushed when Khan Elias Crichell's logistics officer confirmed they would soon provide a new water-purification plant from the Clan Homeworlds. With this news, the soft glove was gone, and the hard steel of the Falcons' talons tore Alba and its purification plants apart. The Scorpius Collective was disbanded shortly after, when a high-ranking Elemental strode to the military advisor's seat, flashed a Star League emblem around her neck, and declared the government null and void.

Clan Jade Falcon's focus on excavating the contents of the rediscovered depot shocked the Antareans, but the attention wouldn't stop there, as Clan Steel Viper trialed to live on the world. At first the Falcons raged at the idea. The Vipers eventually landed on the planet, declaring Trials of Possession against the Falcons for territory on Antares, followed by whatever contents the Falcons could pull from the Alba depot.

Life under the Clans was brutal and orderly. The Antarean scientists were treated with skepticism and outright execution during the Wars of Reaving. With the eradication of the scientists, the culture of Antares shifted from one of discovery to servitude. The planet was famous now for holding a depot the populace hadn't even known about, and its manufacturing capabilities were paltry at best. During the Falcon civil war, known as the Rending, the planet threw support to Malvina Hazen for multiple reasons: one being her WarShip in their orbit and another being their hopes that Malvina's direction would give them some importance once again.

Now, as Chingis Khan Hazen's death is known on Terra, Antares has reached a historical moment. Jiyi Chistu's Falcon Remnant signed a treaty on 10 June 3152 with the Magistracy of Antares, binding their futures to yet another Falcon, hoping the outcome will be different this time.

TERRAIN TABLES

Though Antares is mostly water, it possesses a broad range of environments, so the Mapsheet Tables on pg. 263 of *Total Warfare* can be used to represent the world's landscapes.

To represent the Tibullus archipelago, use *Map Pack: Box Canyon* and treat every hex under Level 8 as underwater; treat Woods hexes that are underwater as clear hexes.

ACE DARWIN AND THE GREAT SMALL WORLD PRANK WAR

JAMES BIXBY

Special thanks to my friends who served, and whose stories inspired the shenanigans therein.

D. Andrews, USAF; J. Montambeault, USAF; P. Pacheco, US Army

THE DEALERSHIP
HARLECH CITY
OUTREACH
FEDERATED COMMONWEALTH
17 JUNE 3054

The life of anyone in a military capacity is often characterized by long stretches of boredom punctuated by minutes of bowel-voiding terror. I am no coward by any stretch of the imagination, but my mercenary career has been made up of finding the kinds of contracts where the boring parts are as long as possible, and the terror is either nonexistent or only exists for the fools who cross the sights of my *Panther*'s particle projector cannon.

So after a year-long stretch on Solaris VII, where a stint as holovid stuntmen turned into putting a ComStar acolyte in his place, and a very confusing whirlwind romance with one of the O'Bannon sisters led to a proposal and a broken heart, I felt the need to reevaluate myself. Thankfully, we managed to secure a DropShip whose charter ran along a command circuit back home.

These days, "home" was the Dealership: Hap Hazard's Sunflower WorkMechs. It was a decent setup, all things considered. The main office space had a meeting room that served for briefings, while I'd converted the showroom into a recreational area for hirelings, and the entire upstairs became my personal apartment. However, the nice, flat rooftop was my secret space, where a lawn chair, picnic umbrella, and drink cooler allowed me to neglect my duties to the WhipIts—or what was left of them anyway—in peace.

The majority of my unit had dispersed. After three consecutive contracts, Nicky Danserau decided he liked show business better, and took his group and several others to form a mini-stable and consulting firm for future holodramas. Other WhipIts took subcontracting jobs as we hopped between Solaris and Outreach. So I returned to the Dealership, which was down to my indelible partner and technician Andrew Sevrin, the dark-skinned and overly muscled Nyla, and a couple Striker tanks whose crews insisted they had signed with me when I established the Dealership. Nyla was spending most of her free time with Sevrin, supervising the refitting of a *Black Knight* she had claimed as salvage from the renegade ComStar adept. A few of the remaining MechWarriors rented space out in the Dealership's repair facility, which at least made sure my finances remained in the black, even if they weren't going to stick around for the next contract.

As for me, I spent most of my days feeling sorry for myself at Elizabeth O'Bannon turning me down. If I wasn't bare-knuckling a heavy bag or toothbrush-polishing my neon-pink *Panther*, I was probably half-asleep somewhere with a computer screen full of unread contracts in front of me.

"Okay, loverboy," Nyla said as I was napping in a hammock I'd installed on the roof of the Dealership, "we're going to work!"

She dropped a noteputer on my lap, and once I depleted my knowledge of expletives in French, Farsi, and English, I glanced at the device. "So what do I owe the pleasure, my Amazonian XO?"

"I got us a contract, and more assets signed on," she replied.

I wiped the sleep from my eyes and glanced at the screen. "Small World? What's there?"

"Not much, but it's on the way to everywhere in the Sarna March. Sixth FedCom is ostensibly stationed there, but a regimental combat team usually TDYs over half its force the next two planets over."

"So who's hiring us to make up the difference?" I asked while cracking a can of coconut-water Coolant Flush. "The AFFC, local nobility, or some CEO looking to appease shareholders?"

"Believe it or not, the AFFC. The local noble was raising a ruckus, and this is supposed to appease him. We are doing palace and spaceport duty in the warmer equatorial regions."

I glanced at the world data and saw how the arctic zones reached down almost to the thirty-fifth parallel. Equatorial temperatures were warm enough, but I had a hard time imagining twenty-four degrees centigrade as "tropical."

"I suppose we need to work," I said. "We're basically floating on indies and small-timers renting out the repair bays."

Nyla smiled as she crossed her well-developed arms. "Well, to be honest, Ace, I'd like to get paid, too. You got Sevrin's soda business, and I don't mind the room and board, but fixing that *Black Knight* is eating up C-bills."

She wasn't kidding. Turned out that *Black Knight* was a type reserved for the Star League's elite, using large pulse lasers and double heat sinks. Both technologies were only recently coming back into the general marketplace, and demand was extremely high. High demand meant high prices, and high prices for a struggling-to-get-by outfit like ours? Well, you do the math.

"Sounds like an emergency. I'll call Sevrin and get us paid." I stood up and stretched, grabbing my beloved jacket off a wall hook. The engagement ring in the inside pocket still felt like a ball of lead against my heart.

Despite it all, Nyla was right. Work was what we needed, the Whiplts weren't going to survive by floating along.

NEW MARIOTTA
SMALL WORLD
FEDERATED COMMONWEALTH
10 AUGUST 3054

To say Small World was unimpressive was an understatement. Perhaps growing up in the Lyran Commonwealth, surrounded by people who were "really rich" instead of "kind of rich" had numbed me. Everything, from the architecture to the food to the local culture, screamed the same kind of "showing off money" feeling you get with the kind of folks who live in large pseudo-mansions that, behind the polymer brick facade, are really just multiple modular housing units stuck together like the studded building blocks I played with as a child.

Even the base we were stationed at was built to look as expensive and impressive as possible while using the absolute cheapest materials. Despite that, the guide from the planetary militia carried on about how it was the most important base on the planet. The last bastion before the governor's palace and how the parliament building and the "Grand Duke's" palace would be overrun without it.

Glancing at the planet's topography and mineralogy, I saw the truth of the matter. Mariotta City seemed located in the least important, but most aesthetically pleasant patch of dirt on the planet. While there was plenty of commercial interest around, there wasn't one lick of industrial infrastructure, nor was it close to any particular mineral deposits. Something about pollution concerns.

So when I marched my bright-pink *Panther* through, the impromptu tour of the city was uneventful. If anything, it seemed our law-enforcement escort went well out of its way to take the most indirect route to our billet as possible. In fairness, BattleMechs can absolutely destroy even the most hardened streets if they really open their throttle. To my eyes, it seemed the concern was selecting the widest roads possible so the decorative planters and trees dividing the four-lane roads would remain undisturbed.

I supposed it was understandable, given the mass we were hauling. In the week before we departed, Nyla had recruited well. We were sporting three full lances of 'Mechs this contract. Joining us was that pair of Striker tanks as force protection, and a Packrat reconnaissance vehicle Sevrin had refurbished into a mobile workshop.

I took the lead of our procession, joined by some rookies in a mix of medium and light 'Mechs in my command lance. Nyla's newly repainted ebony *Black Knight* was leading a Davion retiree in an *Enforcer*, a Northwinder in an antique *Banshee*, and what essentially amounted to our first chaplain, a Rabbi Yitzchak Wrenn operating a new *Bandersnatch*. Our third lance specialized in long-range patrol, and I was told they were already on station. They'd hopped on the contract via HPG while finishing a different contract on Ozawa.

When I parked my *Panther* and gazed out at the interior of our facility, I was less than pleased. The hangar facility was shockingly cramped, barely able to serve all twelve of our 'Mechs. Rabbi Yitzchak's *Bandersnatch* actually had to park outside the hangar because the 'Mech's girth was so wide it took the space of two cubicles, and the *Banshee* had to park on bended knee to fit under a repair gantry.

Officially this militia base was named Outpost Golf, so named because it was attached to a large park that served as a nine-hole private golf course for the planetary duke and his guests. I was pleased to see Pippa's Patrolmen, one of the lances who had signed on for this contract, were getting us set up, their own techs having already put the signature Whiplts paw-print insignia on their 'Mechs' shoulders so we looked the part of a unified command. Inside the combination barracks and office, Sevrin was directing the redistribution of furniture to make way for the gadgets and gizmos he insisted were needed to keep our unit running.

And that was about it. Another boring security and cadre contract was all ready to go, and I had nothing to do other than inspect everyone's quarters and make sure we were bedding in. When I entered the semi-attached office and barracks building by the 'Mech hangar, I was pleased to see the "Pippa" in Pippa's Patrolmen was, in fact, a very old friend of mine from my contract on Second Try.

"Pip, what in God's name made you come out here?" I asked.

Pippa had grown her hair out since I'd last seen her. On Second Try she had buzzed it down to less than a centimeter, sporting a bit of an androgynous punk-rock look. Now, her dirty-blond hair was pulled into a bun I'd seen on some old Terran propaganda poster somewhere. The top of her MechWarrior coveralls was pulled down to her waist, the sleeves forming a makeshift tie-around while she painted a giant pink paw print that served as the unit's logo on a blank wall of the office space.

"Ace! You son of a bitch!" She hopped from her crouch and gave me a big hug. "No messages since Second Try, I don't hear hide nor hair until you show up on *Solaris Tonight* with two champions on your hip and Duncan Fisher making comments about how he wants to switch places with you?"

I laughed off the reminder of that crazy year. "Well, I'm here now, and you took the contract, so...no hard feelings, I guess? Come on, let's chat."

I grabbed a sixer of Watermelon Dream Coolant Flush—which tasted nothing like watermelon or dreams if you ask me—and marched us out to the unmanned guard post at the front of the tiny base. We sat on a bench and regaled each other with tales of our adventures since we'd parted company on Second Try several years prior.

"I tell you, Ace, it's hard for me to figure out what has been more expensive—upgrading my *Hermes II* or my wardrobe."

"No comment," I replied, since I usually wore the same cargo pants and boots until they were no longer wearable and stole whatever stack of printed shirts I could from the Coolant Flush marketing department. Given that, I really was the last person to make fashion choices. We both laughed and clinked our beverages.

Right then a courier approached our lounge point in the immediate perimeter of Outpost Golf. "Commander Darwin?"

"That's me." I stood up and approached the young man. "How can I help you?"

"The duke sends his regards, and invites you and your officers to a banquet tonight." The lad extended a cream-colored folder, again embossed with the duke's seal. Without a chance for me to thank him, he bowed curtly and walked back to his vehicle.

"Black tie..." I muttered under my breath, scanning the invitation and accompanying protocol documents. "Pippa, you get any practice walking in heels lately?"

"More than you think, less than I'd like. But fortunately, I have a dress with me this time."

One of the disadvantages of having neither a permanent roster nor a formal rank structure was figuring out who out of the five extra tickets I could bring with me. So with my selections made, the half dozen of us exiting from Sevrin's Packrat made for a motley group, to say the least. Sevrin slapped one of the valets on the back and whispered something in his ear that made the poor man blanch.

Nyla and Pip were both dressed in evening wear more suitable for a date night than a formal ball. The juxtaposition of the muscular and dark-complected Nyla in a multicolored skirt and blouse contrasted against the lean and pale Pippa in her cyan pencil dress. For my own attire, I pulled out the electric-blue suit I'd had expressly tailored on Solaris for a gala event. My white shirt had not been pressed in some time, and I was relying on a hot-pink tie to cover that fact up. Sevrin, meanwhile, had put on a brand-new flight suit with a tweed sport coat, clearly showing he was ill-prepared for this event. Much to my shock, he had actually trimmed his beard for the first time since we'd established our operations on Solaris. The once long, bushy mass of facial hair was now shaved down to a couple centimeters, brushed and oiled. Rabbi Yitzchak wore his formal vestments, and as a treat, I'd brought along the youngest of the rookie MechWarriors, who wore ill-fitting academy uniforms of some place or another.

Once the Packrat peeled off, clearly stressing the pavement of the inner palace, I turned to yet another flunky with his hand out. Poor man must have been the fifth person I showed the invitation to that evening. Once through, our rabble-rousing bunch was met by a short, bald man with a full beard and an almost comically deep voice.

"Commander Darwin, good evening." The man offered me a handshake. "My name is Justin Finkel Okerlund III. I am Grand Duke Blake Small's aide."

"Pleasure to meet you, sir," I replied. "Please, just call me Ace."

The toady wrinkled his nose at the insistence of informality before continuing. "Please help yourself to the duke's hospitality. How shall I introduce you to the court?"

"Given our state compared to some of the guests present—" I waved my hand at some member of the planet's idle rich who'd just walked by, dressed like a wedding cake. "Perhaps we can forgo the formal introductions and just slip right in." I took the arms of my female compatriots, playing up the playboy routine. "Ladies, shall we?" And I gave Sevrin and Rabbi Yitzchak a wink before walking right in.

The main hall of the palace was decorated in a manner that made Callicoat's Cathouse on Outreach look classy. Growing up in the "new money" hierarchy of the Lyran Commonwealth, I was used to seeing facades of stucco, faux wood, and overworked molding on the baseboards. With the classic columns, gilding, and embossed artwork you can see in any given noble mansion, this whole thing just felt more like a parody of nobility than the real thing.

Pip and Sevrin made for the table of comestibles right away, and I grabbed a pair of flutes from a waiter walking by, handing one to Nyla. "*This* is why I wanted to get into the business," I told her.

"Overdressed stuffy inbreds so far up their own tailpipes they don't know they're suffocating themselves and everyone else?" the Amazonian MechWarrior asked.

"Exactly. The pocketbooks, wine cellars, kitchens, and occasionally spouses of the idle and paranoid rich are a playground. This is life."

Nyla let out a hearty laugh, but before the gaggle could turn around to glare at her for being a loud and large woman, the duke's aide slammed a staff of some sort on the stone floor.

"Ladies and gentlemen, may I present to the Grand Duke our newest defenders! Stationed right here on the palace grounds, ensuring the defense of his lordship and the people of Small World, representing Second Battalion of Harlock's Warriors, Captain Kenneth Petruzzelli, and his officer cadre!"

Polite applause rang through the court as four officers stepped through the doorway. They sported dark blue uniforms cut in a Draconis Combine style, with the usual braids, weaves, and medals one would expect of serious warriors. Captain Petruzzelli himself looked vaguely familiar. I was later reminded we had trained together in anti-Clan tactics on Outreach several years prior. The two women and man he was with—his executive officer and lance commanders, I assumed—held themselves with the same confidence I associated with my peers in the mercenary profession.

"Wait, *we* are supposed to be stationed here," Nyla whispered to me.

"Yeah, but our post isn't on palace grounds," I said. "We are several kilometers away, next to His Richness' golf course."

After several hours of mingling, drinking, and gathering up the rumor mill, the coin dropped.

"Commander Darwin?" a voice called to me.

Up close, Captain Petruzzelli was not as impressive as his entrance seemed. He was about six centimeters shorter than me, though he was more muscular than my comparatively lean build. Despite the clean uniform, his hair was slightly unkempt, held in place more by how close cut he wore it, and he sported the kind of three days' growth of a man who always told himself he would shave tomorrow. His handshake demonstrated a firm grip that said he didn't feel the need to compete by squeezing as hard as possible. Right off the bat, I decided I liked the man, which I probably thought back when we were on Outreach.

"Captain," I said. "Welcome to Small World! It looks like you lot and the Whiplts will be working closely together."

Petruzzelli looked confused. "My understanding is we were here to relieve you, and this was a farewell reception for your service—"

"That is a mistake," Nyla interjected, a pair of highball glasses in hand. "We just got here. Our contract with the AFFC officially starts tomorrow morning."

The switch seemed to flip behind Petruzzelli's eyes. "Oh no. Our contract was with the duke's household. It's why there's only a company of us here instead of the whole regiment."

"Are you supposed to be stationed at Outpost Golf?" I said, a lead weight dropping from my stomach all the way to my pelvis.

Petruzzelli nodded. The facilities could barely handle one company with all the support assets it possessed, and now there were *two* occupying the same space.

"We gotta talk to the duke," Petruzzelli and I said simultaneously.

One of the things that helps when you're not a permanent fixture of a planet's society is that protocol can be broken with little future consequence. So when Petruzzelli and I physically grabbed an initially dismissive Duke Small from his gaggle of hangers-on, there was more indignation than insult taken.

"Sir, there has been a serious error," I said.

"I agree!" Duke Small said. "You don't just grab the planet's sovereign and drag him to a meeting! If you'll excuse me..." He made for the door Petruzzelli just shut, but paused midstride long enough that I had to suppress a chuckle.

"Duke Small," Petruzzelli said, "it seems our contracts were mixed up. Both Darwin's command and mine are assigned to Outpost Golf. We think this overlap happened because we were hired by different parties."

"So what?"

"Sir, whoever built that outpost didn't keep in mind the needs of a single BattleMech company. There are only enough gantries for twelve 'Mechs, no secure vehicle park for the support equipment, and insufficient storage for everything from hydrogen to foodstuffs. And now you have two companies with the same-sized logistical arm claiming responsibility for it."

"How is this *my* problem?" the duke asked.

I could have punched him in his royal face, but Petruzzelli had it in hand. "Sir," he said, "you hired the Warriors, so it is your responsibility to provide us with the facilities we need."

"And I have. Outpost Golf is your station."

"Except my contract is with the AFFC," I countered, "and the authority of the Department of Mercenary Relations supersedes your own in matters of military jurisdiction. So I was assigned to Outpost Golf, fundamentally, under the authority of the Archon-Prince. Captain Petruzzelli is correct. Under the chain of command, Outpost Golf is mine, but that does not change the fact that he needs a different billet."

"I still don't see how this is my problem. Either settle it with your contacts, or work it out yourselves. Now, if you will excuse me."

Two bodyguards walked into the room, presumably summoned by a silent chime or the commotion we had caused. It was clear both of us had overstayed our welcome anyway.

Needless to say, when Petruzzelli's retinue and I got back to the outpost, our respective direct reports were not happy. All of the general command of the planetary militia was off doing some diplomatic garbage to Small World's neighbors, and with no field-grade officers able to give authority for a transfer, we were both stuck. Fortunately, no violence broke out between WhipIts and Warriors, thank goodness, but there *was* a whole lot of yelling.

Petruzzelli and I vainly attempted to raise our voices and get everyone's attention, but the arguments drowned out our presence, let alone voices. It was Sevrin who managed to evoke silence. He pulled a drill instructor's whistle from his pocket and blew a nice, hard blast. This shrill shriek is known to anyone who ever survived a high-school gym class, let alone military life, and even slackers like my crowd immediately snapped to attention and turned to face us.

"ALL RIGHT, PEOPLE! LISTEN UP!" I shouted. "If you think *you* are unhappy about this situation, we had to put hands on the duke himself over this, and his response was complete apathy. Don't be mad at each other, be mad at *him*!"

Petruzzelli took the cue without slipping; I was liking him more and more. "We got a facility here that can barely handle twelve 'Mechs, and we got twenty-plus support. Tents and cots are already being set up for support staff, so everyone is just gonna have to bunk up like we are in the field."

Groans came from the gathered crowd. At this point it was just whining, and any commander learned to live with that.

"Captain Petruzzelli and I are going to work out a rotating schedule for 'Mech maintenance," I continued. "If any concerns regarding facility access require immediate remediation, please come to both of us so we can work it out. This is a great big pile of suck, but right now it is *our* pile."

OUTPOST GOLF
SMALL WORLD
FEDERATED COMMONWEALTH
12 AUGUST 3054

I awoke to the sound of a woman screaming at the top of her lungs. Dashing down with barely any attention paid to modesty, I had just thrown on a tank top when I beheld Pippa Marcus shouting a variety of creative language directed toward Harlock's Warriors. The Whiplts hand-painted paw print logo on the wall of the common area was covered up by a large collection of fist-sized stickers emblazoned with the ax-head logo of Petruzzelli's command.

I placed a hand on Pip's shoulder, interrupting her directives on where precisely she wanted to place her *Hermes II*'s flamer. Behind her, on the other side of the dormitory, I could see a gaggle of Petruzzelli's people smirking, giving fist bumps and shoulder pats. A not-so-subtle clearing of the throat got them to look at me with expressions of having clearly been busted.

"Okay, kids," I said. "It is 0530, and we are a paraprofessional force in ostensible peacetime. It is far too early for this malarkey." I pointed to the gaggle of our unintentional roommates. "You lot are gonna scrape this garbage up and repaint our logo before I can be bothered to get back out of bed. If you can manage it, I won't take this to Captain Petruzzelli."

"Thanks, Ace," Pip said to me.

"I'm not done, Pip," I said. "We got to share this facility for the time being. I want you to get some proper paint, and put that ax either alongside it or on another blank wall. No arguments. We are in this pile of suck together. We gotta act like it. Am I clear?"

A gaggle of reluctant agreement satisfied me, and I went back to my quarters to dress. Bile was too high for me to go back to sleep, so coffee was in order. As I stood there still in my drawers and tank top, Kenny walked up.

"I thought I heard someone get stabbed," he said. "Everything good?"

"Inter-company rivalry. Some of your guys made a statement, I told them to fix it before I take the first patrol out, or I would take the matter to you."

"So, I did not hear or see anything?" Kenny asked. It was so relieving to see that for all the spit and polish his unit showed at the banquet, he understood how MechWarriors behaved.

He still made a show of going out to the common hall earlier than expected to see what was happening. I couldn't resist the show: listening hard through the door, I heard him admonishing his people.

"So let's rewind here. You stuck a bunch of zaps over their hand-painted logo and expected to get away with it?" Kenny was clearly relishing the silence of his MechWarriors. "Can you imagine what would have happened if we were supplementing a Davion Guard or Donegal regiment? The hell we would have to pay for it? Never mind they would've just muscled us out. Darwin is making more of an effort than we probably deserve here. Now, if you need to be *ordered* to follow Darwin's instructions, fine. You are so ordered to extend your full cooperation. Get it done."

OUTPOST GOLF
SMALL WORLD
FEDERATED COMMONWEALTH
15 AUGUST 3054

A few days later, I was sitting on a customary lawn chair, preparing assignments for the daily patrols both in the city outskirts and rural the regions surrounding it, while Kenny's company took over the urban patrols.

The two of us had a private dinner together and got to know each other fairly well. He asked me to call him Kenny in private, which was easy enough, considering only a fool would think "Ace" was on my birth certificate. Beyond that, it was a bunch of shop talk, and I told my third favorite lie about my *Panther*'s origins.

Outside, the local sunset, slated to last about six or so hours, was beginning to turn the sky orange. Some of the Warriors were engaged in an impromptu soccer match at the far side, using the hull of a Striker as a goal. None of my people were visible though, and I should have seen that as a sign of trouble. It didn't hit me that something was amiss until I heard a loud revving of diesel engines.

Two lightweight mobility vehicles tore down from a stretch of road that led to the outpost's namesake golf course. Four people were clearly visible in the back of each truck, each carrying large bulky pipes with back-mounted canisters.

The outpost's general alarm sounded, and I immediately got to my feet just as I saw Kenny storm out of the barracks. By the time he

turned toward the *Starslayer* he piloted, clearly ready for war, it was all over. Eight Harlock's MechWarriors and techs were covered in a mass of foamy gunk, and the truck—one of *my* trucks—was driving off past the main gate, the steel bar meant to prevent unauthorized entry or exit of light vehicles retracted.

As I approached, I saw the gunk was a pink-tinted spray string normally sold at toy stores, but my people seemed to have manufactured it in industrial quantities. I heard a wheezy Sevrin run up behind me, a wide smile on his face. "Well, hot damn, it worked."

I could feel the blood pumping up to my ears. Sevrin was my personal tech, the only tech permanently attached to the WhipIts. His confessed involvement in this implied my approval of this prank.

"Oh, it is ON now!" one of Kenny's MechWarriors screamed. And frankly I could not blame him.

"Mr. Sevrin," I said, the first time I had referred to him formally since we first met, "kill the alarm. Get the others who used my trucks without authorization inside. Now!"

I turned to Kenny. "Captain, I owe you an apology for the behavior of my troops. Will you follow me to observe the proceedings?"

It only took about fifteen minutes to gather the perpetrators of the drive-by foaming. Andrew Sevrin stood at ramrod attention, alongside the patrolmen and some of the other independents and contracted techs who'd gotten roped into this mess. If I was honest with myself, I thought the whole thing was funny as hell, and completely harmless in the end. Kenny, however, had seen the trucks from around the corner, thought it was infantry with flamethrowers, and had hit that general alarm. So the incident flat-out could not be let go. That's why I let Nyla perform the *lostech*-quality ass-chewing.

"I am sure the local kiddie palace appreciated the business you gave them procuring this *garbage*," she bellowed in a baritone pitch I was genuinely surprised she was capable of. "Now if I find out it came out of our operations budget, I'll have you polish all of our BattleMechs with your toothbrushes!" As part of the show, she was tensing her well-muscled body to the point that veins were visible along her biceps and bare shoulders. Were I in the position of the people in front of us, I would be genuinely unsure whether I would walk out with my head still attached to my shoulders.

"This whole spat was supposed to be over *days* ago—Ace made it that way. But you jackasses took it on yourself to ensure your idea of justice was enforced, without consulting or even warning your lance commanders."

Pippa stepped forward to speak, and Nyla shut her down immediately. "You do not count!"

Pippa stepped back, clearly diminished.

"As of right now, Pippa, for the duration of the contract, you are grounded, and Sevrin will lock down your *Hermes* unless we are expecting combat. You are now assigned as his assistant. All day and weekend passes are revoked, and every patrol will include at least one of you clowns, under the direct command of a Harlock lancemate."

Groans came from the assembled crowd.

"Now get out of my sight," Nyla finally said after making sure she bored eye lasers into each individual face.

"Andy, you wait a minute," I said as the rest of the rabble-rousers excised themselves from the spot they were glued on for the prior hour.

Sevrin, knowing this was talking shop rather than an ass-chewing, relaxed and sat down, lighting his usual cigarette.

"Look," I said, "MechWarriors gonna be MechWarriors, and I can see the contractors getting roped in. But you?"

"They needed some technical assistance with the spray string," he said through the smoke.

"Meaning they were gonna just hose 'em down with water and you thought to kick it up a notch?"

"I can't say who came up with the idea, but I knew how to mix the stuff and pressurize it in the fire equipment. Again, gotta keep it safe."

"And the reason it was a drive-by and not standing and delivering, or circling back to barracks?" I held my sense of decency in check at this answer.

"Come on, Ace, ask any aerojock and they'll tell you you *never* go for a return pass."

A bout of laughter erupted from me despite the seriousness of it all. Officially his pay had to be docked, not that it mattered to him at this point. He followed me around 'cause he liked it, making more off his new businesses than I could pay him.

Still, we came to an understanding, and went to bed.

OUTPOST GOLF
SMALL WORLD
FEDERATED COMMONWEALTH
16 AUGUST 3054

There was no such luck that this was the end of it though. When I woke up at 0630, moon still high on the horizon from the planet's fifty-some-odd-hour rotation, my morning reverie was rudely interrupted. The driver of one of the Striker tanks—Sopp, I think his name was—barged through the kitchenette door.

"Ace, we got a—"

I held my hand up, one finger raised, and shushed him, while preparing my coffee with the other hand. I made scrupulously sure it was prepared to my satisfaction and from the steaming mug, I took a pull that was much longer and louder than it needed to be.

"*Now* you may speak," I said to the tanker.

"The tanks are gone," he said. "Trucks and Sev's Packrat too."

"Gone? Gone where? Andy take them out to the FedCom for maintenance?"

"No, sir. Sevrin is in the shop, having a fit."

At this news, I walked out to the impromptu car park that served as the staging point for these vehicles—still inside the fence, but isolated. Plain as day, there were half a dozen gaps, spray-painted lines and numbers to indicate where the Striker tanks would go, with clear drive paths to avoid clipping the light trucks. Sevrin's Packrat was normally parked next to the 'Mech bay, and I had no reason to distrust the report that his baby was stolen, given I could vaguely hear him chewing someone out.

"Guess I gotta do something about this," I said.

It took only six minutes to mobilize and put both WhipIts and Harlock's Warriors in parade formation. Frankly I was impressed with the improving time, considering how often this was becoming an occurrence. A clearly red-in-the-face Ken Petruzzelli joined me on the crates that served as a stage. While the assembly was happening, Kenny assured me he had no knowledge of the theft and would have stopped it, had he known. At this point, to be honest, I was just bored with this whole prank war.

"*Listen up*!" I shouted to get the attention of the rabble. "Before, I found this tit-for-tat amusing, even harmless. But it ends TODAY!" I pointed to the conspicuously empty vehicle park. "Over yonder is a car park where two fire-support vehicles and a quartet of light trucks were parked for the use of everyone stationed here. And my poor crew chief also has an empty parking space where a Packrat patrol van once stood."

The gaggle of Harlock's Warriors clearly suppressed giggles.

"You idiots may've thought you were having fun, but those tanks represent a very real asset, and going missing affects our readiness, peacetime or not. Same goes for that Packrat. That's not a patrol vehicle; it is a field workshop. Sevrin spent a *long* time ripping out the missiles and flamer so he could install the gear he needed to keep the Whiplts in fighting trim in the field.

"You jackasses stole our wheels, I want them back. You got six hours, or I am going to the Mercenary Review and Bonding Commission. *Am I clear?*"

Petruzzelli, in just as much a mood as I was for this jackassery, snapped a parade-ground salute and shouted a "Yes, sir!" to serve as an example. Harlock's side followed suit, and suddenly I felt very uncomfortable. Honest to goodness, I had never been saluted in my life until that point.

"Six hours, I want those vehicles back where they belong, intact, ammunition stocked, full fuel tanks. Every single one of them needs to be combat ready. You twits go *slightly* out of bounds, there'll be hell to pay. Whiplts, same for you. All combat personnel are confined to barracks until those vehicles return. This is *OVER!*" I bellowed.

And the rank and file shuffled off.

"Kenny, Andy, Nyla, with me," I said. "We need to make sure this ends once and for all, and I got just the way."

HALLBROOK GOLF COURSE
DRIVING RANGE
SMALL WORLD
FEDERATED COMMONWEALTH
16 AUGUST 3054

By the time the Strikers, Packrat, and trucks all rolled back into base and parked, the Whiplts and Warriors were back at each other's throats again. Pink paw prints adorned every Harlock 'Mech in some usually inappropriate place. Likewise every Whiplt 'Mech was painted, poorly, in the same midnight-and-yellow scheme as Harlock's crew, even my *Panther*. Everything was going according to plan.

"Clouseau, this is Dryfus. The stone is missing," Sevrin said over the handset radio in my lawn chair's cup holder.

I picked up the handset, and pulled out the best imitation of my grandfather's accent I could muster: *"Oui, monsieur!"*

Behind me, Kenny asked, "Is the French really necessary?"

Sevrin apparently had his thumb on the transmission switch and was weaving a wild yarn about Kenny and I having engaged in a fistfight. If anything was going to get a bunch of grunts to stop fighting each other, it was a throwdown between officers. I knew it would take about ten minutes at a full run to get from the 'Mech bay to the driving range of the duke's golf course, and Kenny and I were already three beers in.

Like Tennyson's poem, there was a gaggle of about fifty or so people just running headlong up the hill to where we were parked. Instead of a fistfight, they saw Kenny and I sitting in lawn chairs, sipping drinks, and listening to power rock over a speaker system. A bonfire was lit, and a buffet was set up, loaded with smoked meats and sides. Cases upon cases of cola, beer, and a cooler full of liquor bottles were stacked up neatly on another wide table.

As a coup de grâce, a wide, bright-orange circle was spray-painted on the turf off to the side, surrounded by bug-repellent torches. Behind the lawn chairs Kenny and I were seated on was the ceremonial halberd every company commander of Harlock's Warriors received as a symbol of office, and my trusty leather jacket was draped over the blunted ax head. The logo of Harlock's Warriors was freshly sewn on the right breast, right above where I put the Gemini design of the O'Bannon sisters' embryonic stable.

"WELCOME, EVERYONE!" I shouted as I stood up, arms spread wide as though we were hosting a family reunion.

"We began this series of emotional events because we were both wronged," Kenny said as he rose to his feet, taking over the narration, just like we practiced. "And like every other arrogant noble, the duke counted on us either sorting this out or killing each other in the process."

Then I took the speech over again. "As commanders, we could either tighten the screws to get this mishap over with, or we could take the fight to the real enemy. That enemy is *right there*."

I pointed to the ducal palace, just visible on the horizon.

"So here's what we are going to do. Today, we are going to enjoy a great meal. I found a barbecue place that basically cleared out their entire pantry for us."

I smiled as a cheer rang from the gathered and exhausted mercenaries.

"We are going to drink. And if that's not your thing, we got Coolant Flush and local colas as well."

More cheers.

"We will pass around the Stick of Destiny—and yes, this is literally a fallen tree branch I found while setting this up!—and we are going to take turns to speak our truth, tell each other our damage, share jokes and limericks, and air our grievances."

"If anyone feels words are insufficient, there is an impromptu ring over there." Petruzzelli pointed to the spray-painted circle on the turf. "Wrestle it out, officer referees. The rules are known in every military across the Inner Sphere. Bring no rank in, take no grudges out."

"No injuries, because we have a war to get to," I said. It was a touch dramatic, but it got everyone's attention. It was almost tradition that before combat an elaborate and well-apportioned meal would be given to the troops, and suddenly the coin seemed to drop. I had them where I wanted them, I do not mind admitting.

"We go to war against Duke Small! Beginning tomorrow, Ace Darwin's WhipIts and Harlock's Warriors will be engaging in combat-maneuver exercises. And I got just the space for it. Like everything on this cheap-ass planet, very little money was spent on this course. It's only nine holes, so we only got about a square kilometer of space, but I think we can tear it up real nice with a couple of lances of 'Mechs, don't you?"

A cheer rose from the assembled mercenaries.

"Before I cut you all loose, Rabbi Wrenn, if you please?"

The short, stocky young man in black vestments and a white shawl around his neck walked through the crowd, standing in front of the buffet with a hand raised. "Oy vey, I take it the ribs are kosher?" he joked while he flipped to the appropriate page of his book. "*Barukh ata Adonai Eloheinu melekh ha'olam borei minei mezonot.* In the spirit of brotherhood all warriors share, regardless of flag, color, or circumstance, let us feast on this day, and tomorrow, let's give the schmuck who passed this buck onto us an ulcer!"

The gaggle shouted various affirmations and made for the meal. As promised, there was an airing out of dirty laundry, more than a few wrestling matches, and by the time the so-called Stick of Destiny came around to me, I genuinely had nothing to say.

"Okay, so I am a fairly surface-level guy," I said anyway. "Only Andy here and a gal far away really knows too deep into my heart. And as these things go, that gal far away is the source of my damage these days."

Laughter came forth.

"In that case, Ace, why don't you tell us how you got that godawful *Panther*?" Sevrin called out, and the gathered mercs all laughed again and roared assent.

There was only one thing I could do. So, with a smile on my face and the perfect story in mind, I said, "Well, no kidding, there I was, hip deep in the Ronin War on Rasalhague…"

UNIT DIGEST: OBERON GUARDS

ALEX FAUTH

Affiliation: Oberon Confederation (Periphery)
CO: Colonel Jackalyne Bane
Average Experience: Regular/Questionable
Force Composition: 1 BattleMech battalion, 2 vehicle battalions, 1 infantry battalion; full DropShip and JumpShip support.
Unit Abilities: One 'Mech per lance may be assigned the Headhunter SPA (p. 96, *Alpha Strike: Commander's Edition*) at no additional cost.
Parade Scheme: A mixture of flat black and gray. The unit has no standard pattern.

HISTORY

The third nation to bear the name, the Oberon Confederation (often mistakenly referred to as the New Oberon Confederation by outsiders) emerged in the wake of the Clan withdrawal from the Barrens in the 3080s. The Oberon Guards were formed in 3086, and while they claimed the legacy of the original Oberon Guards, this new unit had little in common beyond the name and imagery. Allegedly raised for self-defense, the Guards were almost immediately employed to impose the Confederation's will on several nearby worlds.

Initially, the Guards consisted of a collection of cast-off Hell's Horses tanks and poorly trained infantry, led by a perishingly small amount of BattleMechs. For much of their existence, they maintained this standard, the result of an unspoken agreement among Inner Sphere powers not to supply BattleMechs to the nations of the Barrens. Save for some occasional adventurism aimed at the Republic of the Barrens or menacing small, otherwise overlooked colonies, the Oberon Guards remained a low-level threat, hampered by their inability to project their power.

Two events in the early 3140s saw that all change. The first, and most important, was the entry of a new player into the Barrens region. While they did not identify themselves, this group was willing to sell the Confederation the BattleMechs and DropShips they so desperately wanted, with no questions asked. The Confederation gladly accepted the offer, willing to overlook big questions regarding the supplier's identity and aims. Even if this equipment comprised mostly older models that were far from the cutting edge, they were still better than nothing.

The second was the rise of Jackalyne Bane to the command of the Guards. An ambitious and driven officer, she claimed to be a descendent of the Grimm family who had ruled Oberon before the arrival of the Clans. While her claims couldn't be verified, her combination of skill, charisma, and sheer ruthlessness meant few were willing or able to stand up to her. Once she had secured command, Bane cast a baleful eye toward the Confederation's neighbors, seeing them as ripe for exploitation.

Compared to the Oberon Confederation, the Republic of the Barrens was relatively peaceful and stable. While Hell's Horses saw the Republic as an ally, events in the Inner Sphere had seen the Clan rotate its forces away from the Republic's borders. This created an opening for the Confederation to exploit. During the 3140s, they sent BattleMech raiding parties both to test the enemy's defenses and blood their own forces. Bane ensured these units were not wearing Oberon markings or anything else that could link them to the Confederation, a move aimed as much at covering her tracks as sowing confusion among her enemies. These attacks were by and large successful, allowing her to begin development of a grander plan.

By 3147, the Confederation was ready to make its move. The nation's leadership had long seen the Republic's worlds as being historically theirs, and now, their new forces allowed them to make that claim a reality. The Oberon Guards, now acting openly, struck at worlds across the Republic of the Barrens. Initially their assaults went well, with their forces destroying much of the Republic's militia. Having secured some of the Republic's worlds, including Crellacor and Gustrell, the Confederation engaged in widespread looting of their conquests. This ranged from the usual theft of resources and valuables all the way up to trying to strip Crellacor of its entire agricultural output.

Unfortunately for Bane, the arrival of Clan Hell's Horses put an end to her plans. While the Guards performed better than could be expected against the Clan (even if part of that was due to external aid), they were ultimately driven out of the Republic and suffered considerable losses. While for the moment they have been forced to rebuild, Bane remains determined to expand her nation at the cost of her neighbors. However, her suppliers appear to be willing to provide the Confederation with new equipment to make up for their recent losses.

Recently she has gained an unexpected ally in the form of the Red Hunter; while he has no loyalty to the Confederation, his knowledge and hatred of the Clans makes him a potent asset Bane is willing to temporarily trust.

UNIT COMPOSITION

Having long ago abandoned their pseudo-Clan trappings, the Oberon Guards are organized along traditional Inner Sphere lines. While on paper the unit possesses a combined-arms regiment, due to the amount of area they control and their dearth of resources, more than one battalion is rarely present on a single world at a time. Even then, some evidence suggests the Guards are even bigger than their on-paper size suggests. Bane gives her commanders considerable leeway to act, but still expects loyalty from them. While she is wary of the Red Hunter and his aims, she also has been grateful for his aid and, at least for the moment, sees him as an ally.

The equipment used by the Oberon Guards represents a broad range, based as much on what their supplier provided them as what salvage they can take. While most of their BattleMechs are older Inner Sphere models, their ranks also include IndustrialMech MODs, RetroTech, and even salvaged Clan 'Mechs. Their combat vehicles represent a similar range of capabilities. Finally, the Guards' infantry units are clearly their least important asset, and they are mostly made of conscripts, the hopeful, and the desperate.

Where possible, the Oberon Guards will try to cripple enemy 'Mechs rather than disable them, in the hopes of acquiring salvage. While they usually aim to capture resources, the Guards are not afraid to attack civilian settlements to distract opponents or cover their escape.

CAMPAIGN:
DEATH OF A DREAM
THE BATTLE FOR BARCELONA

ERIC SALZMAN

"Our Khan and our *touman* may have departed into the unknown, but this is no time for despair. Recall the lesson of *The Falcon Vision*. When Founder Elizabeth Hazen, alone and unarmed, faced defeat in the Pentagon, great Turkina, the spirit of the Jade Falcon, appeared and exhorted her to keep fighting, rending her foes with talon and beak. Turkina's words strengthened her spirit, and Turkina's gifts armed her against the foe. In our time of need, Turkina calls out to us once again! On Barcelona, we shall rally and rearm. Together, we shall spread forth our wings and reclaim our honor as the Turkina Ascendancy!"

—Falconer Commander M'oko, Somerset, 13 June 3151

When it became clear that Chingis Khan Malvina Hazen's denuding of the Jade Falcon Occupation Zone had left too few warriors to effectively defend the Clan's civilians and critical infrastructure, Falconer Commander M'oko, commandant of the Military Academy of Somerset, engineered a plan to ensure the survival of his cadets and his Clan. Offering the Golden Snapdragon Free Guild exclusive trading rights in exchange for transport, he executed a scorched-earth withdrawal across the coreward border of the occupation zone, taking garrisons and critical resources and leaving sufficient chaos to slow any invader seeking to assimilate those worlds. Their destination was Barcelona, one of the Clan's first conquests in the Inner Sphere, possessing both the industrial base and military infrastructure necessary for M'oko's Turkina Ascendancy to rise from the ashes of Malvina's folly.

BARCELONA

Barcelona's arid southern Moira continent and its wet, stormy northern Norn continent are linked by a narrow land bridge. Due to the frequent atmospheric disruptions, the main spaceport lies on Moira, but the bulk of the populace works in the world's industries and mines on Norn.

One of the earliest colonies of the Rim Worlds Republic, Barcelona was turned into a "hedgehog world," with massive fortifications built atop the soaring northern mountain peaks dividing the Vigrid Plains and the mining city of Su Filla from the industrial centers and planetary capital at Skuld. The Jade Falcons drove the Skye Rangers from these ancient fortresses in 3049, but Falconer Commander M'oko hoped to make Barcelona unassailable by restoring the facilities with Clan technology, holding enemies at bay while the industrial base was put on a war footing and restructured to support the Turkina Ascendant Cluster. He had everything necessary to make the Ascendancy a contender for control of the Hinterlands. All he needed was time.

And then Clan Hell's Horses arrived...

TRIAL BY COMBAT: ASCENDANCY'S CRUCIBLE

This is a campaign intended for use with the *Total Warfare* (*TW*), *Tactical Operations: Advanced Rules* (*TO:AR*), or *Alpha Strike: Commander's Edition* (*AS:CE*) rulesets.

Campaign Objective

Claim sole control of Barcelona through victory at Skuld (Hell's Horses) or Atropos (Turkina Ascendancy).

Starting Forces

Turkina Ascendancy (Force Strength—BV: 125,000 or PV: 3,000)

> **Turkina Ascendant Cluster (Green/Reliable):** The Turkina Ascendant Cluster has been cobbled together from falconers, cadets, paramilitary police, *solahma*, and militia.
>
> **Assets:** Heavy OmniMech Star, Medium OmniMech Nova, Assault BattleMech Star, Medium BattleMech Star, Light BattleMech Binary, OmniFighter Star, Medium Aerospace Fighter Star, Light Aerospace Fighter Star, Combat Vehicle Trinary, Conventional Infantry Binary.

Hell's Horses (Force Strength—BV: 125,000 or PV: 3,000)
  Fifth Rangers Cluster (Green/Reliable): The Fifth is configured for
  high-mobility field maneuvers. It predominantly fields light and
  medium equipment, with nothing exceeding 75 tons. Speed is also
  a must, with all units having a minimum Walk/Cruise speed of 5
  MP (10" for *Alpha Strike*). The Fifth does not field any modular
  Omni equipment except for Galaxy Commander Julian Vewas'
  Doom Courser and his Command Star.
  Assets: Heavy OmniMech Star, 2 Medium BattleMech Stars, Light
  BattleMech Star, Medium QuadVee Star, Light QuadVee Star,
  Heavy Combat Vehicle Star, Medium Combat Vehicle Star, Light
  Combat Vehicle Star, Assault Aerospace Fighter Star.

  Seventh Rangers Cluster (Regular/Reliable): The Seventh fields
  fast units with a minimum Walk/Cruise speed of 5 MP (10" for
  Alpha Strike) and lacks Omni equipment. Its battle armor Binary
  Supernova uses dedicated transport vehicles (Indra, Svantovit).
  Assets: Medium BattleMech Star, Light BattleMech Star, Light
  Combat Vehicle Binary Supernova, Medium Combat Vehicle
  Binary, Heavy Aerospace Fighter Star.

Playing the Campaign

Sequence
Every campaign day, an engagement takes place, advancing the
campaign timeline. Each engagement consists of the following phases,
played in this order:
  - Reconnaissance Phase or Air Superiority Phase
  - Strike Phase
  - Repair Phase

Front-Line Tracker
The campaign begins at Position 0 in the Bosque Forest Reserve.
Depending on the outcome of the Strike Phase, adjust the Tracker
to reflect the shifting front lines. This will affect weather conditions
and terrain.

Forces
Players keep track of each side's total force strength, calculated in
Battle Value (BV) or Point Value (PV). When a unit is destroyed, its BV/
PV is subtracted from its faction's total Force Strength. Players may
choose to fully develop both sides' rosters at the start of the campaign
or generate them as they are assigned to battles, noting each unit's
weight class and unit-type restrictions, as well as the BV/PV cap.

Consult www.masterunitlist.info for the ilClan-era equipment available to the Jade Falcons and Hell's Horses. Players may also randomly generate rosters from the appropriate Random Assignment Tables (see pp. 122–125, *Tamar Rising*). Once a unit is generated, record it for future use.

Victory

Moving the Front-Line Tracker above 5 or below –5 concludes the campaign.

Engagements

Time

Each engagement takes one day. The campaign begins on 13 January 3152.

Storm Season

The storm season ends on 22 February 3152. During the storm season, aerial reconnaissance is unavailable, and both armies rely on forward scouts to identify enemy troop positions.

For Front-Line Tracker positions 1 to 5, Level 0 Clear terrain is Deep Snow (see p. 39, *TO:AR* or p. 56, *AS:CE*), and modifiers for Heavy Snowfall (see p. 58, *TO:AR*) apply.

For Front-Line Tracker positions –2 to 0, Torrential Downpour (see p. 58, *AS:CE*) modifiers apply.

Engagements during this period consist of a Reconnaissance Phase and a Strike Phase. Once the storm season ends or when the Front-Line Tracker is –3 or below, the Reconnaissance Phase is replaced by the Air Superiority Phase.

Reconnaissance Phase

Both sides commit up to a Star (five Points) of ground forces to an engagement with the goal of degrading enemy scouting capabilities and slipping past enemy pickets to identify their positions. For each Point that crosses the enemy's Home Edge while the enemy still has active units, score one victory point. Forced Withdrawal rules (see p. 258, *TW* or p. 126, *AS:CE*) apply. Units may not retreat until they have suffered crippling damage. For each Point of enemy forces destroyed (round up), score one victory point. Determine the margin of victory by subtracting the smaller total from the larger.

9: Overwhelming Victory: the winning side achieves total tactical surprise and may ambush the losing side in the Strike Phase by fielding 200 percent of their Base Strength and starting the battle with every unit as a Hidden Unit.

6–8: Major Victory: the winning side may field 150 percent of their Base Strength in the Strike Phase.

3–5: Minor Victory: the winning side may field 125 percent of their Base Strength in the Strike Phase.

0–2: Draw: neither side gains any advantage in the Strike Phase.

Air Superiority Phase

Both sides commit up to a Star (five Points) of aerospace forces to an engagement with the goal of achieving air superiority over the front lines. Forced Withdrawal rules (see p. 258, *TW* or p. 126, *AS:CE*) apply. The side with the only remaining units on the map wins air superiority, allowing their faction to deploy 150 percent of their Base Strength in the Strike Phase and call in airstrikes from surviving members of the victorious aerospace Star.

Strike Phase

Select two mapsheets appropriate to the Front-Line Tracker position's terrain, and have each side select a home edge. Both sides enter from their home edge on Turn 1, deploying ground forces with a Base Strength of ten percent of their total remaining Force Strength, with the Reconnaissance Phase winner applying any bonuses earned. Forced Withdrawal rules apply. Units may not retreat off the map unless they have suffered crippling damage.

The Strike Phase concludes when one side no longer has any forces in play, and the Front-Line Tracker is moved depending on which side won the battle.

If the Hell's Horses control the battlefield, add 1 to the Tracker.

If the Turkina Ascendancy controls the battlefield, subtract 1 from the Tracker.

Repair Phase

Permanently remove destroyed units from each side's roster, and decrease the total force strength (BV or PV) accordingly. Units without crippling damage will be available for deployment within two days. Units with crippling damage will be available for deployment within four days. Omni configurations may be changed, but the BV/PV cap may not be exceeded.

FRONT-LINE TRACKER POSITIONS

5: Norn: Skuld (Urban), both sides may deploy all their remaining forces.

4: Norn: Vacuum Ridge (Mountain), defending infantry may deploy in Hardened bunkers (CF: 120).

3: Norn: Mariah's Pinnacle (Mountain), defending infantry may deploy in Hardened bunkers (CF: 120).

2: Norn: Su Filla (Urban)

1: Norn: Vigrid Plain (Grasslands)

0: Norn: Bosque Forest Reserve (Woods)

–1: Norn: Värmskog Jungle (Jungle)

–2: Norn: Land Bridge (Grasslands)

–3: Moira: Limnos Desert (Desert)

–4: Moira: Atropos (Urban)

–5: Moira: Atropos Spaceport (Port), both sides may deploy all their remaining forces. The Hell's Horses player may additionally deploy an *Outpost Defender*-class DropShip on the map closest to their home edge.

ZEALOT'S NEST

BRYAN YOUNG

HUNDEPALAST
OLD CONNAUGHT
ARC-ROYAL
ARC-ROYAL LIBERTY COALITION
1 JANUARY 3152
0036 HOURS

The clock had struck midnight, and many of Grand Duchess Callandre Kell's guests had begun filtering out of the palace to sleep off their pending hangovers and get ready for the work that had to be done. The ducal palace was an old, German-style castle that had been the pride of the capital city. When "Calamity" Kell—leader of the Kell Hounds—had taken Arc-Royal back, she also took back the seat of government and all its trappings. As much as Callandre's priorities were to get revenge against the Jade Falcons and to free those who had lived too long under Malvina's tyrannical yoke, she had to admit it was nice to set herself up in a castle overlooking the placid glass surface of Lachan Lake. She took a hearty gulp of champagne from the bottle, rather than a flute and smiled at the Kell Hounds and local dignitaries saying their goodbyes.

For a grand duchess, she dressed in a black cocktail dress like any party-going merc on Galatea might, rather than in the ornate fashion of Arc-Royal. But the more she thought about it, the fashion of Arc-Royal was more and more becoming the fashion of those she brought to liberate the planet. Everyone wanted to look like the people who had brought freedom from the Jade Falcons and their cruel occupation.

Callandre Kell smiled as Brendon, her gunner, staggered over, a bottle of Old Connbrau gripped in his fist like a pistol. "Happy New

Year, Boss!" His eyes widened in panic as she arched an eyebrow and pulled another long draft from the oversized bottle of champagne. "Is it Duchess? Your Highness? What do I call you at these things?"

"Boss is fine, Fievel," she assured him. "Even here. Boss is fine."

"Well, Happy New Year, then, Boss!" He raised his bottle of beer and clinked it to her comically oversized bottle of champagne.

"Happy New Year, Fievel," she said. But her voice lacked mirth. She didn't feel it. She drank. She laughed. She'd done all the things she was supposed to do on a holiday like this, where the customs had barely changed from planet to planet over the centuries—for as long as there had been years, there had been celebrations to usher in the new one.

They both took drinks and smiled, but then Brendon saw someone else he wanted to wish well and nodded to her. They had a good relationship for being in the same tank crew, but she was still the boss, which kept him at arm's length to a degree.

Adopting the title Grand Duchess of Arc-Royal as a legitimate political posting had done nothing to bridge that gap.

So he left Callandre to herself and her giant bottle of champagne. With everyone leaving, she thought some rack time sounded perfect and headed for the grand staircase at the center of the room, plush with red carpet, and ascended it.

Leaving the party behind and beneath her, Callandre sought the right corridor—there were too many hallways in a castle this big—and ambled through it as soon as she found it.

Alone, walking slowly, she wondered about what it would have been like for her grandfather to have walked these halls, as surely he had. Or his uncles. Or any member of her family that had settled on Arc-Royal. Would they have approved of her course of action and set out to carve their own empire from the ruins of what the Jade Falcons left?

She didn't know.

The heavy red drapes along the walls stirred, giving her pause.

She stopped, wondering who would be up here. Those she would have expected from the staff or command crew were still lingering in the ballroom.

For a split second, she wondered if it were a pair of Kell Hounds taking the opportunity to take cover behind the curtains for some carnal pleasure, but the chill at the top of her spine told her something must have been wrong.

"Hello?" she said, as though she were in a horror vid waiting for a horrific avian-creature to pop out and attack her with a spear.

But it was no avian alien.

It was just a kid.

He looked no older than seventeen or eighteen. Brown hair in a tight crew cut. Held himself like a warrior.

And in his hands, he held a needler pistol aimed right at her.

"That will be far enough," he said, firm but quiet.

She made no move, but her mind, addled with the booze as it was, fired its synapses. First to try to recognize the kid, remember him from wherever she'd seen him, and also to plot out some retaliation or survival plot. Because surely, this appeared to her to be an assassination attempt.

He wore a caped suit in Kell Hounds colors, but he didn't have the loosened buttons at the top to denote a night of drinking and he didn't have the wrinkles or beer stains to match the revelry. He was fastidious, the pressed lines in his attire were too perfect.

And then Callandre had a flash of recognition. Not an avian alien, but a bird nonetheless.

"You're one of the Falcon cadets."

"*Aff*," he said.

"I thought you left all that behind. Turned your back on it."

He shrugged.

"And you're not going to challenge me or anything? Just going to find a dark corner and kill me?"

"This is the best way," he said, his mouth a grim slit, his bright-blue eyes sparkling with hate.

Callandre smirked. "I always knew if one of you bastards were going to kill me, you'd be the one to do it. So let's just get it over with, yeah?"

MAKESHIFT HOLDING FACILITY
OLD CONNAUGHT
ARC-ROYAL
FORMER JADE FALCON OCCUPATION ZONE
4 OCTOBER 3151

THREE MONTHS EARLIER

Cadet Cypher stood at attention alongside the rest of his *sibkin*, waiting to learn their fate.

The Kell Hounds had taken Arc-Royal. They had killed the Star Colonel. They had declared all the spoils of the planet *isorla*, and given the remaining Clan elements just days to depart. But the cadets *she* wanted to talk to first.

Cypher didn't know what Callandre Kell looked like before he saw her standing there in front of him. He'd never seen a picture or a holovid. After he'd heard she took the Star Colonel down in nothing but a hovertank, he expected her to be some sort of mad monster, foolish enough to go against a 'Mech in a tank.

But standing there, with her mane of wavy brown hair and storm-gray eyes that missed nothing, he could have sworn she was a devil rather than a monster. The red-and-black Kell Hound uniform had helped with that part of the illusion.

"The Kell Hounds have taken Arc-Royal," she said, bright and clear. There was no waver to her voice, and it had a strength and conviction Cypher's Falconer told him belonged only to Jade Falcons. For what his Falconer had called a "filthy lucrewarrior," she sounded like an *actual* warrior.

"Though, I'm sure you all already knew that." The leader of the Kell Hounds looked each of them in the eye as she passed, never flinching, showing no signs of weakness. "But that means you all have a choice. It's going to be a difficult one, but it's a choice nonetheless. You can leave with the rest of the Falcons we've granted *hegira* to. I suppose you could stay with the *solahma* infantry standing trial for the massacres of this planet, but I can't imagine that will end any way you want."

Cypher and the cadets around him were too disciplined to even murmur at this suggestion. They were all young, and hadn't yet seen real battle beyond the skirmishes they'd been used for during the invasion by the Kell Hounds. They were too young to be put to death for nothing, at least to Cypher's mind, so that felt like no choice at all.

"The only other choice you have is to remain with the Kell Hounds." Cypher furrowed his brow. *Become a mercenary?* That felt just as wrong as the other choices, which left them with no real choice at all. But on some level, they were the bondsmen of the Kell Hounds.

As if she knew what they were all thinking, she shook her head. "Not as bondsmen. You are warriors. Make your own choice; ilKhan Ward may be in a forgiving mood. If you stay, all I promise is a chance to make up for your complicity against the citizens of Arc-Royal. If that doesn't mean anything, then the hell with you."

Cypher blinked, unsure of what to think.

The leader of the Kell Hounds turned on her heel to leave and one of the other Kell Hounds stepped forward to fill the void the Kell woman left. She didn't make that easy; her presence was outsized. "You don't have to decide right this very second," the other Hound said, his eyes light and skin dark. "The other Jade Falcons are departing tomorrow, so you'll have at least that much time to decide if you want to go with them or stay here. If you want my advice, I'd stay. There's a future for you here, and we can use you. You'll be MechWarriors. If you go, I know how much Alaric Ward loves Jade Falcons, and it's anyone's guess how he might treat all of you showing up on his doorstep."

The Kell Hound had the name M<small>ANDVI</small> written on his name patch, and he kept his arms folded tight. Cypher could only guess he was some high rank or another—the rank pips and designations for the Kell Hounds read like a different language to him.

The ranking Hound looked right into Cypher's eyes when he said, "You'll be treated well here. And you'll get plenty of chances to fight. Only this time it'll be *for* the people instead of against them."

And hearing that sentiment caused Cypher a great swell of confusion. Had they not been fighting for the people already?

He supposed now he was not sure.

"Genuinely, I do not know," Cypher said to the *sibmates* gathered around his bunk.

A handful of the *sibko* were huddled in corners around the room, trying to make their decision, just as the group surrounding Cypher was. Most had decided with little hesitation to leave. They would take their chances with Clan Wolf, but do their best to remain Jade Falcons. There were some on the proverbial fence, and those were the ones talking the loudest, trying to come to their decisions.

"What will you do here, then?" a cadet named Jaron asked.

Another cadet, Bella, said, "I would rather be Hound than Wolf."

"They are lucrewarriors," Cadet Anson reminded them.

But then Cypher cleared his throat to take the floor. "I do not know which life is going to be the one that gives us the life we trained for, the life we deserved. What concerns me is the idea we have done something wrong and must make up for it. What did we do wrong? We only did what we were told."

"Why would that concern you?" Jaron said. "If we were ordered to do something, we have nothing to make up for."

"Star Colonel Riss did everything in his power to protect the planet. And Khan Hazen did the same for our push to Terra," Anson said. "If the Spheroids think they did something wrong, they can take it up with them."

"The Chingis Khan is dead," Bella said.

Jaron shook his head and lowered it. "We could be the last of the Jade Falcons. I am not going to let our Clan die because of this offer. I will take my chances with the rest. Surely Jade Falcons remain on Terra."

Cadet Cypher took in a deep breath, trying to put into words what he wanted to say. "If Khan Hazen failed, who is to say there are any Falcons left at all? She was known for her fury and battle acumen. Would she have not fought to the very last with everything she had?"

They all nodded, some more hesitantly than others.

They continued their discussion back and forth, seeking pros and cons of staying or going. Ultimately, for what he decided was for the good of the Clan, Cypher decided to stay. If he could "make up" for whatever it was the Jade Falcons were accused of doing wrong, he could bring honor to his Clan in that way. And if he died in battle in the process, all the better.

In the end, only five cadets from the Solitude *sibko* academy decided to stay. Cypher was the first. Bella stayed, naturally. The others—who Cypher knew less well than Bella, were named Shade, Aurum, and Hunter. There were more than forty others who decided to take the promise of *hegira* and go.

There were no tearful farewells. Those who left—to Cypher's mind—harbored resentment toward those who stayed.

That didn't make staying any easier.

Having determination matched against the shame he felt left Cypher with many complicated feelings to resolve for his new life.

But he was confident he could work that out for himself.

**SOLITUDE SIBKO ACADEMY
GRUNGURTEL JUNGLE
ARC-ROYAL
ARC-ROYAL LIBERTY COALITION
9 OCTOBER 3151**

The academy felt empty. None of Cypher's comrades were there, save the four others that had remained. They weren't moved anywhere else. And it was still too soon to know what would happen to them. They were told to stay here in the meantime.

Armed guards prevented them from leaving, though if Cypher and the other four cadets put their minds to it, leaving would have been no issue. They knew all the secret ways through the Solitude Academy, and could have left the grounds without violence. They had also been trained extensively in the trade of combat, and would have had no problem taking the guards out and leaving at their whim.

The five of them had agreed among themselves to be on their best behavior until they knew exactly what their fates would be.

A few days into their confinement, they were finally summoned to the academy's 'Mech bay.

There *she* stood in the center, with her arms folded, looking up at one of the 'Mechs in the bay. Her back was turned toward them, but her silhouette was unmistakable.

Callandre Kell herself.

Guards marched the five of them into line near her and when they stopped and stood at attention, she dropped her arms and turned to regard them.

Looking each one in the eyes before she spoke, she began with Bella, then moved to Shade, then Aurum, then Hunter, until finally her gaze shifted to Cypher.

"So," she said. "It's just the five of you?"

"*Aff,*" Cypher said automatically.

"That's what, a Star in Clan reckoning?"

"*Aff,*" Bella said. Of the group, Cypher got the distinct impression Bella and he were the two most enthusiastic to be there. The others all spoke and acted in various tones of "begrudging."

Colonel Kell stepped up to Shade, sizing him up. She stood half a dozen millimeters taller than him, and looked down her nose to meet his gaze. "You take your trials yet?"

"*Neg,*" Shade said grimly. Very serious.

She cast her eyes across the rest of the lineup, still close into Shade's personal zone. "I presume you all have experience with a 'Mech?"

"*Aff,*" they all said.

"And you're willing to use those skills for the benefit of the Kell Hounds and the Arc-Royal Liberty Coalition?"

It took a moment, and the response was far less concordant, but they all repeated the word: "*Aff.*"

"Then I have a mission for you. See how well you do. Call it your Trial of Position if you like, I don't really give a damn about that. Whatever you need to tell yourselves to be willing to do what it takes is fine by me."

"What is the mission?" Anson asked before Cypher could.

And Colonel Kell took in a sharp breath with an unnervingly sly smile.

CLONARF MOUNTAINS
OUTSIDE DENTON
ARC-ROYAL
ARC-ROYAL LIBERTY COALITION
10 OCTOBER 3152

Cypher marched through the mountains in a *Mist Lynx* F, side by side with Bella and Anson. Shade and Hunter were left in *Flamberge* Cs on the outskirts of the town of Denton, which was encircled by the Clonarf mountain range. Equipped with Arrow IV missiles, they had the job of acting as artillery. The *Mist Lynx*es, agile and jump-capable, were equipped with active probes and targeting lasers for the purpose. It was on them to find the resistance in the hidden bunkers in the mountains.

Not that there had been many signs of active resistance, but the colonel of the Kell Hounds felt sure there were Jade Falcons hiding in the network of hidden caves and 'Mech bays in the mountains. It had been left to the cadets to find whoever it was and flush them out. If it were Jade Falcons, they were ordered to shoot on sight, since they had been given the option to get off the planet.

Those orders felt antithetical to every instinct Cypher had been trained to feel. Especially if their foes were indeed Jade Falcons. But if they were, by remaining they had declared an act of war against the Kell Hounds and the Arc-Royal Liberty Coalition.

Cypher cursed himself.

He and the rest had to stop thinking of themselves as Jade Falcons now. They were working with the Kell Hounds as part of the military of the Arc-Royal Liberty Coalition. There were still many things that had to be organized about this new government, but that was no concern for him. All he had to do was find the enemies—he'd tried his hardest to stop referring to them as fellow Jade Falcons in his head—and take them down.

He felt up to the challenge.

And he hoped the others would be as well.

"I have something on my scanners," Anson said. "Sending telemetry."

"Receiving," Cypher said. As the information loaded on his map, he saw there was indeed a nest of activity hidden in the mountainside.

"Repositioning," Shade said from the valley. He would need to get in range with his missiles for the target spotting to mean anything. So would Hunter.

"Aff," Hunter said, complying as well. But there was a growl in his voice. Like he was pained.

Cypher tried filing it away as nothing, but he understood where it came from. There was a cruelty in forcing them to go after their former comrades who were likely vastly more experienced than they. They were warriors, though. They were not supposed to have feelings of conflict over who had decided to be their enemy. All they had to focus on was firing in the right direction and attacking those they were ordered to attack.

Perhaps it could have been a good Trial of Position after all.

"How do we draw them out?" Anson asked.

"We can offer a *batchall*," Bella said.

"*Neg.* We were told specifically no *batchalls.* Rules of *zellbrigen* do not apply because they are out of compliance with orders, and we are no longer Jade Falcon." Cypher chewed on his bottom lip. "I can jump in, see what there is to see, blast at the entrance and jump out. There is no guarantee we are even facing Jade Falcons."

"They *are* Jade Falcons," Hunter said, that anger still tingeing his voice.

"They are the enemy," Bella reminded them.

"Even if they were Jade Falcons," Cypher said, further rationalizing what had to happen, "they were given *hegira* and ordered to leave. If they chose not to take it, we are not responsible for their actions. I am going in. Keep me covered."

Cypher activated the jump jets on his *Mist Lynx* F and aimed at the opening their scans and probes had discovered. There was no metal door covering it, just several trees, spaced apart enough that the shadows at this time of day covered the mouth of the cave, giving it all the appearance of an abandoned mine.

"Nothing so far, but there is definitely activity on the inside," Cypher said.

"Caution," Bella told him.

But Cypher knew to be cautious. "That is my watchword."

He edged his *Mist Lynx* F forward. It was a spare 25 tons of 'Mech that packed a punch with three heavy medium lasers, four heavy small lasers, and a TAG laser designator.

Upon Cypher reaching the opening, tension rose in his gut.

"I am coming close behind," Anson said. As promised, Anson's red dot on the HUD's mini-map appeared behind Cypher and to the right.

"I will go in, you wait here," Cypher said. "I will see if I can draw them out."

"They must know we are here," Anson said quietly.

"They may not."

"If they are truly Jade Falcons, do you really think they would allow themselves to be caught unawares?"

"It matters not. All we must do is lure them out. Let the Arrow IVs do their work."

"*Aff.*"

Cypher stepped into the cave, large enough to admit a 'Mech twice as tall as his *Mist Lynx,* at least. Thinking of 'Mechs that large forced a spin of dizziness. He had imagined dying a hundred times in a hundred different engagements, but none of them ever looked like this. For a fleeting second, doubt flooded him. Would this just be a way for the Kell Hounds to ambush them?

He reminded himself that his thought made no sense. Why would they have put them in 'Mechs if they just wanted to kill them? They surely would have just murdered them in their sleep. Or killed them in a public execution if they meant to simply get rid of them.

If there was an ambush, he felt confident it was not one of the Kell Hounds' making.

Rounding the corner in the darkened cave, using his magres imaging to see in the dark and keeping his probe active, Cypher blinked. His console flashed with the light of half a dozen contacts, and the magres scans finally cut through whatever had been interfering with them. The outlines of a few 'Mechs and a couple battle-armored Elementals appeared across his screen. According to his instruments, a wall still stood between them.

"I have contacts," Cypher reported. "Three 'Mechs and two Elementals."

He had no idea what sort of team had such a makeup. Mixed Stars did exist, but the numbers were all wrong here. Were they licking their wounds from a different engagement?

Cypher had no idea.

"We should punch a hole through the wall," Anson said. "And then we run, lead them out, and let the artillery handle them."

"As good a plan as any," Cypher said.

"They know you are there," Bella said. "They have to."

Whether they did was immaterial, and Cypher said so. "It does not matter if we tripped sensors or appeared on their scopes. We must complete our mission."

"Opening fire," Anson said.

It did not help that they had no formalized command structure. They were all equals, doing what they thought was best. This had been another mark against the Kell Hounds, that they did not assign any one of them as a definitive leader. As the old saying went, the buck had to stop somewhere.

Anson's lasers shattered the quiet of the bunker as they cracked through the crumbling wall. Cypher joined in, adding his own arsenal to the cacophony. The viewscreen flashed white as the walls and rocks heated and exploded, but they still had no way in. Cypher switched to IR, hoping to see better in the cave's darkness. The door seemed no worse for wear, but it began parting in the center.

"We did not do that," Cypher told Anson.

Anson's *Mist Lynx* stepped backward. "They are coming."

"Sending target and telemetry data," Cypher said, calling out to Hunter and Shade.

"Get them out of the cave so we can open fire."

"I am aware," Anson called out.

Cypher wasted no time backing up either, hoping he could get a shot at the 'Mechs before they were obliterated in the fire and brimstone the

Arrow IV barrage would bring. The doors spread wider, revealing their enemies. Cypher's computers tagged two of the 'Mechs as *Gyrfalcon*s. The third was an *Ion Sparrow*. The Elementals charged with the fury and rage of a caged jade falcon.

Taking aim, Cypher opened fire with his small lasers, the lights cutting outlines around the Elementals in the dark.

Anson joined in, but they weren't nearly accurate enough to stop them.

The Elementals split up, each leaping onto a different *Mist Lynx*.

"Run," Cypher warned. Sweat beaded on his forehead; Elementals were something to keep at a distance. Their armored hands could tear apart a 'Mech, or their flamers could force it to overheat. Or they could just punch a hole in the cockpit and rip out a pilot. They were vicious.

Anson and Cypher spun around, turning their poorly armored backs to the enemy 'Mechs. Hopefully, getting out and leading them into the trap would be worth more than a stand-up fight, though the retreat pained Cypher. The *Ion Sparrow* would have been a good match against his *Mist Lynx*.

The Elemental that had latched onto his leg tore into his knee actuator, slowing Cypher's movement. The metal joints screamed. He was going to fall over soon if he could not get rid of the Elemental.

Once he crested the entrance, he swapped out the IR view for something more resembling reality and called out to his *sibmate*. "Bella, take the Elemental."

"I will hit you," she radioed.

"You will hit them, too."

It was more difficult to target something as small as an Elemental in the first place, and one that had attached itself to a moving 'Mech felt almost impossible, but there was little he could do about it on his own. With Bella opening fire, he twisted his 'Mech's torso to do likewise for Anson. Anson's Elemental had climbed up the back of his 'Mech and clawed at the *Mist Lynx*'s head. Cypher lined up a shot with his lasers. When the targeting reticle glowed gold, he thumbed the firing stud and pulled the triggers, letting loose with everything.

The lasers burned a hole right through the Elemental, and they dropped to the ground behind Anson's 'Mech like a rag doll.

Unfortunately, Bella's shots missed, and the Elemental attached to Cypher kept pounding at his 'Mech's knee. The metal screamed in agony, and his damage readout flashed from yellow to red.

He would not be able to walk farther if they let the Elemental continue. But he also had to keep moving to lure the other 'Mechs from the bunker, so he just kept moving. It did not matter that it was toward the steep decline leading to the city of Denton.

He just had to keep going.

"Bella, forget the Elemental. Focus on the target spotting."

"Aff," she said with no hesitation; a proper Clan warrior.

She pivoted while Cypher kept moving forward.

He really only heard the rest of what happened.

Anson shouted. "They are clear!"

"Target data incoming," Bella said.

"Missiles incoming," came Shade's voice.

"Missiles incoming," Hunter said, after another hesitation.

And then that was when the world collapsed in front of Cypher. The knee actuator crumpled under the weight of the beating it took. Then the *Mist Lynx* slipped.

He could not keep the 'Mech upright, and it fell into the bowl, sliding toward Denton.

At some point, Cypher realized he must have hit his head because one second he was there, conscious of his surroundings and panic spiking in his chest, and the next there was nothing but blackness.

INFIRMARY
SOLITUDE SIBKO ACADEMY
GRUNGURTEL JUNGLE
ARC-ROYAL
ARC-ROYAL LIBERTY COALITION
12 OCTOBER 3151

The first time, it took only a few minutes for Cypher to come to. A combination of the shift in his blood pressure from the 'Mech's fall, the concussion he got falling, and the second concussion he got landing had hurt. But in those few, dark minutes, the fight was won.

When the Elemental that had been harassing Cypher realized they had downed the 'Mech, they turned to Anson. According to Anson, he was practically looking the Elemental in the eyes when he killed him.

Thanks to Bella's target spotting, the barrage of artillery exploded the *Ion Sparrow* in a single, brutal hit and blasted chunks of slag from the *Gyrfalcon*s. After Anson finished with the Elemental and another volley of Arrow IV missiles fired, he turned to their flank. His laser batteries lanced into the first *Gyrfalcon* and carving into its armor, taking it down. Then the rest of the Star had combined their fire to turn the final *Gyrfalcon* into a pile of slag.

After everyone had opened fire, there was nothing left other than a pile of metal confetti.

Or so Cypher had been told.

Though he had regained consciousness, he hadn't exactly kept control of his mind. Dizziness took him. And with his 'Mech down and suffering double concussions, he went right back out after straining to get his 'Mech back up onto one foot.

Then he'd woken up in the infirmary.

Only one of his *sibmates*, Bella, remained at his side through any parts of the ordeal he could remember.

She was beside him then, too. "It seems they will let you out today."

"Good," he said, satisfied. "Any word from the Kell Hounds about whether we behaved admirably enough?"

"Neg," she said. "We received a message that said 'Good work,' but aside from that, nothing other than the order to return here."

Cypher smirked. "I suppose I remain in the dark."

"I am sure something will come of it."

"How are the others?"

"Angry. Betrayed."

Cypher tentatively nodded his head, and when the swirling dizziness did not return, he realized he was recovering. "I felt much the same. It is understandable."

Bella nodded back at him.

Cypher realized that feeling had not lasted for one simple moment. It lingered. He felt cruelty in the Kell Hounds' decision to force them to fight other Jade Falcons under less than honorable circumstances. But they had agreed to stay and were essentially bondsmen, even if the Kell Hounds didn't count them as such. They were bound to the Kell Hounds, and the only thing less honorable to do than fight their fellow Jade Falcons in such an engagement would be to turn their backs on their new oath to the Hounds.

He only wondered how long that feeling would last.

KELL HOUND BARRACKS
GRUNGURTEL JUNGLE
ARC-ROYAL
ARC-ROYAL LIBERTY COALITION
20 DECEMBER 3151

What had once been known as the Solitude Sibko Academy—the place Cypher had learned to think of as home—had been transformed into a barracks for a mixed company of Kell Hounds.

The building felt less empty, but also less welcoming.

The Kell Hounds held resentment for Cypher and his *sibkin*, and he supposed that was understandable. With each passing day, he learned more of the truth about how the Jade Falcons had hunted the Kell Hounds down, and how the former Khan's actions had cost so much to the civilians. He understood finally why Colonel Kell had offered them a chance to "make up for what the Jade Falcons had done." Quite frankly, some of the Khan's actions seemed *dezgra*, a thought that shocked him.

He had to balance that truth against the fact that he was getting a Kell Hounds perspective on things, which was hardly unbiased.

In the mess, the Kell Hounds who were true mercenaries stayed on one side of the room, and Cypher and his *sibmates* were relegated to their own table in the back corner. It did not seem intentional, but that was just how the social hierarchy played out.

When Cypher entered the mess, he was not surprised to see Shade and Hunter in a fistfight with another Kell Hound.

"Spheroid scum!" Hunter shouted.

The Kell Hound, a big man named Kaneda with a mop of black hair and the sort of build Cypher would have expected more from an Elemental than an Inner Sphere merc, had a fist raised. He lunged at Shade and Hunter, reaching his arms wide as though he were going to crack their heads together.

The other Kell Hounds stepped in to stop the fight, but it took an increasing amount of them to actually keep the Falcons from the Hounds.

"Enough!" came a voice from the edge of the room.

It was suddenly so quiet the silence could be torn with a whisper.

The voice came from Callandre Kell herself. With the news they'd received, Cypher was not sure how to refer to her. Was she still just the colonel, as she had instructed them to refer to her? Or was there something else they should call her to reflect her new title of grand duchess?

And why would the Grand Duchess of Arc-Royal be in a mess, breaking up a fight in the first place?

The whole thing beggared belief.

"We have enough people out there to fight without fighting each other."

Kaneda scoffed and glared at Hunter and Shade. "I thought we were killing Falcons and liberating people from them."

"We are. Those aren't Falcons anymore. And I've already told you that once. If I have to tell you that again, I'll boot you from this unit so fast you won't know what hit you. And it'll be from an air lock."

Hunter stepped forward. "I request the ability to fight this *surat* in a Circle of Equals."

"Neg," the colonel said, hinting with sarcasm. "You aren't Jade Falcons anymore, and you're certainly no longer Clan. Leave that shit behind you. That's an order."

Hunter clenched his jaw, but muttered, *"Aff."*

Shade looked from Hunter to Kaneda and Cypher saw the anger in his eyes. Not only did he see it, Cypher felt it. Looking to Bella and Anson, he knew they felt that burning, too. They were being forced too quickly to become something they had spent their lives learning not to be.

"But that's not why I'm here," the colonel said, walking closer to them with a swagger. "I wanted to personally invite everyone to the New Year's celebration we're holding at the Hundepalast. We deserve a party."

She turned her head to the group of former Falcons, catching Cypher's gaze. "That includes you all."

Cypher nodded, seeing that it would be proper and expected. *"Aff,* Colonel. If our presence is requested, we shall be there."

"Oh, it isn't mandatory. But I want you to know it's an option. You have an invitation. You're Kell Hounds. Through and through." The colonel glanced back and forth across the assembly. "I'd like to see you *all* there. In the meantime, knock all this infighting off. Save it for the Falcons."

She looked around the room, and her eyes met with everyone, both Falcon and Hound. At least that's how Cypher had begun to think of things; they were separate, but still somehow together.

The colonel tightened her jaw. "We're all going to have a good time, and that's an order. You get me? Because after that party, the real work begins."

KELL HOUND BARRACKS
GRUNGURTEL JUNGLE
ARC-ROYAL
ARC-ROYAL LIBERTY COALITION
31 DECEMBER 3151
0740 HOURS

For New Year's Eve, a celebration Cypher was aware of but still did not quite understand, he dressed in the fashion he was expected: a caped suit in Kell Hounds colors. He surprised himself in the mirror: the red and black suited him just as well as the green and yellow of the Jade Falcon dress uniforms.

The others were dressed in the same getup. The four men of the group almost looked identical, with their buzz cuts and etched, clean-shaven jaw lines.

"Shall we go then?" Bella asked them all. She was the only one with a notable difference to her, with her blond hair tightened into two old-fashioned buns on top of her head. Her face was much more angular, but the Kell Hounds uniforms hid the differences in her body shape.

"I still cannot believe we are doing this," Anson said.

Shade shook his head. "It is just one dishonor after another."

"She should have let me fight that *surat*," Hunter said. "I will never live that down."

"Agreed," Shade added.

Cypher understood that humiliation. That Kell Hound had mocked them and had not suffered any consequence. Among Jade Falcons, if one mocked another, they had better have the strength to back it up. Instead, the colonel had just strolled in and ended it.

The five of them had debated this furiously since it had happened. Unless they did something about it, Cypher wondered if it would ever cease.

They had to defend their honor. How else would they be taken seriously?

"I am sure we will find a solution to this somehow," Cypher said.

"We will," Shade said grimly.

Breaking up that line of thought, Bella led them to the hovercar that would take them to the palace, where the party was just beginning.

HUNDEPALAST
OLD CONNAUGHT
ARC-ROYAL
ARC-ROYAL LIBERTY COALITION
1 JANUARY 3152
0016 HOURS

After the countdown to midnight and the plethora of alcoholic beverages, Cypher better understood why they would have gatherings such as New Year's. He also felt much closer to the rest of the Kell Hounds. He might be a Clanner who had been told he possessed superior genetics, but letting loose with that much booze relaxed him.

Hunter and Shade stood arm in arm, singing an old Jade Falcon war song: "Eden's Zealous Nest."

It was the most natural thing in the world when one was drunk.

Singing felt positively normal in those situations.

Except Kaneda Ito was there and took offense.

He threw the first punch right into Hunter's face. The second punch—this one from Shade—took Kaneda in the kidney.

By the time Cypher had tossed his glass and sprinted into the fray, the colonel whistled loud enough to shatter windows from the base of the grand staircase.

Movement stopped.

All eyes turned to her.

"What did I tell you? *All of you?* Knock it off. We're *done* with this. We're going to have a Happy New Year, and anyone who doesn't is going to get written up for insubordination. I told you all tomorrow is when the work begins, and I wasn't kidding; 3152 is going to be the most important year we've ever had. And you all need to get on board. Now say your goodbyes and get the hell out of my palace."

Hunter raised a hand. "But what about—"

"Get. *Out!*" she said, cutting Hunter off sharply. Her eyes were made of the very fires of hell itself.

Cypher felt the same burning humiliation Hunter felt, and he knew something had to happen.

0042 HOURS

Callandre's free hand twitched as she formulated her plan for the fight she found herself about to take part in. She could throw the bottle at the Falcon cadet and hope she knocked him out cold with it. Or she could crack it in half and use it as a weapon.

"I didn't think a song was going to cause so much trouble," she said.

"This has nothing to do with the song," he said. His face turned red, and he looked smaller and smaller with every word he uttered.

"Do tell," she said, creeping forward slowly, hoping to close in enough to make a move.

All she had to do was keep him talking.

"You damned our honor. I thought I was doing the right and honorable thing by staying, but you twisted it against me."

Cursing herself, she couldn't remember his name. Callandre couldn't always remember the names of everyone in her command. And since she'd taken over Arc-Royal and established the Liberty Coalition, there was an unending stream of bullshit to deal with that had kept her from getting as close to the Hounds as she wanted. "How have I done that?"

"Back," he said, pointing at her with the needler.

"How did I twist anything from you, kid?"

"I honored my commitment. I expected to be treated like a bondsman, but you refused. I thought our honor meant something, and you forced us to kill our fellow Falcons."

"You aren't a Falcon anymore. That *was* me treating you like a bondsman. With honor. If you got snatched by the Wolves and you were their bondsman and they ordered you to fight against the Falcons, would you do it?"

"*Aff*," he admitted begrudgingly. "That is the Way of the Clans."

"Do you think I'd have put you in a 'Mech at all if I didn't respect you, let alone against other Falcons? It wasn't a test of loyalty. I knew you'd perform, and you all did admirably."

"You refused to let us fight in a Circle of Equals to defend our honor."

Her memory, still fuzzy from the wine, focused in. Not just to the song, but the fight from before. Kaneda Ito was involved in that one, too. "I don't tolerate fights in my command."

The kid growled.

Callandre took another hesitant step forward as, from the corner of her eye, she saw another one of the ex-Falcon cadets dressed identically, lurking in the hallway. He padded softly, as though sneaking up on the hothead with the needler rather than coming to help kill her. She tried not to look at him directly, for fear of giving him away. And she cursed herself again for not remembering their names.

That was something she'd have to correct ASAP.

She took in a deep breath and took a tentative step forward.

"It is the Clan way," the cadet said.

"The Kell Hounds aren't Clan. Never have been."

"Phelan Kell was Clan."

She rolled her eyes and hoped she was pouring on the charm, but through the booze she didn't know. "Don't even get me started on him."

She crept even closer. Just a few meters separated them. She was ready to swing the bottle if she had to.

Her eyes flitted to the approaching cadet, close enough to reach the aggressor. Then her eyes flitted back to the wronged party.

His curiosity tagged him, and he turned to look over his shoulder.

That's when she and the second ex-Falcon pounced.

Charging with a tackle, she discarded the bottle and went for his middle. The other ex-Falcon wrestled away the needler.

"Let go!" one shouted.

"This is *dezgra*!" the other responded.

The needler clattered to the ground, and both of them wrestled to reach it, but she extricated herself from the fray, snatched it, and stood, aiming it at the pair of them. "Get up. Both of you."

They stopped and did as she commanded. Their Kell Hound uniforms were rumpled from the effort. They didn't look so sharp anymore.

"What's your name?" she said to the offending cadet.

He wiped blood from his mouth. "Hunter."

The other stood at crisp attention. "Cypher."

"Hunter and Cypher what?"

They both looked to each other, confused, and she realized her mistake.

The one called Cypher tilted his head slightly. "Colonel, we would take the name of the Clan who took us as bondsmen until we earned our Bloodname, if ever."

She knew that.

But she'd been too busy thinking of more important things.

"What's your Bloodhouse then?"

"Hazen," they both said in unison.

Callandre suppressed a shudder. "I'm sorry I didn't sort this out sooner. I'll work on it. In the meantime, you're going to go as just Hunter as long as you're in the brig. Maybe you can earn a last name of some sort. You, though—" She looked over to Cypher. "Get used to Cypher Kell. You get me?"

"Aff," he said.

And she saw a change come over him. He stood a little straighter and filled out the uniform a little better.

Maybe they just needed to be told they belonged, and *feel* it for a change.

"Guards!" she shouted.

The fight had been quiet enough that they hadn't been alerted. And why they hadn't seen the situation on surveillance was something she would scream at them about later.

They arrived quickly with plastic wrist cuffs and laser pistols, faster than she expected. "Toss 'Just Hunter' here in the brig."

She and Hunter shared a knowing look. Almost as if he were pleading with her.

Callandre broke eye contact with him and looked to the guard. "Let him sleep it off, and we'll decide what happens tomorrow." Then she looked back to him. "We'll see if he can behave himself."

"Yes, Colonel," they both replied and gathered Hunter up.

That left her alone with Cypher.

"I'm sorry about that," she said to the kid, still at attention.

She wondered if he felt much different than she did when she'd to step in and take over the Kell Hounds; out of her depth in a world different than what she knew. Granted, her situation was a lot less drastic from point A to point B than his, but it was comparable.

She smirked when realizing the kid didn't know how to take an apology. "It means I appreciate what you did. Keep it up, and you might make it in this outfit yet."

"Yes, Colonel," he said, nervous and unsure.

"Now get out of here. You sleep it off, too. I wasn't kidding about tomorrow. Understand?"

"Aff," he said.

And he left the way she came, by the grand staircase.

She watched him go, her heart still thumping with adrenaline. She hadn't expected any of those Falcons to join the Kell Hounds, but despite what just happened, she knew it could be a good thing.

She had plans for them.

But they were going to have to wait for those.

Callandre Kell wasn't kidding. 3152 was going to be a very big year for the Kell Hounds.

BATTLETECH ERAS

The *BattleTech* universe is a living, vibrant entity that grows each year as more sourcebooks and fiction are published. A dynamic universe, its setting and characters evolve over time within a highly detailed continuity framework, bringing everything to life in a way a static game universe cannot match.

To help quickly and easily convey the timeline of the universe—and to allow a player to easily "plug in" a given novel or sourcebook—we've divided *BattleTech* into eight major eras.

STAR LEAGUE
(Present–2780)

Ian Cameron, ruler of the Terran Hegemony, concludes decades of tireless effort with the creation of the Star League, a political and military alliance between all Great Houses and the Hegemony. Star League armed forces immediately launch the Reunification War, forcing the Periphery realms to join. For the next two centuries, humanity experiences a golden age across the thousand light-years of human-occupied space known as the Inner Sphere. It also sees the creation of the most powerful military in human history.

(This era also covers the centuries before the founding of the Star League in 2571, most notably the Age of War.)

SUCCESSION WARS
(2781–3049)

Every last member of First Lord Richard Cameron's family is killed during a coup launched by Stefan Amaris. Following the thirteen-year war to unseat him, the rulers of each of the five Great Houses disband the Star League. General Aleksandr Kerensky departs with eighty percent of the Star League Defense Force beyond known space and the Inner Sphere collapses into centuries of warfare known as the Succession Wars that will eventually result in a massive loss of technology across most worlds.

CLAN INVASION
(3050–3061)

A mysterious invading force strikes the coreward region of the Inner Sphere. The invaders, called the Clans, are descendants of Kerensky's SLDF troops, forged into a society dedicated to becoming the greatest fighting force in history. With vastly superior technology and warriors, the Clans conquer world after world. Eventually this outside threat will forge a new Star League, something hundreds of years of warfare failed to accomplish. In addition, the Clans will act as a catalyst for a technological renaissance.

CIVIL WAR
(3062–3067)

The Clan threat is eventually lessened with the complete destruction of a Clan. With that massive external threat apparently neutralized, internal conflicts explode around the Inner Sphere. House Liao conquers its former Commonality, the St. Ives Compact; a rebellion of military units belonging to House Kurita sparks a war with their powerful border enemy, Clan Ghost Bear; the fabulously powerful Federated Commonwealth of House Steiner and House Davion collapses into five long years of bitter civil war.

JIHAD
(3067–3080)

Following the Federated Commonwealth Civil War, the leaders of the Great Houses meet and disband the new Star League, declaring it a sham. The pseudo-religious Word of Blake—a splinter group of ComStar, the protectors and controllers of interstellar communication—launch the Jihad: an interstellar war that pits every faction against each other and even against themselves, as weapons of mass destruction are used for the first time in centuries while new and frightening technologies are also unleashed.

DARK AGE
(3081-3150)

Under the guidance of Devlin Stone, the Republic of the Sphere is born at the heart of the Inner Sphere following the Jihad. One of the more extensive periods of peace begins to break out as the 32nd century dawns. The factions, to one degree or another, embrace disarmament, and the massive armies of the Succession Wars begin to fade. However, in 3132 eighty percent of interstellar communications collapses, throwing the universe into chaos. Wars erupt almost immediately, and the factions begin rebuilding their armies.

ILCLAN
(3151-present)

The once-invulnerable Republic of the Sphere lies in ruins, torn apart by the Great Houses and the Clans as they wage war against each other on a scale not seen in nearly a century. Mercenaries flourish once more, selling their might to the highest bidder. As Fortress Republic collapses, the Clans race toward Terra to claim their long-denied birthright and create a supreme authority that will fulfill the dream of Aleksandr Kerensky and rule the Inner Sphere by any means necessary: The ilClan.

CLAN HOMEWORLDS
(2786-present)

In 2784, General Aleksandr Kerensky launched Operation Exodus, and led most of the Star League Defense Force out of the Inner Sphere in a search for a new world, far away from the strife of the Great Houses. After more than two years and thousands of light years, they arrived at the Pentagon Worlds. Over the next two-and-a-half centuries, internal dissent and civil war led to the creation of a brutal new society—the Clans. And in 3049, they returned to the Inner Sphere with one goal—the complete conquest of the Great Houses.

SUBMISSION GUIDELINES

Shrapnel is the market for official short fiction set in the *BattleTech* universe.

WHAT WE WANT

We are looking for stories of **3,000–5,000 words** that are character-oriented, meaning the characters, rather than the technology, provide the main focus of the action. Stories can be set in any established *BattleTech* era, and although we prefer stories where BattleMechs are featured, this is by no means a mandatory element.

WHAT WE DON'T WANT

The following items are generally grounds for immediate disqualification:

- Stories not set in the *BattleTech* universe. There are other markets for these stories.

- Stories centering solely on romance, supernatural, fantasy, or horror elements. If your story isn't primarily military sci-fi, then it's probably not for us.

- Stories containing gratuitous sex, gore, or profanity. Keep it PG-13, and you should be fine.

- Stories under 3,000 words or over 5,000 words. We don't publish flash fiction, and although we do publish works longer than 5,000 words, these are reserved for established *BattleTech* authors.

- Vanity stories, which include personal units, author-as-character inserts, or tabletop game sessions retold in narrative form.

- Publicly available *BattleTech* fan-fiction. If your story has been posted in a forum or other public venue, then we will not accept it.

- Multi-part stories. Your story must be a self-contained stand-alone story with a clear ending, not Part 1 of a series

- Stories that go beyond the current timeline in published *BattleTech* products. As of this writing, any stories set after June 3152 will be automatically rejected.

MANUSCRIPT FORMAT

- .rtf, .doc, .docx formats ONLY
- 12-point Times New Roman, Cambria, or Palatino fonts ONLY
- 1" (2.54 cm) margins all around
- Double-spaced lines
- DO NOT put an extra space between each paragraph
- Filename: "Submission Title by Jane Q. Writer"

PAYMENT & RIGHTS

We pay $0.06 per word after publication. By submitting to *Shrapnel*, you acknowledge that your work is set in an owned universe and that you retain no rights to any of the characters, settings, or "ideas" detailed in your story. We purchase **all rights** to every published story; those rights are automatically transferred to The Topps Company, Inc.

SUBMISSIONS PORTAL

To send us a submission, visit our submissions portal here:
https://pulsepublishingsubmissions.moksha.io/publication/shrapnel-the-battletech-magazine-fiction

BATTLETECH™

The march of technology across BattleTech's eras is relentless...

BATTLETECH TLETECH 'TLETECH 'TLETECH TLETECH

RECOGNITION GUIDE: ILCLAN VOL. 01

RECOGNITION GUIDE: ILCLAN VOL. 02

RECOGNITION GUIDE: ILCLAN VOL. 03

RECOGNITION GUIDE: ILCLAN VOL. 04

RECOGNITION GUIDE: ILCLAN VOL. 05

RECOGNITION GUIDE: ILCLAN VOL. 06

Some BattleMech designs never die. Each installment of *Recognition Guide: IlClan*, currently a PDF-only series, not only includes a brand new BattleMech or OmniMech, but also details Classic 'Mech designs from both the Inner Sphere and the Clans, now fully rebuilt with Dark Age technology (3085 and beyond).

STORE.CATALYSTGAMELABS.COM

Printed in Great Britain
by Amazon

47378618R00129